IN TIMES OF RAIN AND WAR

also by

CAMRON WRIGHT

Christmas by Accident

Letters for Emily

The Orphan Keeper

The Other Side of the Bridge

The Rent Collector

IN TIMES OF RAIN AND WAR

A NOVEL

CAMRON WRIGHT

Visit us at shadowmountain.com

This is a work of fiction. Characters and events in this book are products of the author's imagination or are represented fictitiously.

Library of Congress Cataloging-in-Publication Data

Names: Wright, Camron Steve, author.
Title: In times of rain and war : a novel / Camron Wright.
Description: Salt Lake City, Utah : Shadow Mountain, [2021] | Summary: Seventeen-year-old Audrey Stocking, a German-born Jew, hides in 1940 London, hoping someday to reunite with her family while pretending to be a British citizen. American Lieutenant Wesley Bowers arrives in England the same day as the beginning of the Blitz, which is also the day a bomb penetrates Audrey's apartment—and doesn't explode. When they meet Audrey must decide whether or not to reveal her true identity and past.
Identifiers: LCCN 2020044993 | ISBN 9781629728544 (hardback)
Subjects: LCSH: Jewish teenagers—England—London—Fiction. | Ordnance disposal units—England—London—Fiction. | World War, 1939–1945, setting. | Nineteen forties, setting. | London (England), setting. | LCGFT: Historical fiction. | Romance fiction. | War fiction. | Novels.
Classification: LCC PS3623.R53 I5 2021 | DDC 813/.6—dc23
LC record available at https://lccn.loc.gov/2020044993

Printed in the United States of America
Publishers Printing

10 9 8 7 6 5 4 3 2 1

To the brave who keep trying.

It's always worth it.

"I feel we are approaching dangerous times. What a great thing it is to have been born in the 20th Century. This supreme moment in the nation's history did not come in my great-grandparents' time, it is not something lying in wait for my great-grandchildren, but it is here in *my time.* When the victory comes what a day for those who are here."

—PAM ASHFORD, 1940, in *We Are At War: The Remarkable Diaries of Five Ordinary People in Extraordinary Times* (compiled by Simon Garfield)

PROLOGUE

September 7, 1940, London, England

Eins! Zwei! Drei! Vier!

Four bombs dropped from the plane in succession, chasing one another—though the fin on the last caught on a rivet in the bomb bay, delaying its liberation until the pilot briskly pulled the aircraft's nose up to nudge the explosive free. Loose at last, the devilish missile gained speed as it dove earthward. Faster, closer, wilder, causing the wind to exhale, the sky to shiver, the clouds to arch aside, all fleeing its frightening shrill, a battle cry to *remember the Heimat*, the cherished German motherland.

The bomb, an SC 250, was named for its weight—250 kilograms to the Germans who built it, just over 550 pounds to the civilians who would be killed by its blast—and equipped with an EL25 fuze,* designed to arm with electrical current after the bomb left the plane and then detonate instantaneously upon impact.

The distance now between its metallic nose and the ground

* In military usage, the term *fuze* refers to a sophisticated ignition device designed to initiate a main charge, such as a bomb. The spelling differentiates it from a simple burning fuse.

below rapidly closed—a thousand meters, nine hundred, eight hundred. Gray squares transformed into rooftops, tiny blocks became cars, the large snake cutting through the city was clearly the River Thames.

It was a proud day for the Luftwaffe, for Hitler, indeed for all of Germany. With the beginning of a strategic bombing campaign on England's capital, British forces would soon be brought to their submissive knees.

Five hundred meters, four hundred, and then three, as the bomb's rage bore down on the roof of an innocent three-story flat planted on the corner of Gosset and Durant in London's East End.

Time would allow for more sophisticated bombs to follow, some set to explode in the air above a crowd to rain down a storm of fire, others armed with a delayed fuze that would let the ordnance penetrate deep into the belly of a building before detonating, instantly killing most of its occupants and burying alive the rest. Yes, there would be ample opportunity to terrorize England. The obliteration of London was only beginning, and Germany would prevail.

Two hundred meters, one hundred . . . and then, with a crash of furious thunder, the shell shattered clay tiles, sheared through a roof beam, severed apartment walls, and collapsed once-sound ceilings. Shards of brick, wood, mortar, furniture, and other fragmented belongings shot in all directions as the bomb pummeled through the building's upper three stories and came to rest in the floor of the ground-level flat.

The pilot had misjudged his altitude, flying his plane too low, not giving the fuze enough time to arm properly before the bomb struck. But it didn't matter—the bomb would wait. Though hastily assembled, it was equipped with a secondary fuze that would arm once the bomb had come to rest. If the bomb was then tipped, touched, or turned—even slightly—electrical current would rush down its wires, meet resistance, glow hot, and ignite a charge. In less time than it would take to scream, the building where the bomb was lodged would be blown to bits, along with everyone in it.

For now, the bomb lay wedged in the floor, having pulverized the plastered walls, spitting up so much dust and debris into the room that for the next few minutes, it was going to be almost impossible for anyone to breathe. The bomb may kill British enemies after all, and without even exploding.

Except the girl in the room now gasping for her life wasn't from England.

Audrey Stocking, age seventeen, was a German girl—a German girl in London, trying her best to hide.

CHAPTER 1

Audrey Stocking had been having vivid dreams of late in which she was about to die: tumbling off a towering cliff, being swept out to sea in a churning swell, or having a hand gripped forcefully across her mouth, strangling away the last of her air. On every occasion, at the very moment her death seemed imminent, she had always startled awake—until now.

This time the bed where Audrey had been napping flung her to the floor like a tantruming child discarding an unwanted toy. The bedroom walls and ceiling that boxed in her modest flat thundered, bent, and cracked. A cloud of grit blasted into every crevice, driving away light and life.

Was ist los? Hilfe!

Audrey's panicked cry caught in her throat as she choked for air. She arched her head forward and then back, awkwardly twisting as if craning her neck might open her airway and help her inhale. Outstretched fingers begged for help to no one and then dropped down as she scratched flailing fingernails across the uneven grain of the floorboards. The muscles in her chest were stiffening into stone, triggering not only panic but pain.

Death by suffocation wouldn't be easy. Her veins bulged, her pulse pounded, her lips turned a sickly shade of blue. Sensing that time was short, she felt a profuse stream of tears begin to leak from her eyes, stirring with the air's soot to cement her lids.

This was no dream—Audrey was dying.

Can't breathe!

She pushed herself up and tried to stand, frantic to flee the suffocating dust, but teetered sideways, collapsing back to the floor.

This is how my life will end. My struggle stops today.

She quit thrashing and lay still, cheeks clenched, lungs on fire, arms quivering, until her dirty but delicate fingers brushed against the leg of her "siren suit," a one-piece garment she'd been given almost a year earlier by the Women's Voluntary Services when she had first volunteered for wartime work.

Siren suit: its design would always look horrid—there would never be an argument there, even from those less caring about fashion. It was a practical, all-in-one outfit that a woman could pull speedily over nightclothes before escaping to an air-raid shelter. She hadn't put it on in weeks, since before the bombings in England's coastal cities had started. But there had been no bombings in London, and so she had tucked it away in the wardrobe beside her bed, never needing it . . . until now.

As dust dredged the room, Audrey clutched the precious garment, mashing the fabric against her knotted face, using it as a filter to draw in swallows of saving air, heaving beautiful breaths that tasted of splintered wood, ground plaster, and chaos.

Audrey rolled achingly over onto her back, still coughing, still forcing sifted breaths through the lifesaving cloth, grateful to still be alive.

You can do this, Audrey. Don't quit.

Her muddy eyes cracked open in teeny slits. While the room, in shambles, teemed with billowing debris, it seemed to be settling as the surrounding walls groaned and shuddered. Above her, sirens shrieked, thunderclaps boomed, aircraft droned, all contributing to the obvious chorus: the bombing of London had started.

Think! Think!

And then, amidst the rumbling, an unexpected sensation swept across her skin: a breeze, arriving like a surprise visit from a friend who had decided to drop in and help tidy up the place.

Another explosion, and then another, more distant than the one before. The floor beneath her shivered, but with less strife, as Audrey pushed herself up into a sitting position. She lowered the filthy fabric from her mouth, tested the clearing air with a couple of shallow, sullied breaths, then pulled the cloth back into place.

The gust had strengthened, shooing away the besetting cloud of grime from the room and letting the breeze carry her stare toward the ceiling. Her head lifted but slanted sideways, her brain doing its best to stitch pieces of the shadowy scene together. There was a hole in her ceiling, and in the ceiling above that, and in the ceiling above that, and at the peak of it all . . . a patch of . . . was it *sky*?

The openings in the ceilings above her were not perfect circles, but close, exposing the inside of her flat and those above it to the outdoors. It looked as if a giant poker had been plunged into her stately structure, aiming for its heart, and then was yanked away when the building remained standing and refused to die.

As the dust in the room settled, Audrey stood to get a better look, her slender legs newborn shaky. As they steadied, she sluggishly tracked the ascending openings in reverse order: roof of the building to the upper floor, second-story ceiling to the middle floor, and then her ceiling to her floor, where . . .

Shouldn't there also be a hole?

Something across the room moved—or did it? She peered hard toward the door, turned her ear a crumb to better listen. In the space of a cough, her toes tensed, her body rocked backward, and her grip on the siren suit stiffened. Three meters away, protruding from her broken and displaced floorboards, were the saluting fins of a leering German bomb.

It wasn't moving, but it looked as if it wanted to, like a crazed animal that had sniffed her out but had gotten tangled up in a trap, unable to move, but still craving to rip her apart with its teeth into jagged little pieces, if it could only set itself free.

Audrey let her eyelids close, not to hide from the creature across the room, but to protect herself from something equally dangerous—herself. Since being flung to the floor by the blast, she had felt a familiar distress lunging within her, eager to slash at her heart with razor nails, and she knew from experience that giving in would be dire.

She widened her feet, set her jaw, silently pleaded, and then demanded that the menacing onslaught of sorrow back away. It didn't withdraw but paused its advance, and as Audrey debated what to do next, a voice called out.

"Audrey?" It was the frantic cry of a woman, followed by a cough. "Where are you? I think the building has been hit."

Audrey's next logical step should have been to call back to the voice and suggest they both run, or at least yell out a warning about the bomb and then hunch down to take cover. Instead, just her eyelids moved.

The unseen voice tremored again. "Oh, Audrey, please tell me that you're alive."

This time, as the pleading penetrated more deeply, Audrey lowered the fabric and followed the sound to the floor above her.

"Yes . . . YES! I'm . . . I'm all right, Aunt Claire. I'm down here. And you . . . are you hurt?"

Seconds strained before the woman answered. "My leg is injured . . . but I don't think . . . no, it's not bleeding. Let me try to stand."

Audrey heard shuffling, scraping, and a whimper. "It hurts, but it's not broken. I . . . I can walk." Concern crept into Claire's next question. "Audrey? Audrey, how are you doing? Is everything . . ."

"I'm fine, Auntie. Honestly."

"Are you sure?"

"I promise." She waited in silence, listening to see if her aunt believed her.

"That's good. I knew I should have stayed downstairs with you instead of—"

"Can you get out? Is the way free?" Audrey asked, cutting Claire's sentence short.

"I . . . um . . . yes. I believe so," Claire replied, her wobbly words trickling over the edge of the hole and down to the floor below. "But we need to hurry. I don't know how much longer this building can stand."

As the whir of war planes still hummed above them, the anger of another explosion sounded a street or two away. The walls in the flat rumbled and shuddered but held against the quaking ground.

Be strong, Audrey. You can do this!

A gasp, another gaze toward Claire. "Very good. Let's meet at the stairs."

Audrey shook the dust from the crumpled siren suit, then pulled open the inside of a sleeve and used it to wipe away the silt that had camped in the corner of her eyes. Her golden hair, now more dusty silver than blond, clung to her head like wet clothing. Her fingers held the grit between her joints like they'd been dredged in sugar.

While the breeze from above was doing a stellar job of finally clearing the air, it also carried a chill. Shivering slightly, she unzipped the siren suit and clumsily slipped it on.

Think, Audrey.

She was in a fix for certain. She'd told her aunt that she would meet her at the stairs—and she fully intended to, but for the pesky problem of a rather large bomb that blocked her path to the flat's door.

Worse, when the bomb had pummeled through her ceiling, the force had ripped away part of a supporting wall, a piece of which dangled limply as an odd-shaped triangle of embedded lath and fractured plaster. It swayed above the bomb, looking as if one more rattle might cause it to let go. It was a good six feet across, and if it fell, it would knock into the fins of the waiting explosive . . . and then what?

Audrey breathed in, exhaled, and then edged toward the bomb as quietly as a child might sneak back to her room after midnight curfew.

Is it warm? Could it still detonate?

As she got closer, she fought the urge to lean over and touch it. Two of its four fins, once held in proper position by a welded stabilizing bar, were badly mangled, though her eyes moved past the bomb to scan the ravaged room that encircled it.

So much damage . . . and without even exploding.

But she couldn't keep her eyes away from the bomb, its presence hypnotic, almost daring her to reach over and give it a little shove.

Did it quiver? Was it ticking?

"You didn't explode," Audrey whispered.

When the bomb offered no response, she answered for it. "Not yet . . . is that what you're thinking?"

She should have kept gliding watchfully toward the door, making her way to safety, but she had more to say. "Of all the flats in London, you came from Germany to hit mine."

Oddly, the looming threat of death had delivered more courage than grief, and Audrey found herself sharing a secret with the beast that until now she had kept tightly tethered. "My life is not what it seems. But you know that." Her tiny voice filled with a tremble. "Is that why you're here? Am I being punished?"

Audrey wanted to be brave, but a sense of sadness was welling up inside her. Feelings she'd been trying to hold at bay were now firmly pushing back, causing an odd thought: she and this metal menace that had landed here so unexpectedly to administer death to strangers had something in common. It was a notion that stuck in her throat, a truth not ready to break free.

"Are you here to kill me? If so, then do it!" she said, pausing long enough to give her sharpened directive time to reach the bomb's metallic surface and knock. "EXPLODE! I AM READY!"

While she'd hoped her affirmation would sound defiant, it was a vow that also roused regret—regret dusted in memory. Still, she must have called the bomb's bluff because the metal didn't move, the fuze didn't ignite, the casing didn't detonate into a burst of molten shrapnel shards that would instantly obliterate her petite frame. It simply waited.

A noise from outside startled Audrey, reeled her back to reality, reminded her that she shouldn't be conversing with an inanimate enemy bomb, that Claire would be waiting by the stairs, and that others in the building may still be in danger.

Her eyes darted around the room until they found a single shoe and then its mate, which she knocked together and slipped on. Next, facing the door, she edged past the bomb as if excusing herself from a Sunday social gathering. "Claire needs my help," she said, as if to make clear to the beast why she was ending their little chat so abruptly.

The wail of a fire engine passed on the street to join in chorus with the urgent air-raid sirens, all directing Audrey's attention to the door that offered the room's sole escape. She pushed steadily toward it, finally gripping its grimy handle, fighting her body's demand to celebrate her impending freedom by obeying a single, straightforward request: *RUN!*

Audrey didn't listen, didn't flinch. Would it really matter? If the bomb lingering behind her were to explode while she was nearby, whether standing inside the room by the door or being twice the distance away on the other side, she would die as quickly. Hurrying faster would not save Audrey Stocking today.

Instead, she tugged the door inward as gently as a woman leaving for afternoon tea, but it would open only partway, being blocked by strewn debris on the floor. She readied to kick the rubbish aside but paused when she noticed, mingling among it, a shattered gilded frame that had held two photographs. The photo on top, the one that would have been visible to anyone who might have previously entered the room, was of Audrey's family: Audrey, her father, and her two younger brothers, Jessey and Lewy. A second photo, one that had once been hidden beneath the first, had slid free and was staring up through the dust. It was a photo of Audrey with her aunt, taken in Stuttgart, Germany.

The broken frame must have held memories that wanted to remain concealed, because when Audrey reached for it, a slivered piece of glass sliced the tip of her finger.

The sound of scraping nudged Audrey backward as the wooden door swung inward, scooting the glass and pictures aside out of her reach. No matter—it was better that Claire not see them anyway.

"There you are!" Claire cried, relief limping in with her. "You weren't at the stairs, and I was worried something was wrong."

Claire Bergmann was a serious-minded woman with chiseled cheeks, straight hair, and a studious brow. A good dozen years older than Audrey, she sometimes acted like a mother, other times like a protective older sister. At the moment she was carting an overnight suitcase, every bit the woman who would pack for a disaster and looking frustrated that Audrey hadn't thought to do the same.

"I was looking for my shoes," Audrey stammered. "How's your leg?"

"It's sore, but it will be fine." As Claire's reply edged sideways through gritted teeth, not only did she not notice the blood dripping from Audrey's cut finger, but she also missed seeing the outline of the lurking bomb.

Audrey reached for her coat, now crumpled on the floor beneath the hook where it normally hung, shook it, and then pulled it on. She held her wounded finger against her thumb and sleeve to stop the bleeding.

"I tried the lift," Claire said, as she tottered forward, "but it wasn't working. Luckily I managed to get down the stairs."

"Come, Auntie, let's get ourselves outside."

Audrey led, and Claire followed. But as they escaped the building's foyer for the freedom of the street, they found the area flooded in chaos. Sooty plumes of smoke rose from far-off fires as the drowning drone of air-raid sirens clamored for attention. In the background, a defiant crimson sun sagged low in the late afternoon sky, as if loitering long enough to see what was happening to the frightened residents of London.

"Pardon us, please! Make way!" A young man in a soiled topcoat bumped past them, followed closely by a woman towing a toddler—a trio of terrified faces staggering eerily toward the protection of a public shelter several streets away.

Claire reached for Audrey's hand, noticed her cringe, then looked at her finger. "You're bleeding!"

"It's nothing," Audrey assured her. "Let's keep moving. There's a shelter on Teale, but it's small. I think we should head for the Underground."

An enemy bomber rumbled overhead. Claire grimaced but nodded as she limped forward, biting at her lip with such ferocity that Audrey was sure the woman would draw blood. It was bad enough that she was hobbling, but every time bombers passed overhead—and they were doing so relentlessly—Claire insisted that the two crouch in building doorways or lie flat against the rows of sandbags that snaked London's sidewalks.

By the time the pair reached the Underground entrance, their tired limbs twitching, the stairs down seemed steeper than normal, as if the platform were trying to inch away from the danger. Audrey was two steps from the bottom when her foot jerked to a stop.

"What is it?" Claire asked.

Audrey's free hand rushed to cover her mouth. "I forgot the list," she exclaimed, every syllable throbbing. "I have to go back."

Claire's voice curdled. "Audrey, the planes are attacking! We need to take shelter. We can get our things in the morning."

Audrey's wobbling head knew otherwise. Claire hadn't seen the bomb. She didn't understand. "If we wait until morning, the bomb could go off, and then it will be too late."

Claire's cloudy eyes scrunched. "Bomb?" She took a labored step closer. "Audrey, what bomb?"

Audrey gulped in a deep swallow of air but tasted only despair. How could she explain? "It's in our flat, Claire, past the door. It hit our building but didn't go off. If it had, it would have killed us all. I'm telling you that tomorrow could be too late."

"Audrey, you can't . . ." Claire's mouth moved, and words followed, but Audrey was no longer listening. She reached out for Claire's shoulders like a child grasping her mother to ensure she'd be heard.

"*Ruhe bitte!*" Audrey nearly shouted.

Fear halted all sound as Claire spun nervously around to see if any strangers had been close enough to hear the German command to be quiet.

Audrey didn't wait for a reprimand. "Claire, listen! After the bombing stops, go and find Cora Holden. Tell her about our flat. She'll be able to help. I know that we need to be careful with what we say, but you also need to find someone from the Royal Air Force. Tell them we have a bomb in our building." She hesitated, unsure whether the next bit of information was worth sharing. "Tell them that as I stepped past the bomb when I was leaving . . . I was a little distracted, but . . ."

If Claire had been cross, it soon pirouetted into panic. "Tell them what?"

"Tell them that I think I heard it ticking."

Then, before Claire could reach out, knowing that the woman would never stand a chance of chasing anyone down with her injured leg, Audrey bolted back up the stairs toward home.

Claire shivered as she groped her way across the platform, every part of her unsteady—leg, head, heart.

That girl, Audrey, was impossible to control, never considering consequences before running off like a jilted bride. Now, with bombs dropping from above and stress stewing in her gut below, Claire was left, as usual, to wait, worry, and then try to piece their lives back together.

Having arrived at the Underground station so long after the bombing had started, she expected there to be no room in the inn—and she appeared to be right. The pickle-packed platform was littered with bundled bodies seemingly tossed in all directions, covering every smidgen of space. It looked as if East End Thrift had been gifted truckloads of clothing that they'd strewn across the floor for a warehouse sale, but had forgotten first to remove the clothing's occupants.

"There's room at the far end," a woman said as she patted Claire's arm and pointed.

"Thank you," Claire answered, then stepped politely around people—some resting, others anxiously watching—as she eased deeper into the musty bowels of London's Underground. She was happy the platform was well lit, with incandescent lamps hung every thirty feet in the ceiling, leading to a slight bend where a dark tunnel would normally either swallow or regurgitate trains—though certainly no more would run tonight.

Claire aimed for the far wall, listened to the abounding chatter around her—a quiet cough, a despondent murmur, a child whimpering here and there—but she also heard occasional laughter. It was a strange reaction perhaps, from people huddling in shock while their homes were being bombed by an enemy invader, but down here they were alive, they were together, they were still friends and family. They might have been huddling, but few were cowering.

While some of the city's displaced residents napped alongside their belongings—a suitcase here, a duffel bag there—many had come clutching only a coat and the hope that these inhospitable arrangements wouldn't last longer than a single evening. That was Claire's desire as well.

She was a strong woman in every sense, but tonight she helplessly lumbered through the swarm with lonely exhaustion. Finding an open space, she positioned her suitcase to use it as a makeshift stool, but as she sat, the concrete quivered—more German bombs, dropping from German planes, flown by German pilots.

The thought transformed into a palpable question that poked her in the cheek: could one of the pilots be Kaden Froe?

Kaden was a soft-spoken man with perpetually tousled hair. Claire had met him in Hamburg when he'd stopped at Audrey's home to review a set of her father's drawings. Claire was there working and had struck up a polite conversation with the man while stalling for Walther. However, politeness soon gelled into genuine interest, and by the time Walther had arrived, almost an hour late, the wall clock was being ignored, eye glances were interlocked, and a dinner invitation with the stranger had already been set.

In the months that followed, Claire had never been happier. She and Kaden were seldom apart, their future was being penned in full rhyme, and even icy days, those she typically dreaded, had warmed into sunshine. There were even whispers of wedlock.

Claire's chin lowered. *Verdammter Krieg,* she thought, silently cursing the war. Kaden was an experienced airplane mechanic and pilot, so with the rise of the Nazi Party in Germany and the repudiation of the Treaty of Versailles, the Luftwaffe had come knocking—and the man knew better than to turn them down. She hadn't seen Kaden since she'd left Germany, but had she stayed, it wouldn't have changed anything. She had considered trying to get a message to him to let him know that she was in London, but how would that have made any difference?

Kaden Froe was the only man Claire had ever loved, and now she was in London, and he was likely overhead, flying a German plane, dropping a bomb at this very instant that could unknowingly kill her.

The senseless ironies of war.

A man's voice interrupted her thoughts. "Ma'am, are you all right?" It was a policeman walking the platform to help out where he could.

Claire wiped at her eyes. If anybody found out that she and Audrey were German, that they'd used false papers to enter the country, it would not go well. Worse, if anyone discovered that Claire's fiancé was a German pilot and that Audrey's father owned a German factory, they would be locked up for certain.

Claire stood and then leaned so close that only the policeman could hear. "I'm a bit unsettled," she said, using her best English accent.

"How may I assist?"

"It seems I need to report an unexploded bomb that is sitting in our flat."

The streets in London's East End were a war zone in every sense of the word. The ominous roar of enemy bombers continued to violate sovereign skies above as a cadre of antiaircraft fire defended the beloved English capital from below. The concussive combination was both deafening and relentless—*boom, boom, boom, boom*—a thunder that was traumatic enough alone, but when stirred with the screech of air-raid sirens and sprinkled with the sporadic cries of panicked people as they sought shelter, it set Audrey to checking her pockets for anything that she could cram into her ears. Sadly, the more sinister sound for Audrey wasn't coming from the outside, but from a swelling inner commotion that couldn't be quieted by tiny twists of tissue. As if to thwart her good intentions to rush back to their flat as fast as possible, misery had chased Audrey from the Underground station, caught up to her on the way, and was now crushing her courage.

Turn back! Give up! You won't make it.

She passed another stretch of street and took a second squint behind her, every stride slower than the last. Up ahead, along the path where she and Claire had recently passed, furious flames now belched from the bank building, keeping an amassing horde of firefighters at bay. Between the heat and the brave men futilely combating the blaze, the most direct route home was blocked, forcing her to head left down a side street.

"Let me make it to the flat," she pleaded to no one in particular, her voice so soft it scarcely surfaced. "There are things I need . . . the list . . . the letters . . ." Yet even before the last word had slipped out, she knew it was too late. In the handful of seconds that it took her to step down from the curb, cross the pavement, and climb up the opposite side, a feeling of deep dread that had been clinging to her clothes now itched across her neck and crawled inside, clawing at her core.

She coiled around, almost longing to see a menacing stranger stalking her in the crimson haze, as that would at least add reason to her concern. But except for the firemen battling the flames behind her, she was alone.

Please, please!

With steps so belabored she barely budged at all, she shuffled to the back of a building and propped her frame against the bitter brick. Her legs were shaking, her skin was pale, her chest was heaving in deep and piercing gasps. That was the worst part, being hungry for air, wrestling to suck it in, but feeling like an iron hand had covered her mouth and nose, squeezing away life.

It was difficult to describe these *attacks of melancholy,* as she called them, that had been occurring over the last several months. The spells of anxiety manifested so rapidly and acutely they would physically paralyze her for a time. She worried enough that, after the third episode, she had gone to see a doctor. The man listened impatiently as she listed the symptoms, sneered at her like she was making it all up, and then diagnosed her with asthma, for which he prescribed the smoking of stramonium leaves.

She never went back.

The only other person she'd told was Claire. When Audrey finally sat her down to explain how the bouts felt, it was hard to find words both broad and jagged enough to define the depth of her grief. The closest Audrey could come was to have Claire imagine that all the earth's sunlight had been snuffed away, leaving her bone-chilled, naked, and overcome.

"There is an echoing darkness," she'd added, "where you play a demon's waiting game to see if you can summon the strength never to blink as you wait for the light to return. Because if you blink, Claire—even once—then the fiend tears you apart and you've lost."

The attacks had been sporadic but unrelenting, about two per week since she'd started keeping track—but not always. Despite the nightmares, eight days had passed without one, letting her harbor a modicum of hope.

Tonight, her trembling legs gave way, and she collapsed to her knees, bent over the gutter, and threw up. She'd been clenching her cut finger so hard the wound was again dripping blood.

Other than the handful of minutes that she'd rested before the bomb had crashed through her flat, it had been hours since she'd had any sleep. Now, with dusk turning red from the flicker of indignant flames, she transferred the burden of her tired bones and body to a yard-high sandbagged wall that was safeguarding a small market. Once seated, she clamped her hands against her ears to muffle the bombs and despair that rained down like fire both in her head and from the skies above, and then released a breath so deeply from her lungs that she wondered if it would be her last.

Stay calm, Audrey. You have to make it!

She had told Claire that she needed to return to their flat to retrieve a list, a directory of children she'd been helping scurry out of London as part of her work with the Women's Voluntary Services. She had been compiling the list for Cora Holden, the woman taking charge of the London Region of WVS and personal assistant to Lady Reading, the organization's founder. And the urgency was real—without the list, children could be in danger.

But there was something equally important that she'd left in her flat, and she berated herself for rushing away without it—bomb or no bomb. Hidden beneath her mattress, near the head where she could keep it close, was a rectangular wooden box made of carefully carved and stained ebony. If the letters inside this box were discovered, it would ruin everything.

As buildings burned around her, her pointed pleadings swirled into the darkness of the disparaging night sky.

"I'm sorry, Father," she repeated faintly. "I'm so very sorry."

CHAPTER 2

Skies above Northamptonshire, England

Second Lieutenant Wesley Bowers, an American who had played fullback on his college football team, could deadlift twice his weight, and had defeated every man in his squad who would dare race him, had never been airsick a day in his life—until today.

The Lockheed Hudson bomber in which he was buckled, en route from Newfoundland to RAF Brackley, an airfield in the East Midlands of England, was intentionally flying through a rain-laden layer of nimbostratus, apparently a safer alternative than risking a run-in with stray German fighters.

The plane jolted, metal rattled, and rain pelted, all while Wes's one-handed grasp tightened around a dirty steel cup he'd been given in case of nausea.

"We're just reaching the coast of Ireland. It won't be much longer now." The man talking above the engines through his headset, now seated beside Wes in the aircraft, was the copilot, Captain Jonathan Grassley, a chatty sort from North Carolina who'd come back to report on their status. "Are you well?" he asked Wes. "You look a little . . . ill."

Wes shrugged with his eyes. "Crazy how a rattling plane in a rainstorm will do that to a man, right?" His feeble frown let Grassley smile for the both of them.

"I've been through worse," Grassley replied, though the moment his lips closed, the plane took a violent bump, causing both men to clutch their seats.

Wes returned a compulsory smile. "It appears the plane disagrees. And to think I was uneasy about going to England."

"What's wrong with England?" Grassley asked, no doubt making conversation to divert their attention from the storm.

"I'm joining one of the British bomb disposal teams."

Grassley chewed on the news. "If I were a betting man—which I'm not, 'cause my wife won't let me gamble—I'd say you'll come through it just fine."

Wes had just met Grassley when boarding the plane, but he already felt like an old friend, the kind of person whom one could trust with anything. "That's because you don't know about the memo."

"Which memo is that, son?"

Wes placed the cup he'd been cuddling at his feet. "When I was called to this assignment, the commander was interrupted and had to step out of his office, and a folder was open on his desk. I know I shouldn't have looked, but I couldn't help myself."

Captain Grassley turned his smile toward Wes. It was clear that he loved a good story. "Well, what did it say?"

"It said that the average life expectancy of those working with British bomb disposal is ten weeks—*ten weeks.*"

"And that's why you're scared," the captain replied, more as a statement than a question.

When Wes answered, his voice was brittle. "I'd say more like apprehensive, but whatever it is, does it make me less of a soldier?"

Grassley leaned in, spoke with as much reassurance as the crackly intercom would allow. "Son, I'd say it makes you human."

As the plane dropped out of the clouds, Grassley glanced forward. "That's my cue. We're over land. I hate to cut this discussion short. If you want, we can continue once we arrive. Otherwise, all I can suggest is that you greet each day with honor and then leave the rest up to Someone of a higher rank, if you know what I mean." His warm Southern drawl wrapped Wes like a woolen scarf.

Wes shook the man's hand, stretching the moment. "Thank you, sincerely. I guess my single saving grace is that I'll be training at Brackley, so I just have to best the ten-week average there. After that, I head to London."

"London?" Lines on the captain's forehead pinched into rounded rows.

"Yes, sir. What's wrong with London?"

Grassley drew up tall. His words were slow to come out. "You haven't heard, have you?"

"Heard what, sir?" Wes's head had tipped back as confusion wormed its way through the rumble of the engines.

"Do your best to stay at Brackley."

"Why? What is it?"

"I'm sorry. I thought you knew. Hitler's advance has started. London is being bombed!"

The aircraft taxied to a fortified concrete revetment and was swiftly draped with a massive camouflage net to blend the plane into the countryside. Wes was ushered off and led to an adjacent bunker where he expected to meet Captain Landen Trumble, commanding officer of 34 Section, Bomb Disposal Company Royal Engineers, to which he'd been assigned. But when the door opened, and he was steered inside, there was only a boy waiting.

The lad was wearing a uniform of sorts, though it had missing buttons, ragged sleeves, and oversized shoulders, looking a lot like he'd found his pop's World War I garb and tried it on for size. Wes would have guessed the kid was about fourteen but for the cigarette that drooped from his mouth.

"You the Yank?" he asked Wes, his words wrapped in a thick Cockney accent. He tossed Wes a nod but never bothered to salute.

"That depends," Wes replied. "I'm here to see Captain Trumble. Can you take me to him?"

The kid didn't miss a beat. "Well, mate, that's gonna be a bit of a stink for ya."

"A stink? Why is that?"

The boy took a drag from his cigarette as if he'd been looking forward to this moment all afternoon. "You see, Trumble an' his sapper was blown up yesterday. I heard they 'ad a thousand-kilogram beast that missed the bunker and they should've set up sandbags an' blown it up in place, and not try to extract the fuze, but they didn't. An' too bad, 'cause I met 'is sapper once and 'e weren't half a good bloke." He delivered the news as casually as if the two men had simply been delayed on holiday.

"Trumble's dead?" Wes repeated, not because he hadn't understood or didn't believe the boy, but because the words were simply the first to dash across his tongue.

"The parts they found jolly well were." The boy's bluntness spilled to the ground, where he let it wallow in a moment of silence. When he looked up, he flicked ash in Wes's direction. "You've been reassigned. Colonel Moore sent me. You're going to be part of 5BD 37 Section."

"And you are?"

The kid snuffed out his cigarette on his boot, then held out his hand toward Wes for the first time. "I'm Private Dekle Dinn, chief, but everyone calls me Driver."

"Driver Dekle Dinn. That's a lot of Ds," Wes said, taking the kid's grip, still deciding if he could take him seriously.

"Definitely."

"Can I ask how old you are?" Wes added.

The kid's stare was as prodigious as a pit bull's. "Nineteen."

"Nineteen?" Wes aimed a doubtful glare squarely at the kid's eyes. What was the youngster going to do, lurch forward and bite Wes's leg?

There wasn't even a flinch. "Yes, sir. Nineteen proper."

There was no argument; the kid could lie with the best of them. Wes blinked first, picked up his duffel bag, and then thumped the boy once in the chest. "Well, Driver Dekle Dinn, which way do we go?"

Driver pointed east. "There's a truck out front. I'll take you to the barracks to meet the colonel an' the rest o' the bleedin' section. Right. 'e couldn't come 'cause 'e's 'elpin' to load up. We're packin'."

"Packing?"

"Quite. We've been reassigned from Brackley. We leave tonight. We're all drivin' to London."

On their ride to the barracks, Driver volunteered a bit of history on their commander. "Moore's a good bloke, but 'e wears 'is Great War gear 'cause 'e says it's mint. They gave 'im a Military Cross in the last war, excep' 'e won't say why—oh, and 'e's a gaffer."

"A gaffer?"

"Yeah, a pensioner. You know . . . 'e's *old*!"

Wes joked that, compared to Driver, everyone was old, but the boy didn't seem to follow the humor. When the truck chugged to a stop in front of the barracks of 37 Section, Bomb Disposal Royal Engineers, soldiers were scurrying: two men were loading a box into the back of an idling truck, another was wiping down the windshield with a rag, yet another was removing a painted wooden sign that had been bolted to the side of the building.

Driver switched off the ignition. "I'm guessin' the fellas look 'bout ready." He nudged with his nose toward the man laying the sign to the ground in the faint light of the truck's headlamps, barely bright enough to cast a weak shadow. "There's the colonel."

Wes stepped from the truck and approached the man, then offered a salute.

Colonel Russell Moore saluted briskly back and then brushed the formality aside with a flick of his wrist. "It's good to meet you, sir," he said, offering Wes a welcoming handclasp.

"Likewise."

Driver's description proved precise. The colonel, in his mid to late sixties, wore a close-fitting four-pocket tunic, straight-leg trousers, and puttees that wrapped snugly from his ankles to his knees. It was as if he'd been discharged at the last war's end but merely stumbled off and never found his way home. His uniform was aged, but not tattered. His eyes were wrinkled, but not weary. He seemed experienced, but not old. Most prominent was his gray, woolly mustache, which looked like two plump, elderly caterpillars had attached to either side of his upper lip and were now hanging on for dear life.

"I'm sorry about the change of plans," the colonel said, his voice gravelly.

"Not as sorry as Captain Trumble, I'm sure." Wes didn't intend to sound flippant, but once the quip had skated out, it was too late to get it back. He was speaking, after all, about a man who was dead.

The colonel took it in stride. "Yes, he'll be missed." He stooped to pick up one end of the sign he'd been repairing. Wes followed his lead, hoisted up the other end, and helped him lug it to the truck. The colonel talked as he worked. "I received orders from your CO. You'll want to confirm with him, rightly, but you've been reassigned to my section, and, as you've heard, we're heading to London. We'll drive in tonight, but with masked headlights due to the blackout, so the going will be slow."

Once the sign had been loaded into the truck, the colonel assembled his men and then turned to Wes. "Let me introduce you, and we can be on our way."

Just four men gathered with Driver and the colonel.

"I'll make this quick," the Colonel said. "This is Second Lieutenant Wes Bowers of the United States Marine Corps. He'll be joining our little group as part of . . . well, an educational mission. He's here to learn how we defuse bombs."

A stocky soldier across the circle snarled with his eyes, directing his chilly assertion toward the colonel as if Wes were standing distant. "The Yanks won't join the war, but they send us this sod?" He spun toward Wes. "No offense, chap." Though plainly *offense* was his main point.

"That's enough," the colonel said, tamping down the attitude. "I expect you all to make him welcome."

Before the disgruntled soldier could complain, the colonel motioned to the officer at his right. "Lieutenant Duke Hastings here is my second-in-command, a good bloke, so if you have any worries when I'm gone, see him."

Wes and the lieutenant were already locking eyes, but with curiosity. Hastings was in his mid-thirties, the oldest of the men in the circle besides the colonel, but wearing the newest uniform along with a peaked cap, though all of the Brits' uniforms seemed a bit tatty compared to the gear Wes had brought along. After a moment of mutual sizing up, Hastings welcomed him with a nod and a single-word greeting, "Mate."

The next soldier in line, rocking back and forth on his feet, was dressed in a Royal Air Force uniform. He was about Wes's age, though smaller in frame, and, most noticeably, he had a badly disfigured right eye.

"This is Aircraftman Second Class Patrick Pillman, though we call him Gunner," the colonel said. "He served as a gunner on a bombing crew, but as you can see, he took some shrapnel to the face—which he thinks improved his looks, and nobody here will disagree—so he was discharged. Still, he couldn't quite leave the comforts of soldierly life, and so he's serving with us."

Gunner took a long step forward, almost to the circle's center. Above a tautly stretched grin, his scarred eye was twitching. It was only when Driver started to snicker that Wes realized Gunner was trying his best to wink.

The colonel, unfazed, bumped Gunner back into position before facing the soldier who'd first objected to Wes's presence. "This is Private Croydon Snee, but he prefers to be called Badger. He's one of our sappers, the lads who dig out the unexploded bombs so we can get to the fuzes—and he's one of the best you'll ever see."

Snee's nickname was accurate: he was wide-bodied, with short legs, muscular arms, and undersized ears that made his head look abnormally large—and he was gawking at Wes with equal amounts of anger and disdain like he wished the two men could step away then and there and have a personal *chat.*

Wes tossed him a nod as if passing an acquaintance on the street whose name you don't recall and so you move quickly on.

"You've met Driver," the colonel said, gesturing past the boy toward the only man left, "so we'll finish with sapper Scafell, whom we call Pike. He's been with us for just a couple of weeks. He's quiet—which I find refreshing—but he's been an asset, and we're glad to have him."

Pike was also young, older than Driver, but not by much—seventeen, eighteen tops—and the skinniest of the group. He was wearing an army service cap, the fabric type that wilts to one side, but his looked ready to fall off at any moment. Unlike Badger, Pike faced Wes and saluted.

"That's everyone," the colonel announced. "You can chinwag later. For now, Driver, take the Tilly. Hastings, you drive the Hippo. We'll be bunking at a warehouse in Holloway."

Before the men dispersed, Wes roped a glance around the circle. He constantly struggled to remember names. Now, repeating them back, he prayed they'd stick.

Driver: *too young to drive, but who's asking?;* Hastings: *second-in-command and seems likable;* Gunner: *a bad eye and proud of it;* Badger: *a ferocious weasel;* Pike: *two weeks new and still petrified, something we have in common;* and of course, the colonel: *the "pensioner" in charge of them all.*

Wes was promptly grasping the reality that, like almost everything else in the military, his official assignment—shadowing a British bomb disposal squad—read more glamorous on paper than the hard reality now showering him down.

Ten weeks. Could he possibly beat the average life expectancy with this lot?

The group had fewer men than a normal section, and as he tracked them back in the opposite order, his shoulders sagged. Their uniforms were faded and frayed, their boot soles were slim and separating. The helmets two of the men wore were seated so loosely on their heads they looked more like discarded pasta pans than official military gear. In truth, it looked like they were wearing secondhand battle dress that they'd picked up at an army surplus store. There was no way to sugarcoat it: to call this group haggard was to impugn the demoralized.

"Have you slept?" the colonel asked.

Wes had tried to get some sleep on the flight over, but nerves had kept him anxious, and the weather had kept him awake—not to mention Captain Grassley's constant chatter. If counting, it had been twenty hours since he'd closed his eyes, and right now, they burned.

"I'll be okay."

Colonel Moore motioned to the larger of the two trucks. "Throw your bag into the back of the Hippo and catch a couple of hours of sleep on the way." Though his next command was aimed at Badger, he let it float out across the entire group. "I trust you will all be civil. So, if there's nothing more . . ." He thrust up his arm as if cheering. "Bowers, welcome to 37 Section, Bomb Disposal Royal Engineers. Let's get ourselves to London and disable some Nazi bombs."

The Leyland Hippo, like the men it served, was a resourceful military vehicle. It had an open cab in front that was large enough to accommodate two or three soldiers, and a heavy flatbed in the rear, which was typically boxed in with wooden sides and a canvas cover for hauling men, but could be completely removed to cautiously ferry a bomb to a safe location for detonation.

However, the Hippo assigned to 37 Section, Bomb Disposal Royal Engineers, had seen better days. What their extended cargo truck offered in versatility it lacked in reliability. On the outskirts of London, with Wes asleep in the back and the city skyline just coming into view, the vehicle sheared a rod to the transmission's flywheel, and, with a heated huff and a grunt, the Hippo sputtered to a halt.

As Hastings jerked the vehicle off the road, Wes jolted awake. Still groggy, he wiped sleepy fingers against moist eyes and then lowered his listless body down from the truck's bed.

The night was pitch-dark, the ground cold and unfriendly.

Dreaming . . . I'm dreaming, he thought—but what he saw as he looked out toward the horizon felt more like a nightmare. In the distance, an apocalyptic meteor shower seemed to be raining down its wrath across the far city of London.

If there were still enemy aircraft in the skies above, he couldn't see them. His attention instead fixed toward the hazy horizon, where dozens—no, hundreds—of fires traversed the flickering panorama. The enormity of human sorrow that smoldered ghostlike toward heaven was staggering. Under any other circumstance, the scene might be called majestic, even breathtaking, but as Wes steadied himself against the truck to keep from falling, it was a hallowed moment that deserved only silence.

In the stillness, Wes thought back to college and his mythology class, where he'd studied the origins of fire. In the folklore, mystical animals would steal fire from humans and try to use it for their good. But in every case, it would end up back in the hands of man, the fables implying that *ownership of fire* is an inherent human quality.

Tonight, watching the fires in London, Wes was ashamed for his species.

The door opened, and Hastings and Badger stepped down. They'd been observing from inside the truck.

"What do we do?" Wes asked.

"WHAT DO WE DO?" growled Badger. "You tell us, cowboy. Should we run in and piddle all the fires out?"

"I meant about the truck," Wes answered, though he knew that was not exactly true.

The colonel and the other men who'd been in the vehicle ahead had turned around and were getting out as well. A quick inspection of the Hippo confirmed that the repairs would require major parts, so it was decided that they'd bunk by the side of the road for the night. In the morning, Driver would ferry everyone into London in two groups.

The night air was doleful, and little more was said as the men prepared to bed down.

Wes found a patch of grass-covered ground a short distance from the road, and he rolled out his mummy bag. The colonel and Hastings had opted for the back of the Hippo, where there was plenty of room for others, but the remaining men followed Wes's example and scattered to various spots on the ground nearby.

For Wes, little sleep followed; after two hours of fretful twisting, he slipped from his bag and inched quietly toward a thicket of trees past the Hippo where he could relieve himself. But as he got closer to the thicket, something stirred in the trees ahead.

He stopped, waited, listened.

Another one of the men had obviously had the same idea, since it was the perfect spot for some privacy, but just when Wes was ready to slink away to look for a place in the opposite direction, a muffled sound held him motionless.

He squinted toward the silhouette in the dim moonlight.

The man up ahead in the thicket was the colonel—and he was openly weeping.

CHAPTER 3

Audrey spent most of the night curled into a ball on the dirty pavement, shivering under her coat, slipping in and out of restless dreams—explosions have a funny way of disturbing one's sleep. She was never certain what time the enemy truly abandoned their assault of the city. She was caught up instead in sporadic but devilish dreams: ascending an impossibly precipitous cliff, fighting a freezing rain, screaming back to fiendish voices who whispered through the gale that she'd never make it. And they always proved right. "Please, Papa, please help me!" she cried repeatedly on her journey, almost able to make out his form standing above her, but her father never called back, never looked down, never lowered a hand to help his endangered child.

"Miss? Are you injured?"

An elderly man wearing an apron was on his knees, warily shaking Audrey awake, no doubt concerned that the young lady huddled on the sidewalk in front of his shop had been hurt by the bombing.

He was likely surprised when Audrey folded back the jacket and groggily sat up. It took her a moment to take in her surroundings. Rubbing the night's apprehension from her eyes, she peered up at the stranger in the apron.

"Thank you, sir . . . I . . . I'll be fine," she told him. Then, with as much dignity as could be mustered by a young woman who has fallen asleep on a stony sidewalk in her siren suit, she stood, held the man's hand in hers, thanked him for his kindness, and hurried off down the road, leaving him to scratch his bewildered head.

The sun was not yet up, but it was stretching. Audrey paused for a moment to pull on her coat and take a closer look at her surroundings. There was visible destruction to parts of the city—debris in the streets, buildings damaged and burned, some still smoldering—but, like ants repairing their scattered hill, Londoners were already scurrying about.

It was invariably the same for her the morning after an attack—an attack of the emotional variety, not the physical one that was exacted on the city. She was still nervous, a bit disoriented, and it would always take a day or two for the bruises of sadness to completely heal after the mental misery that had so thoroughly pummeled her spirit the night before, but she could at least function, sensing that she would once again find the space to store hope in her heart.

What she longed for most of all was to understand why these bouts of overwhelming sadness kept reoccurring.

As Audrey neared the corner by her flat, a man walked past and then turned toward her for a second look. Any other day she might have been flattered. Today, she understood: she looked like a street vagrant—and technically was, having slept on cement. She didn't need a mirror to know that she looked pitiful and likely smelled worse. Bomb or no bomb, as soon as she sneaked in to get her list and the box, she'd also grab clothes and toiletries, no matter how dusty.

But when she turned the corner, she found her building completely roped off and abundantly signed.

No Entry. Unexploded Ordnance.

She would have ignored the warning, crept past the sign when no one was watching, but the Home Guard had stationed a soldier at the barricade, and, frankly, there was no other way around—so she approached.

Everything about the man standing between her and home felt formal—his straight arms, the way he cradled his rifle, the spacing of his steps as he tracked a narrow line back and forth in front of the guarded building—as if the way he carried out this singular job would determine the war's outcome.

After looking him over, Audrey dropped her gaze to her feet. While she didn't want to cause trouble, she lugged a desperation that wouldn't be ignored. She calmly conveyed to the soldier—a man in his fifties—how the bomb had hit her flat the night before; how, not being in her right mind, she had rushed out without taking a list of children she was compiling for the Women's Voluntary Services; and how, without it, children's lives could be in danger. Her eyes rose to meet his as she reached out and placed her slender fingers on his rigid arm, hoping for compassion. "If you can just let me inside, I'll be swift."

The man brushed her hand aside. "I'm sorry for the little 'uns. I am." His tone was strident, void of any regret whatsoever. "I simply can't let anyone through."

Audrey's voice lifted. "Please, they're children. It's for the WVS."

"Well, unless the WVS outranks the British Army, which they don't, I've been given strict orders. No one enters until the disposal team gets here and eliminates the threat. It's for everyone's safety, including the children."

"But it's been hours!" she protested.

"Miss, the bomb isn't threatening public transportation, it isn't interfering with the army's ability to function, and lives are not in immediate danger. There is an order to these things, and a team will come as soon as rightly possible."

"But when? When will they—"

The soldier's sigh cut her off, pressed against her, caused her to shuffle a step back. He had raised a finger, ready to fling it around freely while berating her, when she realized confronting him had been a mistake.

"You're right. Please forgive me," she said, verbally disarming him. "It's been a formidable night for all of us. I apologize for my rudeness. You've probably been here for hours helping to protect the building, and I should never have been so blunt." She pointed to the sidewalk nearby. "I guess I'm wondering if I may sit . . . to wait for the bomb disposal team to arrive?"

The soldier lowered his arm and eased away. "Well, I suppose you can sit wherever you fancy . . . as long as it's not in the way."

Audrey thanked him again, then ushered herself over to a corner of the sidewalk and sat down.

Tired, so tired.

The guard continued to watch her, but she didn't care. She rubbed at her eyes, certain they were stone. Oh, how she longed for a warm soak and a soft pillow!

"Excuse me, miss," the soldier said, coming close, his tone now tempered. "I was going to pour a cup of tea from my flask, which I know sounds rather savage, but it's all I have—if you'd care for some?" He held the metal flask in the air beside his tin cup.

His offer seemed to have surprised them both, causing a complete loss of words. She managed a thankful nod, waited as he poured the steaming liquid into a cup and then held it toward her. Only after she'd absorbed a bit of its heat in her hands did she speak.

"Thank you. This is lovely, absolutely lovely."

Claire clenched the taxi's back-door handle as if she alone was responsible for keeping it securely attached to the car. Her body was rocking in the leather seat, her eyes squinted and steely. Her cold and darting gaze carried her concentration through the window to pat down every person walking at the edge of the street. She preferred pacing to calm her nerves, but there was too little room in the moving vehicle.

Where on earth could the girl be?

"I don't see her. Let's try again, but go down Mansford Street," she told the driver, an obedient man with a heavy neck, a knobby nose, and an unlit cigar clamped between his teeth. For the past hour they had been circling back from the underground station to the damaged flat, covering a myriad of paths, but so far coming up empty.

And then Claire spotted a familiar bob of wavy blonde hair poking up above a street barrier. "STOP!" she screamed, barely giving the driver proper time to slow down before flinging open the door and bailing from the car, forgetting that her black-and-blue leg wasn't yet ready to support her own weight. She collapsed to the pavement, let out a yelp that some may have mistaken as the cry of a distressed puppy, and then tried to right herself with as much poise as possible.

The taxi had screeched to a stop, the driver already rushing around to help, all creating enough commotion to catch Audrey's attention.

"Aunt Claire?" she exclaimed, and she too hurried over to assist.

Claire brushed the worry aside. "Audrey! Thank goodness I found you. I've been looking everywhere." She was standing now, letting Audrey help her hobble to the sidewalk.

"I've been here since dawn, except when I had to go down the street to the lavatory." Then Audrey's voice quickened. "Claire, I haven't been able to get inside. The Home Guard won't let me in until the disposal team arrives, but they haven't come."

"Do you need me to stay?" the driver asked Claire.

She wagged a hand toward his taxi. "Yes. Please pull up by the curb, and we'll be there shortly."

It was the first time Audrey noticed Claire's clothes. "What are you wearing? Where did you get those?"

"If you wouldn't run off . . . " she chided, reaching toward outrage but finding only relief. "So much has happened."

Audrey's eyes shifted down. "How's your leg?"

"It will be fine. Now listen. I spoke with Cora Holden, and she spoke with Lady Reading. They've made arrangements for us to house in a flat on Columbia. It's one of several they've been preparing for displaced families."

Audrey watched a hesitation crest above Claire's eyes. "What aren't you telling me?" she asked.

"She wants to come and see you. I'm not sure why."

Audrey's eyes clenched. "It's about the list. I knew it—I'm being sacked."

"We don't know that, Audrey." Claire held her hands against her stomach. "She didn't say anything about it, and so it doesn't make sense. I mean, if she was going to sack you, why would she let us stay in the flat?"

As the pair headed toward the waiting taxi, Audrey's fingers couldn't quit fidgeting. "Well, then, what could Cora possibly want with me?"

Claire clutched Audrey's arm, jerked her to a stop. "Heavens, I wasn't clear. Cora Holden is the one who made arrangements, but she's not the one who wants to meet. Audrey, you're meeting with Lady Reading."

As Audrey worked more shampoo into her still dirty hair, attacking the stubborn grit that was clinging for dear life, Claire tapped her knuckles lightly on the door.

"Audrey?" she asked tentatively, as if someone else may have sneaked past and was now bathing covertly behind the door. However, it was the latter half of Claire's question that caused Audrey's eyes to narrow. "May I come in?"

Aunt Claire had never asked Audrey for permission to barge in on her—*ever.*

"Please do," Audrey answered, her timid tone waiting as Claire jiggled the handle, not yet accustomed to the latch that apparently tended to stick.

When the door at last opened, Claire burst in wearing a pasted-on smile. From her nervous glance behind, Audrey could tell that someone else was with Claire . . . and close enough to listen.

"Audrey, dear, if you could hurry, Lady Reading has arrived early. She is here now to see you, and she has only a short window of time."

Lady Reading, born as Stella Charnaud in Constantinople, was the daughter of Charles Charnaud, director of the tobacco monopoly of the Ottoman Empire. She had been educated by private tutors, and in addition to her native English had learned to speak fluent French, German, Italian, and some Greek. Indeed, she had lived a life of privilege that few could fathom—until her father lost all of his money during the Great War.

The demise of her family's fortune, the means that had fueled her burgeoning accomplishments, made for the perfect tragic ending to the young woman's fairy-tale life—but Stella didn't believe in fairy tales. A bout of childhood spinal troubles had confined her to bed for months, and that "lucky" experience had taught her that a meaningful life—one in which you step outside of yourself and make a difference in the world—comes only when you face tribulation head-on with determination and perseverance.

During the war, she joined the British Red Cross Society, and after the war, she found employment in a solicitor's office. In 1925, as a woman of thirty-one, when she was asked to join the staff of Viceroy Rufus Isaacs in Delhi, India, she jumped at the chance. She served first as a secretary to the viceroy's wife, then as chief of staff to the viceroy himself. Soon, she was back in London, helping direct the business affairs of Imperial Chemical Industries, where the viceroy served as president.

Then, in 1931, a year after the viceroy's wife had died, she was asked by Viceroy Rufus Isaacs, First Earl of Reading, a man she'd grown to respect and love through her years of service, to become his wife. Thus Stella Charnaud became Marchioness of Reading—and again, the latest chapter in her life read like a storybook happy ending.

But her joy was short-lived.

Four years later, Rufus Isaacs died, leaving Lady Reading a young widow. She would later admit that the years after his death were a dark time of faltering, of losing her footing, nearly forgetting that, in life, adversity prepares for opportunity. And oddly, war has an uncanny way of pointing humankind back to its purposeful path.

In 1938, with war looming but before formal hostilities had been declared by England, Home Secretary Samuel Hoare asked Lady Reading if she would establish an association of women, a team of female volunteers who would boldly band together to serve during the country's greatest conflict. While generals in the country's army wanted warriors, Hoare trusted that Lady Reading would see the need for a counterbalance of compassion, a society of bold, selfless, determined women who could provide wartime assistance to their fellow countrymen in need.

The invitation was an epiphany to the grief-stricken Lady Reading, as if the flames of her past had been forging the opportunities of her future, and now the whole of her life experience—both triumphs and trials—whispered firmly into her ear: *This is your purpose! You were born for this moment!*

She said yes, of course, the only way she knew how—with a vengeance—and the Women's Voluntary Services, or WVS, was born. Its structure was simple yet effective. England was divided clockwise into twelve regions, London being the last, in which its members would take on innumerable duties, including collecting clothing for the needy, helping the injured, relocating those who'd lost homes, serving food to both soldiers and the destitute, and lately—and currently the most urgent—evacuating children from the cities being bombed to safer locations in the country.

WVS quickly spread outside of England, stretching into Scotland, Wales, and Northern Ireland. Thousands of women were flocking to the group to do their part for country, friends, and family.

As with any organization, there was some administrative overhead, but it was kept to a minimum. Lady Reading wouldn't allow rank among the staff or the volunteers. "It's the only organization," she liked to boast, "where a duchess and a dishwasher can work side by side."

At the end of the day, it was the downtrodden dishwashers of the world, those lugging their hushed hardships and bitter burdens, who concerned Lady Reading the most. She knew from her own experience that wounds to one's spirit slice deep and can't be dressed with pretend joy. But in the WVS, she'd found her answer. She had created a coalition to help others, and thereby discovered—or rather remembered—that service is a salve that can heal all hurt, not just in strangers, but in oneself.

But now, the group's burgeoning size was both a blessing and a strain. It had grown large enough that whenever she attended a meeting in person, the surrounding volunteers would throng around her, making such a spectacle that all work would come to a standstill—and she deemed it all nonsense. Lately, she'd found it more prudent to send Cora Holden, her assistant, to address the groups, letting herself sneak in unnoticed to sit in the back beneath a scarf and well-placed bonnet.

It was while using this tactic that she first noticed Audrey Stocking. Although she had only formally met the fair-haired girl once—a quick grasp of the hands after Lady Reading had spoken to the London Region months earlier—there was something besides the girl's beauty that she found compellingly curious.

The girl was dedicated, even zealous, especially when safely skirting children away from London, an assignment she'd requested with near reverence—unusual, since she had never been a mother. But it was the motive behind the zeal that Lady Reading found perplexing; it was as if Audrey had taken hold of the cause to help steady her own rickety legs and was now terrified to let go and stand on her own.

Lady Reading had also noticed that Audrey spoke with the slightest of accents, imperceptible to most, but not to her trained ear. True, Audrey's English was precise, but an occasional sound would amble out dusted with the slightest German or perhaps even Swiss savor.

She suspected there was more that Audrey wasn't sharing, and while Lady Reading wasn't certain yet what was motivating this girl or what she was hiding, she intended to find out.

Audrey swiftly patted her hair with a towel, brushed it into submission, and then slipped on the donated clothes Claire had laid out for her—a brown tweed skirt with matching jacket worn over a rust-colored blouse that, while stylish, draped a bit large over her narrow shoulders. She commanded her rapid heartbeat to slow, pushed out her chest to fill out the garment better, and then stepped through the door into the flat's entryway where Lady Reading stood.

Hands were extended, held, and gently shaken. Pleasantries were exchanged. Every speck of the woman was genuine: her pin-curled hair, her long-drawn nose, her unpretentious smile. She was wearing a lovely lace top with a navy jacket and a pearl necklace, though each adornment looked privileged to have come along for its own pleasure, and not to enhance the appearance of the wearer.

"It's incredibly considerate of you to come by," Audrey said, dragging fingers through her own wet hair. "I am sorry I'm not better presented. We're getting settled and—"

Lady Reading interrupted with a laugh, the honest kind that begins from deep within one's chest. "Child, you'd look lovely in a mineral mud bath. Nonetheless, I'm having Cora send over some additional clothes and necessities."

"Is Miss Holden with you?" It was a daft thing to ask since it was plain Lady Reading had come alone.

"It's been a hectic day, as you can imagine. Cora is winding down schedules for tomorrow and won't be joining us. Shall we sit?" Lady Reading pointed to a chair. She was never known to dally.

"Goodness, yes," Audrey answered as she and Claire hurried toward opposite seats. An awkward silence then skated into the room as the three women sat circle-staring at one another until, thankfully, Lady Reading stretched out her fingers to shoo it away. "I have a favor to ask of you, Audrey," she said.

Audrey turned, tipped, squinted. There had been no mention of the missing list. Perhaps she wasn't getting sacked after all. "How may I be of assistance?"

Lady Reading bent forward as if to share a secret. "I don't know if you're aware, but I've been watching you, and I sense you're a somber child. I don't know if that's on account of the war or if it's merely your nature, but I will say it suits you. Still, there is a trace of fire in your determined eyes, and, well . . . all this fuss could be that you remind me of myself when I was your age."

Audrey used the moment to take a careful breath.

"But enough nostalgia," Lady Reading added. "While you've been doing a stellar job with the children, there is an additional way you may be of assistance. But first, I have two questions."

"Certainly."

Lady Reading's lips drew tight. "Why are you here in London?

Because I doubt that you are from England originally. And also, why precisely did you join WVS?"

The silence stood as Audrey shot a glance at Claire, who was trying to remain composed though her brows were nearly touching. Her head was methodically bobbing as if to remind the girl they had talked about this already.

Audrey twisted back toward Lady Reading. She picked her words with precision, leaving ample pause around each phrase. "I came to England . . . from Switzerland . . . to study. But when war was declared . . . I wanted to do my part. It seemed the right thing to do."

Claire's nod let her know it was a good answer, and Lady Reading also seemed pleased, until she leaned nearer. "I knew I detected a slight accent, but I couldn't tell from where. I will say, your English is impeccable. I would guess you had private tutors?"

An invisible shrug passed toward Claire. "Yes . . . I did."

"Interesting. So how many languages do you speak?"

Audrey shifted again. "Well . . . I speak . . . um, English, Italian, . . . German, and, well, Swiss German, but I don't count that."

"Yes, child. Indeed, we come from similar backgrounds. Wealthy families, private tutors, only the best things in life with a world of opportunity ahead. But then life around us changed. Am I correct?"

The answer fell timidly at her feet. "Yes, ma'am."

"Look up, Audrey." Lady Reading's gaze was inescapable. "Make life a blessing. But I suppose you already are, since you spend your time helping the children. So let me ask: why did you select WVS as the place to *do your part?*"

These weren't just idle questions. This was an inquisition. What did Lady Reading know? What should Audrey tell her? The truth?

Audrey's hands joined her lips in a tremble. "When Claire and I initially entered London . . . from Switzerland," she repeated, " . . . it was after England had declared war. The first wave of children was being taken from the city and relocated to the country . . . to avoid the enemy invasion . . . which we all knew would shortly come. Well, as we came that day by bus, we passed a group of little ones—possibly a dozen children—and amongst them was a panicked little girl reaching for her mother . . . and both were sobbing. There was a soldier there to help the ARP worker, Air Raid Precautions, and while the good man was only trying to assist . . ." Her voice trailed off, searching for words that wouldn't offend.

"Please go on," Lady Reading prodded.

"Please pardon me for saying so, but that's a job that should never be done by soldiers . . . *ever.* Though I barely caught a glimpse from a distant bus window, I knew instantly I had to help these children. Claire wasn't certain it was a good idea . . . we having scarcely arrived and all . . . but when I saw a poster advertising the need for help, I . . . I had to sign up . . . and in the end, Claire agreed." Audrey let her gaze fall back to Lady Reading. "Does that answer your question?"

It was a long moment before Lady Reading spoke. When she did, her voice was tall and deep. "Thank you for sharing—you're extremely articulate. You're also young, charming . . . and a bit vulnerable. Let me get to the point, Audrey. We have women joining WVS every day, and for that, we are blessed. The majority are housewives—some mothers, many grandmothers—experienced women, many with children of their own. And while that's smashing, to accomplish what will be asked of us, especially now with the bombing of London, I need your help."

"I don't understand."

"Audrey, I am in need of younger women like you. I want the women of your generation to see more than the horror of this war;

I want them to also see the blessings. And so I'd like to ask if you'd be willing to speak to groups of younger women, on occasion, to tell your story, like you've just told me, to inspire them to do what you've done. You could change many lives—even your own. Will you say yes?"

"Inspire others to do what I've done?" Audrey repeated softly. "But what about the bombings, the invasion?"

"Don't give in to fear, child. Have some faith in our future."

Claire clasped her hands, locking her fingers. "That is an exceedingly kind offer, Lady Reading. But as you know, Audrey is very devoted to helping the children get out of London. We wouldn't want anything to take time away from that effort." Claire looked to Audrey for agreement.

"She's right," Audrey added, her eyes observantly lifting.

Lady Reading's head was already shaking. As one would expect, she was a hard woman to turn down. "Your devotion to the children, Audrey, is the reason I will promise to never take you away from your responsibilities at WVS. That is my pledge. In fact, we have two girls who shall need help getting to Somerset tomorrow afternoon. You and Claire can take them if you feel ready."

"Tomorrow?"

"If you're ready. I know you've been through a lot. I will send details over with Cora in the morning, and then you may decide. But won't you please help me convince a thousand, and then ten thousand young women like you to join us? Imagine how many more children we could help if that happened!"

Audrey took a breath, a swallow, then turned toward Claire with every concerned curve in her forlorn face pleading: *What am I supposed to say?*

Her mouth didn't wait for a reply. "Thank you, Lady Reading," she heard herself declare. "I would be honored."

"Please, Audrey, call me Stella."

With her business complete, Lady Reading stood. There was no time to waste, not when one was in the business of helping others. Audrey and Claire walked with her to a sedan that had been idling at the front curb. All agreed it had been a wonderful visit, and with little more said, they all waved their cheery goodbyes.

As the car whisked Lady Reading away, Audrey reached for Claire's fingers. Even before she turned, Audrey's words were begging for mercy. "Claire, I had no choice."

"Did you watch her eyes?" Claire's focus stayed on the car. "She suspects something."

"But what could I have said?"

Claire was clucking her tongue, an unconscious habit when thinking. "It may be a good thing, all points considered. You do love helping the children."

"But what if she finds out about us?"

"Hiding in plain sight has served us well. Is this any different?"

It was odd—Claire was usually the fretful one. But before the thought could be further considered, the shrill of air-raid sirens swept over the city.

Audrey tensed. "Claire, the bombs are starting again!"

"Follow me," Claire directed. "I haven't had a chance to show you, but this building has its own shelter in the cellar. I've been down there, and it's perfect. Come!"

As Audrey quickly trailed Claire back into their building, the distinct rumble of exploding bombs once again assaulted the city of London.

CHAPTER 4

When 37 Section, Bomb Disposal Royal Engineers, and their recovering Hippo limped into London in silence, it was as if they were paying their respects to a dying friend. With good reason: the ruthless reality scattered before them demanded both pity and reverence.

At the city's outskirts, they were relieved to see that the neighborhoods previously alight in the nighttime sky had fared far better than imagined. Yes, there were occasionally burned-out buildings, but there were fewer than expected, with many more structures still standing proud and unharmed.

But then the team rolled through East London.

Near the docks, in the boroughs that nestled along both banks of the Thames—Limehouse, Millwall, Beckton, and Woolwich—it looked to Wes like the devil had come calling.

More than once, Driver was forced to alter course, weaving around impassable streets, circling smoldering rubble, coaxing the chugging vehicle beside disheartened men pushing wheelbarrows full of salvaged belongings.

A fireman spraying water across a pile of charcoaled timbers shared that more than a thousand fires had started, turning the Thames red. They had burned so ferociously at the docks that paint on boats three hundred yards away had blistered and peeled. Even the wooden blocks paved into some of the wharf's older streets had burned.

It was an inferno that had pulverized more than just property: 430 people had died, more than 1,000 had been wounded. A radio program—surely monitored by the Germans—reported that London had suffered only *slight damage,* but anyone living in the East End could view the results firsthand: death, destruction, despair.

The sky was still chalky when the men finally reached the warehouse where they would be billeting. While most of the Bomb Disposal sections in London had been assigned to Chelsea Barracks in Westminster, Colonel Moore's section had been told to report to a building located a bit farther to the northeast.

As they climbed down from the Hippo, they weren't sure if they should feel appreciation or disappointment. On the one hand, the building had been untouched by explosions or fire, meaning they had a place to stay. On the other, it was a space so dusty, dreary, and dank, it needed therapy for depression. By the time everyone in the section had cleaned up, eaten, and stored their gear, the sun was painting the last of its late afternoon shadows across the London sky.

Itching for a way to be productive while casting off the gloomy mood that had fallen over the group, Wes had wandered down to the cellar and was tinkering with their single source of heat: a large, coal-fired furnace. He was hoping he could get it working to battle temperatures that were likely to turn chilly in the coming weeks. He had just repaired the door to the coal chute so it would close correctly when the colonel came down the stairs.

"Are we ready to go?" Wes asked.

"Not yet. The Krauts love their punctuality, which means the bombings will begin again soon."

"And do we always wait until the bombing is over?"

"Since the bombs are buggers to catch, it's the safest approach." He delivered the line in the typical British style, without smiling, but perhaps also feeling the need to lighten the mood. "We'll shelter here until we receive the all clear. I've received notice there's a UXB* in Finsbury Park we need to handle, and another lodged into a flat on Durant."

"Colonel, if you have a moment, there's something I've been wondering about."

"Do tell."

"Most BD sections have a dozen men or more. We've got half that. I can see that you're passionate, and for that I'm grateful, but is your War Office?"

The colonel's jaw stiffened. "Why would you think otherwise?"

"I only ask because of what I see: we're short on coal, and Hastings said this is all we may get for a while. The Hippo is ancient and barely running. Your uniforms are threadbare and falling apart, and the men . . ."

"What about the men?" The colonel stretched tall as his arms folded. Wes had struck a nerve.

"Don't get me wrong. The men are great, but you've got a kid driving who isn't old enough to have a license, another who can't see out of one eye, and even you admitted they hauled you out of retirement to run the section. It seems that bomb disposal here is

---

* Unexploded ordnance

the neglected child with a short arm at the dinner table. That's all I'm saying."

Wes watched as the colonel drew in a new breath of the mushy air, let it settle into his lungs. "I guess there's some truth to what you say," he admitted. "If Driver was older, and Gunner had sight in both eyes, and if I hadn't called in favors to keep Hastings with me—which he doesn't know, so not a word—then all of these men would be fighting the enemy in person elsewhere. Which is where they would prefer to be, and it's where the War Office would send them."

The man wet his lips before continuing. "Instead, they're stuck at home with me, doing a job that comes with less respect but more danger, and so I suppose you can pity them there. But that doesn't make the duty any less important or the men less capable. Frankly, the soldiers on the front lines probably stand a better chance of making it through the war alive. Either place, the boys are saving lives and defending freedom, which sounds pretty noble to my ears."

In the dim light, the colonel's features looked dogged. "I apologize, sir," Wes said. "I didn't mean to imply otherwise."

"And you should know, we're not completely alone out here."

"What do you mean?"

"Well, on its face, the war pits Bomb Disposal sections, with little more than basic tools and the desire to serve our country, against the best scientists Germany has to offer, all designing ingenious ways to ensure that we die."

"I can't say I like those odds."

"Except we have the boffins."

"The boffins?" Wes asked, with a chuckle. "It's not fair that you Brits kept all the good words."

The colonel, not yet ready to smile, enlisted his hands to help explain. "The boffins are scientists, engineers, the technical lads who take the information and hardware we send them and tear it apart, analyze it, and experiment with it, looking for creative ways to defeat the German bombs. So while Hitler has rooms full of engineers scheming ways to make their bombs harder to disarm, inventing fuzes to kill the men who try, we have our own rooms of engineers doing their cracking best to outsmart the Germans. Yes, it means that we are stuck in the middle, and that can be a frustrating place to be, but I sense these boys will rise to the challenge."

"Again, I'm sorry if I appeared harsh," Wes repeated. "I'm just grappling poorly with rejection."

"Rejection?"

"Badger is pissed at me . . . and a couple of the other men seem tentative."

Wes watched the lines stretching across the colonel's cheeks turn upward. "You need to know that in England, 'pissed' means drunk. I believe you mean, why is the chap so miffed that you're here?"

Wes kicked back the smile. "Yeah, why the anger? What did I do to him?"

The colonel's mustache curled tighter. "Keep in mind that Badger hates most Yanks . . . and all Canadians."

"Is that my fault?" Wes asked.

"Not directly. But you've rightly described the deficiencies in our uniforms, so look at your own and tell me what you see."

"I don't follow."

The colonel rested a hand on Wes's shoulder so his fingers could squeeze in rhythm. "I'll spell it out for you. The stitching on your jacket is sturdy, the buttons perfectly placed. The fit is brilliant, almost Italian tailored. Your boots likewise. Of course, they could use a good spiffing up, but they fit well and show little wear. Every piece of equipment in your kit—waterproof combat pack, bayonet, canteen, entrenching tool, first-aid pouch, cartridge belt, and clips of ammunition—it's all posh, all perfect, all issued courtesy of your US government."

Wes's chin began to nod before his words were fully formed. "You're saying he's jealous?"

The colonel swatted the look away, and then his voice strengthened. "I'm saying he's scared. And it's not just Badger. All of us are here with our old, battle-worn gear, standing up to a madman in Germany and his colossal army, while you Yanks in your perfect, pretty uniforms watch from the corner . . . and we're getting weary of going it alone. No offense."

"None taken."

"Tell me—since you've been in the Marine Corps, have you ever failed to collect your wages?"

"No, sir. I haven't."

"These boys have—and they get a servant's pittance compared to what you earn. But they're still here, still on duty."

Wes's shoulders had slumped. If he'd had a white flag, he would have waved it. "Sir, I'm told that FDR wants to help, but he has to get reelected, and people in the States don't want another war."

The colonel had reloaded. "Nobody *wants* another war! But in life, there are times when the war comes to you, when hard decisions need to be made, when you act because it's the right thing to do."

Wes surrendered with words. "I don't disagree. The funny thing is, you sound like my father."

The colonel waited, wielding the silence like a stick. But when he finally spoke, he was no longer swinging. "There's something more you need to hear."

"Okay."

"Last night, when we stopped outside the city and could see London burning, I know that you saw me in the dark sniveling like a bullied schoolboy. I should tell you that I lost my wife of forty-four years, Margaret, a stitch under two years ago."

"My deepest sympathies, sir." It was a whispered condolence that felt small coming out of his large frame.

The colonel continued unfazed. He had things to say. "She was from London, and so we'd spent a lot of time here. Last night, standing in the dark alone, watching this city burn . . . it was a little too much."

"Sir, there's no need for apologies."

"No, but there's a reason to share. It's the lesson I want you to learn. The men won't start trusting you until you start trusting them the same way." His counsel filled the room, almost breathed on its own.

"Thank you," Wes answered. "That's good advice. I'll try . . . and Colonel?"

"What?"

"Your wife, Margaret . . . how did you know that she was the one? I ask because I have a girl back home that I'm writing to, and . . . I have doubts."

The room brightened as new light twinkled in the colonel's eyes. "Margaret and I first met in London at the wedding of a friend, and I didn't know right away either. I'm slow like that. But over time, I realized that aside from her beauty—and I won't complain about it—she would make me a better man. But most of all . . ."

"Yes?"

The colonel pushed off from the old iron boiler where he'd been leaning. "That woman could make a meaty mutton cobbler that would make a witch weep." He finished with his best English grin.

Wes straightened and offered a quick salute. "It will be an honor serving with you and your men. Even if Driver is only fourteen." But then Wes's expression turned solemn. "Sir, to answer your question, I can't tell you why the United States hasn't yet joined the war, but I suspect they'll come around."

The colonel blinked and then pointed a finger. "You asked why our section has half the number of men?"

"I did."

"It was my choice, not the War Office's. I told them I wanted a smaller section to be more nimble, easier to deploy." The man hesitated, as men will do when their words aren't entirely true. "It may also be that I've seen more war than my tired eyes will care to admit, and this old ticker knows it won't be able to handle that much loss if something happens to so many good soldiers. I'll let you choose which to believe."

The colonel stepped forward. "There's one more thing about Badger you ought to know. About a month back, his girl left him for a Canadian soldier, and he's still acting a bit barmy from that." The man's voice quieted. "I asked him more about it, and he said the girl had never been past the outskirts of her village, Chiddingfold, until she recently visited London. She met the Canadian soldier in a pub with her friends and was so taken with the chap's fancy accent and dashing uniform that she hasn't spoken to Badger since. So, I hope you see why he's a tad bent up."

Wes opened his mouth, but his thoughts sputtered, allowing the colonel the opportunity to slide in beside him. "This has been a productive chat, but it's not why I came down to see you."

"Why, then?"

"Typically, there would be an attempt at classroom training before we throw a soldier into the field to do actual bomb disposal work, but it seems the bloody war is going to muck that option up. So, I'd like to start your training here with a little test, shall we?"

"We shall."

"Good, then." The colonel roosted on a nearby stool. He spoke up to Wes. "What is a bomb's main purpose?"

Wes squinted in the low light. The colonel had started with an easy question for the beginner. Fair enough. "To explode . . . to cause damage . . . to kill people."

"Seems logical . . . but wrong," the colonel answered, conveying the confidence of a seasoned professor. "In war, a bomb's primary purpose is to *disrupt.* A bomb that doesn't explode right away—or even one that does—triggers fear and panic and does far more harm to the population psychologically than the physical explosion. This means that our job in this war is to take away that fear, to neutralize it."

"That's fair."

"Bombs are relatively simple devices. They consist of a steel shell filled with an explosive compound surrounding one or more fuzes. So here's your second question: What's the primary purpose of the bomb's fuze?"

Wes shuffled his feet. This query also sounded easy—too easy. "The obvious answer, the one I'll choose, is to set off the explosive compound in the bomb *when planned,* be that on impact or later, letting the bomb cause the greatest disruption." His chin lifted. Had he covered all of his bases?

The colonel stood from the stool, perhaps to add more force to his reply. "What you've described—to set off the bomb when planned—is the fuze's secondary purpose. More important is to keep the bomb from exploding when unplanned. The Germans demonstrate this truth by stamping a number on the outside of every fuze head that tells them—and us—what type of fuze the bomb carries, at least for the main fuze. Why do that? Why make it easier for us?"

Wes presumed the question was rhetorical. His ceding stare signaled for the colonel to continue, his eyes now luminous.

"Imagine the chaos, Bowers, if a German bomber that couldn't deliver its payload due to cloud cover or mechanical problems returned with armed bombs. Their personnel wouldn't have a clue how to deal with them. They'd end up destroying their own planes, killing their own people."

Wes sat humble, silent, listening. Nothing was slowing the colonel down.

"Keep in mind that even though the enemy tells us what fuzes he's used, it doesn't make our job any easier. Which leads me to today's final question. It comes from the Royal Engineers exam administered for Bomb Disposal Units. Of all the questions on that exam, this one has given me the most to contemplate."

Wes crouched slightly, like a catcher waiting for the pitch. "I'm ready."

But the colonel had stepped off the mound and was waving Wes over to a friendlier huddle. "I don't expect an answer tonight. I just want you to reflect on it like I've had to do. The exam stated that each member joining the unit should be of excellent character and be *prepared for the afterlife.* So, Lieutenant Bowers, I ask you: as you take on this assignment to work side by side with the men upstairs—virtual strangers, in a country that isn't your own—are you prepared for the afterlife? Are you prepared to die?"

It was a question too big for the tiny room, pressing promptly against Wes's chest. The colonel understood and stepped toward the stairs to make space, leaving Wes alone to stew in his thoughts. Naturally, Wes didn't want to die, he wanted to live, but that wasn't what the colonel had asked. Wes mouthed the words to make them his own, his uncertain voice winching just above a whisper.

"Am I prepared for the afterlife? Am I prepared to *die*?"

Finsbury Park, in the borough of Haringey, was one of London's first grand Victorian-era parks, offering a splendid mix of formal gardens, mature trees, an arboretum—and one unexploded German bomb.

Four men holding flashlights—Colonel Moore, Hastings, Gunner, and Bowers—hovered over a dark, circular hole pounded through the silty soil. Gunner was on his knees, shining his light into the curved shaft, looking like a one-eyed doctor checking a sore throat.

"Hole swings east," he announced, motioning Badger toward a clump of shrubbery as if it was hiding something.

Badger was already there scouting, stooping beside an elongated bulge in the dirt that had furrowed up from below. "Colonel! I think I found it."

He was standing a good twenty-five feet away, which made no sense. "They go sideways?" Wes asked.

The colonel turned. "Normally, no—but on occasion."

Hastings filled Wes in on the physics. "They hit the ground, mate, at hundreds of miles per hour, so depending on speed, entry angle, soil layers, and density, even how the tail fin sheers off, they can veer in odd directions. We've seen them go as deep as thirty feet or, on occasion, travel horizontally, like this one. They can even resurface."

"Let's all move back," the colonel said. "Badger and Pike, you know what to do."

While retreating to the Hippo, the colonel detailed their division of responsibilities. "The sappers will dig it up, uncovering the fuze pocket on the side of the bomb, and then either Hastings or I will go in and defuse it. We want as few men as possible exposed at any one time."

"I don't mind hard work. I'm willing to dig," Wes offered.

Though they had been walking away from the hole, they were still within earshot of Badger. His reply flashed like lightning. "No, thanks! Last thing we want is a dodgy Yank striking the bomb."

The colonel seemed to agree. "Don't worry, Bowers, there will be plenty of other opportunities. For now, help us fill some sandbags. We build a barrier to absorb the explosion should she blow prematurely."

Two hours later, Badger and Pike, sweaty and smudge-faced, returned to the Hippo.

"Looks to be a (15), sir." Badger said.

"That's what I'd have guessed," the colonel replied. "I'll do this one."

"Sir, can I come? I'm here to learn," Wes reminded.

"You won't want to watch this one."

Wes reached out his arms, his tone aiding in the protest. "Look, I know it's my first day, but give me a chance to help, to do something—anything!"

The colonel rocked forward. His lips carried a coy smile. "It's only a 50-kilogram bomb. We're in a park, there are no buildings, no people, no critical infrastructure around. What I'm trying to explain is that I'm not going in to defuse the bomb. I'm going in to attach some guncotton and blow it up. If you want to be standing beside it when it explodes, so that you can take notes, that's your business. The rest of us will be hunched down behind the sandbags."

The colonel didn't wait for Wes to respond since he assumed there was just one logical answer. When he came running back a few minutes later, everyone else—including Wes—was behind cover.

As the colonel knelt down, he offered Wes one last suggestion. "You may want to cover your ears."

CHAPTER 5

"Audrey, we'll have to try on our way home. Right now there just isn't time!" Claire remarked, clucking her tongue. "We'll be late to meet the children!" Busy mother hen chiding her chick.

Audrey winced. She hated it when Aunt Claire treated her like a child. The woman wasn't her mother, so she should quit pretending. Besides, the two no longer seemed that far apart in age. Couldn't they agree to just be friends? Audrey turned calmly, took in a long breath of patience. "Auntie, the flat is on the way. The driver will only need to stop for a moment. If there's not time, I understand, but let's at least try."

Besides, the trip today was an easy one. They were picking up four children—three boys and a girl—in White Castle and returning them to Marden Ash, an urban settlement in the Epping Forest District of Essex. The children had lived there once with the butcher's family, staying for a three-month stint after war was declared the year before. Operation Pied Piper, carried out at the time by the British government, had moved thousands of children to safer ground. For many of the city's mothers who had placed their little ones far away, anxious days turned into lonesome weeks, lonesome weeks became unbearable months, and with no invasion imminent, families began sending for their children to come home—and they came back in droves.

All was well until the bombing started. According to Cora Holden, their London office was being inundated with requests, and they were doing their best to prioritize the children. She hadn't mentioned Audrey's list, but it was plain that it was still needed, that it would help. So what could it hurt to stop and see if the disposal team had disabled the bomb in their flat?

As they neared, two military trucks were parked outside. Not only was the building cordoned off, but the barricaded area had been extended to include the front and side streets.

"They're here, Claire!" she declared, barely suppressing an *I-told-you-so* tone. Audrey tapped the driver on his shoulder. "Sir, please pull up over there. I will be right back."

The colonel's nails scratched at his mustache like cat claws on a couch. The wretched bomb that was wedged into the floor of the Durant Street flat right behind him was a dodgy one. As commander, he'd gone in first to assess the situation and then asked Hastings in to take a second hurried look, but the bomb's position had Hastings stumped as well.

Now the section's three commissioned officers—Moore, Hastings, and Bowers—were standing in a circle just inside the roped safety zone, talking it through.

"The way that beast was jammed into the floorboards, I couldn't see the fuze pocket," the colonel said. "My guess is that it's an impact fuze that armed late after it was dropped too low."

"Do we take a chance moving it? Remember the rumors," Hastings added.

"What rumors?" Wes wondered aloud.

The colonel tugged at his cap as if it would reverse his frown. "We believe the Germans have developed a timed fuze. But the only way to know for sure what kind of fuze is in this bomb is to get to the fuze head."

Hastings used the pause. "It was packed pretty securely against the floor. We'll have to be careful if we cut it away. It's risky."

The colonel's eyes clenched. "It's sticking almost straight up, and the roof beam above it looked solid. What if we roped it and tried to gently lift it, just enough to see what we're dealing with? We could feed a line in through the side window."

Hastings eyes had also started to glow. "There was that big piece of wall dangling above it. We'd need to wrench that back first—but it's doable."

The two men were lobbing eyebrow shrugs back and forth so quickly it was like watching match play at Wimbledon. "Let's take another quick look. Bowers, we'll be right back." It was the last volley before the two turned their backs on Wes and headed inside. He'd been snubbed enough that morning to know better than to beg a place in the game.

"Excuse me, sir. I'm wondering if you can help," a silvery voice behind Wes asked.

Wes turned to see a young woman calling to him from across the barrier. She was wearing an olive-green uniform that, while official, didn't look military, with a white armband tied around the right sleeve. She was waving her hand to get his attention, but timidly.

Wes stepped toward the girl with the honey-blonde hair and quiet eyes—blue but subdued with a stir of gray. "How may I help, miss?"

"You're an American," she replied, her muddled pitch rising.

"So it seems." He didn't mean to sound snide.

"Are you with the bomb disposal team?"

"Though it appears otherwise, I am . . . or will be, as soon as they decide to include me."

She stepped under the barrier and then lowered her voice as she described the bomb in her flat, how she'd stood beside it on the night it fell, and how in the confusion she had forgotten a list of children who needed to be evacuated from London. And then, in the most softhearted and proper English accent that Wes had heard since arriving in England, she asked him if he would be so kind as to let her inside to get it.

"Right now?" Wes wondered. "I think we should disarm the thing first."

She swayed forward as if to help her struggling words skate out. "It's just . . ."

Recognition danced in Wes's eyes. "You're afraid we may blow it up, aren't you?"

"No, of course not." This woman was a terrible liar. "Though I guess that would be quite dreadful."

"Listen," Wes replied, as amusement battled pity, "I'll check with the colonel when he comes out. Your flat is on the ground floor, right?"

"Yes, it's the one with the menacing gray bomb ticking inside. It has red markings on the tail." Her lips half turned, no doubt aiming for a splash of sarcasm, but something she'd said spun Wes around.

"Did you say it was ticking?"

She shuffled back a step. "Well, I don't know for certain."

It was enough. "Stay here. I'll be right back." And with that, Wes sprinted past the roped-off section of the street to enter the building. He stepped around the rubble, then followed the voices to find the colonel and Hastings coming out through the door.

"Bowers, what are you doing?"

"Sir, I know you wanted me to stay back, but the young woman who lives here says she thinks she heard the bomb ticking. I thought you should know."

"I put my ear against it and didn't hear anything," Hastings said. "I didn't have a stethoscope, so I can't be sure."

The colonel hesitated, weighing his next move. "We're going beneath to have a quick look to see if we can see the fuze head. Follow us, but with caution."

While sunlight was seeping into the ground floor with reckless abandon, making itself at home to brighten up the place, the lonely basement wasn't as lucky. The men reached for their flashlights, pointing them forward to cut through the inky air as they descended the stairs.

"What a mess," Wes whispered, stepping over the debris. "It looks like a bomb went off in here."

Only Hastings grinned. As they neared the spot where the bomb's nose cone poked through the ceiling, the colonel focused his light.

"The floorboards were tight against the bomb on top, right?" The angst in his voice announced that he didn't care for what he was seeing.

"Not tight enough," Hastings confirmed, also spotting the gaps on the far side. "We need to get out of here."

"One second . . ." The colonel was squinting again at the bomb as if doing so would improve his aged vision. "The fuze head is concealed by the floor. Regardless, we've got to get a line hooked to it. If this building were to shake, that bomb could come down."

Hastings repeated the plan they'd been apparently discussing before Wes had barged in. "I'll get both ropes from the Hippo and tie them together so we can reach from the far side of the street. We'll feed an end to Gunner through the flat's window, and he and Badger can take it over the beam and then clear out before one of us secures it to the stabilizing bar on the fins. And then . . ."

"Let me help," Wes said, his voice saluting.

The colonel and Hastings turned in unison as if the pair had been practicing. Wes didn't give them time to say no. "Look, it's against your better judgment and mine because we are talking about roping a bomb, but I want to do more than just watch from the sidelines."

Hastings glanced from Wes to the colonel. He spoke as if Wes had wandered away and couldn't hear his every word. "The kid's awfully naïve, but he's got spirit."

The colonel used the moment to meet Wes's stare. "Were you a Boy Scout?"

"Yes, sir."

"Can you tie a solid knot?"

"Absolutely."

More silence, until it nudged the man in charge to speak. "Let's get out of here, then, and get this one finished."

Wes turned. "Does that mean I can help?"

"Bob's your uncle," the colonel answered, using what was clearly a British phrase, but the way he'd smirked when he said it let Wes know that he had agreed.

Wes was halfway to the Hippo when he remembered that he'd

forgotten to find the list for the pretty blonde woman. He checked the barrier where she'd been standing—not there. He gazed up and down the street—no one. The young woman in the green uniform with the white armband was nowhere to be found.

For the next forty-five minutes, the team prepared and strung the rope, moved back the outside barrier, built a wall of protective sandbags, and positioned the Hippo so the rope could easily be attached.

"Are we ready?" Wes asked, hoping to sound confident, but his voice cracked like cheap crystal. He had wanted to be included and had convinced himself that he wasn't nervous. If that was true, why was he sweating like a cat at the dog pound?

The colonel cast a sympathetic smile. "It's different when you know you'll be standing right beside it, touching it, dancing with it." While his thoughts spilled out in bunches, they were tinged with encouragement. "Your pulse will beat like a kettledrum, your lungs will swear you're sucking air through a straw, and your muscles will snug into what feels like a single knot. But don't worry . . . after a while, it gets considerably easier."

Wes winced. "Is this your idea of a pep talk?"

"Better that, mate, than a farewell."

Wes had felt this way when playing college football—parched tongue, thumping heart, sweating hands. It was a quarterfinal game, the stadium was full of fans, his team was down, and the clock showed less than a minute left to play. In the huddle, his number was called, meaning it was time to perform or lose the game. Except today, in England, with a live bomb, there would be profoundly different consequences.

"Go, team! On three!" Wes mumbled.

The colonel's eyes puckered. "What does that mean?"

Wes spat his next words to the ground like bad tobacco. "It means it's game time. Let's get this done."

While the colonel quickly strung in the rope that Gunner was feeding through the window, Wes tied back the hanging plaster and secured it to the wall to ensure the bomb's fins wouldn't smack into it when the explosive was raised from the floor. Next, he snatched the mattress off the bed to lay over the beam to ease the rope's friction.

"Before we start, I want the other men to move back," the colonel instructed. "We want as few men as possible near the bomb. No sense being foolish."

"Then you should go before I tie it on," Wes insisted.

"No, I'm telling you that—"

"Colonel, I can handle it. It's one rope and one bomb. I can do it. Like you said, no sense both of us being in danger."

The colonel drew a long breath, communicating mostly with his eyes. "Bowers, I'm willing to make you part of this team, but I'm in charge of the section, and I bloody well don't intend on letting you make a hash of this alone. It's your first live bomb, so if you don't mind, I'll be here to make sure you do it right."

With the colonel watching, Wes scanned the room a final time before picking up the rope to approach the beast. Ten weeks was how long his CO's report had said men with this assignment lived. Would he bring down the average on his first real day, with the colonel watching? He wanted to be brave, but his hands were clammy, his mouth was dry, and trickles of sweat were rivering down his back.

Couldn't the colonel just leave and let him perspire in peace? While the man didn't offer that luxury, his directives were quick and succinct. "Drag the rope around the far fin, cinch up the slack, and then tie your knot."

Wes followed his commands, then listened as the colonel continued. "The fin section is usually knocked free on impact. It's unusual to see one mostly intact, but the rivets look good. It will hold."

"Should I tie the loose end to the fin as well, just in case?" Wes could see it would mean he'd have to nearly hug the thing.

A smile flashed. "I like how you think. Do it, but carefully."

Once the rope was adequately fastened and Wes was certain that his old scoutmaster would be proud, he motioned toward the door. "Our work here is done."

Making one final glance around before leaving, Wes noticed a binder lying on the floor by the table. He picked it up and thumbed its pages.

"What's that?" the colonel asked.

"The woman who lives here asked if I could find it and bring it out to her." Wes handed it to the colonel. "Take this. I want to tighten up some of the slack where the rope drapes out the window and then take a last look around. I'll be right there."

The colonel's hand tapped Wes lightly on the back, his message clear. Nobody could argue that the American wasn't diligent. He took the binder from Wes and then stepped through the flat's door, careful not to let it slam.

Once alone, Wes pulled the looseness in the rope taut and threaded it out the window opening. He considered giving it a quick tug to make sure it was secure but then decided a visual inspection would suffice. There was just one more thing he had to do.

When Wes reached the Hippo, the end of the rope had already been fastened to the back of the vehicle.

"We're ready," the colonel called out, signaling Wes to rest his fingers on the rope as it stiffened. "You'll be able to feel when the bomb moves." And then he called to Driver to have him inch the Hippo forward.

"Raise it up about a yard. . . . That's good. A little more. . . . Perfect, now ease it . . ."

As Wes watched the colonel's mouth, the next sound seemed to both gain speed and mushroom until it hit Wes in the chest and then rippled through him with such ferocity that it threw him backward and knocked him heaving to the ground.

There was white light, vicious heat, and percussive pain from a bone-shivering blast that blew out building windows, fractured walls, and crumbled brick. A peculiar silence then followed until a furious rain of pebbled fragments spattered the ground. Just as quickly, what remained of the dying four-story structure toppled inward, quaking as it imploded into a smoking mountain of stone, sticks, and memories that would never be put back together again.

Wes rolled sluggishly over and stood, his skin waxy pale. Panting heavily, he checked for blood and broken bones but found neither. The colonel was picking himself up also, looking right at Wes, miming through his mustache to ask if Wes was hurt. At least that was the question the man's fuzzy lips appeared to be forming.

In Wes's ears, all he heard were the garbled echoes of a heated, hollow ringing.

CHAPTER 6

Cora Holden had sent word that two under-fives—twin girls Berta and Merrilee—in Bermondsey needed to be accompanied to a makeshift nursery at St George's University in southwest London and then taken by car to Glastonbury. It would be a good half day's journey towing the little ones, so arrangements were made for Audrey and Claire to stay the night with the girls' host family, bid goodbye to the tiny evacuees in the morning, and then be back in the city by high tea.

"Are we at the right place?" Claire asked as they approached the flat, and Audrey checked her paperwork.

Although the neighborhood was a tad slummy, the outside of the place was orderly and well kept. Audrey pressed the buzzer.

There was a clatter of movement, and then a child's voice wiggled out through the wood as a disheveled mother squeaked open the door. "I'm sorry," she said. "I've been unwell. I thought you were coming at three."

She invited them in and then guardedly gathered her girls'

things. Eager to hurry the mother along, Claire and Audrey helped dress the shy young ones: two paper-doll-looking sprouts, not quite five, who were charming in their bare little knickers and camisoles but were beyond cherished once they'd slipped into their floral frocks with matching olive buttons and Peter Pan collars.

The tots had the long, rustling hair of girls twice their age, and when the mother interrupted her packing to insist on giving their curls a quick brushing, Audrey could see she was battling back tears. The mother may not have been feeling well, but it had little to do with outside sickness.

After buttoning up their suitcases and collecting their gas masks, Audrey pinned an ID tag to each girl's collar, as if she were tagging luggage—name, address, date of birth, and school attended—a requirement by the government to ensure that any lost children were swiftly reunited. Once their bags were also suitably marked, the little moppets gave their mum a final kiss, surely not understanding what was happening. With nary a peep, they walked away with no fear or fuss whatsoever, as if friends had shown up to take them on a ramble to the park.

"I will guard them with my life," Audrey proclaimed to the sniffling woman as she closed the door. Then Berta promptly took ahold of Audrey's right hand, while Merrilee clung to her left, leaving Claire no choice but to fall in behind with their belongings.

"Don't forget, I have a bad leg," Claire reminded, quieting her voice to not raise alarm with the children. "And I don't like that we're leaving this late."

When Audrey spoke, her words were directed toward the horizon. "The sun is still up. We're on our way. We'll be all right."

Twenty minutes later, it was clear that they wouldn't.

Their plan had been to catch the bus on Albany Road, but they found the stop closed and the route diverted due to street damage from the previous evening's raid. Instead, they crossed and headed toward Kennington Park, hoping to find a bus there—until the unnerving shrill of the air-raid sirens drove them against the nearest building.

It was early for the bombing to start, though perhaps someone had forgotten to post notice to the Germans. The neighborhood was less desirable, so none of the buildings on either side of the street would offer much protection. Worse, before there were even bombers overhead, the pummeling *boom-boom-boom* of antiaircraft guns began to shake the ground as they pounded at the sky from a mobile battery temporarily stationed nearby in a hidden corner of the park.

Berta and Merrilee didn't cry—leastwise, not yet—but the fright on their little faces communicated all that Audrey needed to know. They were terrified.

Audrey drew them close. *What to do?* There was no place to shelter, and the direction they needed to run was directly toward the deafening throb of antiaircraft fire.

Berta tugged on Audrey's arm. "I need my mum," she whispered.

"Don't fret, darling. We'll figure this out." Audrey looked to Claire, raising her voice to be heard. "Let's keep going. We can move past them."

Claire had let go of the suitcases. Her fingers had curled into fists. "It will be too loud. We should . . ."

Then, before she could lay out her plan, with no sound of enemy bombs ever dropping, the guns fell silent, followed by the sirens.

"It's a false alarm, girls," Audrey assured. "There's no danger. We should keep moving."

As they crossed the park, a ring of army vehicles circled around the knoll, protecting the antiaircraft battery. Claire was dragging disgust along with the girls' luggage. "It's not right. We're trying to help the children—and this isn't the first time. You must insist that Cora Holden or Lady Reading talk to their contacts in the army. They must warn us where they plan to station their guns, for the sake of the little ones."

It was nearly midnight when Claire, Audrey, and the children reached the farm in Glastonbury, an apple orchard as quaint as it was quiet. The family who had agreed to board the girls was good-natured at their late arrival and instantly enamored with the children, even with them being lugged in sound asleep.

The twins were put to bed in a room with the couple's eight-year-old daughter, Tillie, while Claire and Audrey were shown to lodging upstairs, a tranquil room with an eastward window, not pasted over with black-painted cardboard like all of the windows in London. The place was idyllic, meaning the most menacing sound to disturb Claire and Audrey in the middle of the night would be an overzealous rooster. There would be no screaming sirens, no shattering artillery shells, no foreboding hum of buzzing bombers.

Out in the country, Audrey should have slept peacefully, and would have if her chest hadn't begun to constrict, her throat hadn't decided to parch, and sweat hadn't started to sheen across her hairline. She clamped her eyes shut, forcing slow, steady breaths, not wanting to disturb Claire, praying that sheer stubbornness would drive her emotional enemies away—and, to a degree, it worked.

Deep breath in. Deep breath out. Deep breath in. Deep breath out.

She let her rhythmic breathing carry her past the panic and

into the waiting arms of her repeating night dream. The setting was often the same: climbing the face of her familiar steep mountain, her father standing on top. Yet, it was puzzling—no matter how desperately she pulled herself up, no matter how fast she scrambled, she could never reach him. A rustle of noise behind would startle her, but before she could turn around, a smothering hand would grasp her mouth, pinch her nose, obscure her sight as it brutally strangled the last of her lingering breath. And every time, at the very moment she was about to die, she would jerk awake, frantic, tossing, panting.

"Audrey! Wake up!" It was Claire quieting the cries, rocking her side to side, reassuring her that everything was fine, that she was only having one of her nightmares.

"I'm all right," Audrey gasped. "I'm awake." And, based on past history, she would be until morning. "I'm so sorry I disturbed you. Go back to sleep."

As Claire turned over and drew the covers close, Audrey also yielded to the warmth of the bed's quilt, except her eyes remained wide. It was all so perplexing.

Was this nightmare a premonition? Was fate offering a glimpse of her future to allow her a proper escape?

As she pondered the scenes that had played out in her head while she listened to Claire fall back into slumber's steady arms, an intriguing insight washed over Audrey, causing her to sit up.

There was something different about this most recent dream, a scene that had changed. While she had started scaling her usual mountain, it had transformed near the end from a craggy cliff into a teetering stack of large wooden crates.

What did it mean?

It was hard to say, but she would get Claire's thoughts on it first thing in the morning.

Colonel Moore had been parked at the table staring down at the same stain on the warehouse floor for so long that Wes set aside his book, sat in the adjacent seat, and jostled the man's shoulder. "Do I need to check for a pulse?" he asked, coaxing up the man's eyes.

"I should ask you the same. How are your ears? Still ringing?"

"I'd call it more of a faint hum, but they're getting better."

The colonel didn't wait to voice his pestering concern. "I can't quit thinking about the bomb in the flat. Why did it detonate?"

"Sir?" Wes asked, packing his words with confusion. "It's a bomb. We moved it. Did you expect a different outcome?"

"Make room," the colonel said, edging his own chair closer. "Let's continue our lesson."

Wes scooted, straightened, watched.

"I assumed the bomb had an impact fuze that was either a dud or it armed late. Gently lifting the bomb like we did shouldn't have set it off. But . . ."

"But what?"

"What if it did have a timed fuze? What if the rumors that the Germans have them are true, and they have put them into greater production?"

Wes's palms turned. "Look, it blew up. I don't see how we'll ever know."

The colonel's fists smacked against the table. "No! My job is to defuse bombs while protecting my men. I can't do either if I don't know what I'm dealing with here."

He stood—and for a man who'd been sitting for so long, he seemed winded. He surveyed his section: Driver and Pike were having a smoke outside against the Hippo. Gunner was snoring coldly in his cot. The remaining two—Hastings and Badger—were camped on the opposite warehouse wall near the window playing cards and arguing, though it took work to tell the difference.

The confusion filling the colonel's eyes squinted into determination as he gathered up his notes that were sitting nearby.

"I'll be back in a few hours," he said. "There's someone I need to see."

The man sitting across from Colonel Moore in Chancy Park was Dr. Herbert J. Gough, Director-General of Scientific Research. He had been heading to a meeting at Whitehall, but he always found a way to make time for his friend. He was a good ten years younger than the colonel, more energetic as he leaned his boyish face close. "Russell, we've got a problem," Gough confided, speaking low as if protecting their words from listening strangers.

Colonel Moore had yet to lay out his theories over the exploded bomb and the possible causes. "What is it?" he asked instead.

"We'll be distributing the specifics soon, but I'll give you the gist."

Colonel Moore had first met Herbert Gough in an untimely yet fortunate circumstance during the Great War. Moore, then a major, was to lead a group of men against the Germans at the Somme Offensive in northern France. Tanks were to be used in battle for the first time, but the new war machines were beset with difficulties. In Moore's opinion, they'd been rushed into combat too early by upper command, well before their design had been sufficiently refined. As such, an unacceptable number had broken down. Voicing his opinion to those of higher rank had landed him the assignment to assess their condition in person and report back—but while in transit, his motorcycle also broke down along the road.

Gough, a captain, was in turn commanding a signal battalion in charge of communications and happened along at the opportune time. Being mechanically inclined by both nature and nurture—having joined the Royal Engineers at the outbreak of the war after coming from the engineering department of the National Physical Laboratory—he promptly diagnosed and repaired Moore's motorcycle using only rudimentary tools.

Moore was so impressed he conscripted the reluctant Gough to assist him in evaluating the faulty tanks, a decision that probably saved both their lives.

The pair were well behind the front line when the battle began, an attack near Albert–Bapaume Road that proved a total failure for the British Army, causing 57,470 casualties and 19,240 deaths, the greatest number of men killed in action in a single day by any army on either side.

After the war, Moore stayed in the military and continued to rise in rank, while Gough returned to his work at the National Physical Laboratory. He became a specialist in metal fatigue and then, in 1938, was appointed Director-General of Scientific Research at the Ministry of Supply.

They'd kept in touch over the years, their friendship cemented in the fact that each had pushed above his middle-class English upbringing through hard work and self-reliance. It was a bond that had proven especially provident for the colonel when the government decided that an Unexploded Bomb Committee (UXBC) was needed to supervise the defusing effort.

Dr. Gough and three associates from the Royal Engineers had dealt in person with the first two unexploded bombs dropped on England in November of 1939, and so he was tasked with championing the cause.

As a lifelong scientist, Gough amassed colleagues of similar persuasion, a group of men fiercely fighting the Germans by donning lab coats instead of uniforms and shouldering ingenuity in place of firearms. Those who knew of the group's existence—which included the colonel—often called them by their sometimes dubious but equally enviable moniker: the Backroom Boys.

"The rumors you've been hearing are true," Gough confirmed. "The Germans have developed a clocked fuze. It's clearly the work of Rühlemann, their leading fuze designer, and it's his most impressive yet."

Colonel Moore was already head shaking. "You sound like the man should be admired."

"He's a scientist. He wants his work to be appreciated."

"Except that he'll be responsible for the killing of thousands of people—there's that."

Gough turned. "I don't disagree, and to think it all could have been avoided."

"What do you mean?"

"Have I not told you?"

"Told me what?"

"Drawings for some of Rühlemann's first fuze designs have been discovered in our patent office."

Surprise latched onto the colonel's words. "*Our* patent office?"

"Apparently, before the war, when Rühlemann and his company

first began designing fuzes, he showed them to Hermann Göring, the German Luftwaffe chief. When Göring showed little interest, Rühlemann brought his work to England, presented it to some underlings in the British War Office, tried to convince them to adopt his designs. It was then that he applied for a patent."

"What happened?"

"The same thing that always happens with government. No decisions were made as his drawings languished and then died in our bureaucracy—but he didn't give up. He finally headed back to Germany, and this time they listened—and now, the Germans are buying all the fuzes his company can produce."

"Such petty decisions forcing such fateful outcomes."

"If we'd have shown the man just a little respect, perhaps history would be different. As it turns out, we'll have to live—or die—with the consequences."

"But you and the rest of the Backroom Boys can outsmart him, right?"

Gough turned his attention back to the fuze. "The Germans have numbered this one a (17). The first one was recovered several weeks ago, but it was damaged and took us a while to piece together. We've subsequently recovered two more."

"What do you know about them?"

"We know the sneaky buggers are relentless. They have Churchill worried. We've got the team working day and night to find an answer."

"How long is the timer?"

"Once the bomb hits the ground, a clock starts that can run up to eighty hours. The problem is, there's no way to tell when it might detonate. It means that if such bombs land near critical locations—hospitals, railways, oil refineries, war factories, airfields—they will have to be abandoned for days. And after all the disruption, they still explode." The man drew a weighty breath. "The Germans have discovered that anticipation can be worse than the actual explosion. It's human nature."

"What do we do? How do we defuse them?"

"New procedure will instruct you to leave any (17)s alone for ninety-six hours."

"And if we don't have ninety-six hours?"

"Then you extract the fuze while it's ticking, knowing the bomb could detonate at any time."

"How confident are you that you'll find a way to stop them?"

"We're working on different approaches. We'll have something soon."

The colonel knew better than to ask for details.

"The Committee is preparing the official communiqué for the teams."

"How is the Committee going?" the colonel asked, changing the current and painful subject.

"It's ego wrangling at its finest," Gough added, introducing a smile.

"Well, if anyone can ride that train into the station, it's you, my friend."

It was a compliment that seemed appreciated but not needed. "Now, was there something you wanted to discuss?" Gough asked.

When Colonel Moore exhaled, his shoulders dropped. "Unfortunately, you've already answered it."

CHAPTER 7

Wes shifted in his cot, repositioned the notepaper he was holding against his book, and then shook his pen as if it might help him form words. So far he'd managed two: *Dear Nathelle,*

After standing so close to death, even touching its hand, with more such meetings likely, anything past a simple greeting seemed rather pointless. What do you say to a girl who may be *the one* when you will probably never see her again?

A knock thumped at the warehouse door. Not wanting to get up, Wes hollered at the only other person with him in the expansive room. "Driver, can you get that?"

"Is that an order?" the boy asked.

"It's a suggestion. I *suggest* you do it or . . . how do you say it here in England? . . . I'll give you a gubbing."

Driver blinked his eyes and then sighed. "Mate, please never repeat tha' again." He picked up the bowl containing his breakfast—boiled oats and sausage—and then walked slowly toward the knock.

Wes could hear both sides of the conversation but could see only Driver's face.

"I'm sorry to bother you," a woman's voice said.

"No bother at all, miss." A coy grin swept wide across Driver's cheeks as his eyes tipped head to toe. It didn't take a genius to see the boy was visually perusing the woman—every glorious inch.

"Please tell me that I have the correct address." Her heightened pitch cut the boy's once-over short. "I'm looking for the American who is working with the bomb disposal team."

"You don't need 'im. There must be somefin' else I can 'elp with?" Driver asked, always the optimist.

"Well . . . no," she replied, in a tone as cold as her smile would tolerate. "Is he here or not?"

Never good at rejection, Driver turned to Wes, who was already on his way to the door to conduct a rescue. "Bowers, you 'ave a visitor. Your mum's 'ere."

"Don't mind him," Wes said, shoving the boy aside and stepping in to greet the lady. "That's Driver. He's been in a mood since we took his blankie away. I see you got my message. I was beginning to wonder. It wasn't easy to track you down. Won't you come in?"

He started to reach out, but then couldn't remember proper salutation protocol in England when meeting a woman. Handshake? Hug? Was it the French who kissed on the cheeks? He stuck with a handshake. "I'm Wes Bowers. We've met, but not formally."

"Thank you." She took his hand, their eyes also meeting in the middle. "I'm Audrey Stocking."

He had more time to study her today, more reason. She didn't yet look twenty, seventeen or eighteen, perhaps—was of petite build, but with a figure that would turn the heads of most soldiers. She was out of uniform, looking less official in a plaid skirt and jacket, but she also proved his point: drab clothing can't hide grace no matter how hard it tries.

"I apologize for running off the other day, when . . ."

"When we blew up your building?"

She touched her hands to her face, holding in the slightest of chuckles. "I wasn't going to put it that way, and I don't know why I'm laughing. I truly cried when I saw the rubble. I couldn't wait for you that day because I was late to pick up some children we were taking out of London."

"You're lucky. I heard nothing but ringing in my ears for hours. Two days later, it's finally getting better." Wes led her inside, presented his surroundings. "Home, sweet home."

The place was both spacious and sparse, a two-story warehouse whose center was filled with rows and rows of double-high racks, longing to be useful but with nothing to hold. Along the outer wall, the men had arranged their array of cots and gear to give each soldier a separate living space on the floor, but without partitions to offer privacy. A solitary lavatory door waited in the far corner.

"There's sadly not a good spot to sit unless you don't mind my cot. The military is planning to use this building for storage, but until they do, it's home."

"I don't mind standing," she said, and then she pursed her lips as if holding in a hesitation.

"What is it?" Wes asked.

"It's something that I've been curious about since our first meeting. You see, I didn't know that Americans were working with our soldiers."

His head nod introduced arm gestures. "I'm here. Although after the start I've had, it may be a relationship that's short-lived—literally."

She smiled again at his wit, seemed to find it soothing. "May I ask one more question?" Her eyes met his as if there might be an army-imposed limit.

"Sure. What is it?"

"The bomb in my flat . . . I had to walk past it the night my building was hit, so close, I almost touched it. If I had, would it have . . ."

She didn't need to finish for him to understand. "We don't know. It had either a secondary fuze or a timed one. I'm still learning about them, but if the bomb was active, which is likely, then yes. If you had bumped it—even barely—we wouldn't be having this conversation." A look of grim understanding crept across her face. "Now, let me get you that list," he added.

He stepped to the side of his bunk, picked up a canvas bag, and carried it to her. As he took out the binder, she reached for it with eager hands.

"Oh, my! Thank you!" She cradled it gingerly, like a newborn baby, then turned its pages one by one. "I thought everything was lost. This is going to help so many children."

Wes could feel himself smile. "I'm happy to assist."

As she closed the cover, she bid another sincere and polite thank you and then turned toward the door.

"Don't you want your other stuff?" Wes called out.

Her pirouette was like a ballerina's. "There's more?"

Wes raised the bag toward her. "You obviously didn't get my entire message. Before I left your flat, I looked around and grabbed a few other things that seemed to be . . . well, important. I hope I made wise choices."

Eyes that had first creased with confusion were quickly growing into saucers as Wes held open the sack so she could reach inside.

It was crowded with her possessions. On top, beneath where the binder had sat, were half a dozen frames bundled together. As she pulled them out, she slid to her knees to lay them on the floor. They were photographs that had been on her bookshelf in the bedroom, pictures she'd presumed were lost forever, including the only picture she had of her mother. Also, loose in between were the photos from the broken frame that had been left lying by the door, images that she now caringly caressed.

He held up the bag, let her reach in again to remove a silver hairbrush. "I was using this before lying down on the bed," she explained.

"If I recall," Wes replied, "it was on the floor. Again, I just picked up anything that appeared valuable." He nudged the bag, urging her to look through what was left.

On the opposite side from where the brush had been, she found a porcelain cup with hand-painted roses. "Claire bought this for me at the market to hold my hairpins."

Wes assumed that meant it was worthless, with no real sentimental value at all—perhaps until now.

"It's absolutely beautiful," she muttered.

From below where the cup had been, she pulled out her purse: a round, chocolate-brown, knitted shoulder bag with a fabric rose sewn to the center. Inside were her passport, wallet, ration book, lipstick—everything exactly as she'd left it.

With each reunited treasure, she offered thanks, though Wes paid little heed as he perpetually pointed her back to the bag until a single item remained. When she reached in, not knowing what to expect, her fingers made a thud against the hard side of a wooden box. A stillness crept across the moment as moisture welled in her eyes, priming a pool of tears poised to trickle across her flushed face.

She drew it out so carefully, Wes wondered if her slowing motion would grind to a halt.

"This can't be," she mouthed almost painfully to herself, holding in her shaky hands a polished rectangular box, one that looked like it may have been used for jewelry. Looking past Wes, as if someone were standing on his opposite side, she asked again, "How is this possible?"

Now seemed a good time for Wes to explain. "When I moved your mattress to put it over the beam to ease the friction on the rope, this box fell to the floor. I don't know what it is, but it looked . . . well, it looked like it was important."

Audrey tried to speak, but only gurgles escaped. She started sniffling like a youngster lost at the market who had at last been reunited with her mother. Wes didn't know what to do, as he was never calm around crying women. The tremors of a rumbling truck outside came to his rescue. It would be the colonel and the men.

"Excuse me, we'll give you some time," Wes whispered to Audrey as he roped Driver with his eyes and then towed him behind so the two could wait outside.

"What did you do to 'er, mate?" Driver asked.

Wes let Driver step ahead and then booted his backside. "Let's be gentlemen and give her some room, shall we?"

Once outside, the two greeted the crew, helped them unload a bale of burlap bags, and then divulged that there was a woman inside whose flat had been destroyed by the bomb and that they needed to give her a little space.

After a dozen minutes, Wes stepped back in to check on her.

"Miss Stocking?"

He looked around. He called out her name again. He tapped on the door to the water closet, and when no answer came, he checked inside. Empty.

It had to have been while they were unloading the truck. Audrey Stocking had taken her things and slipped away.

The girl with the captivating blue eyes was gone.

Audrey was two streets away when the strength in her legs gave way, forcing her again to the cold, hard, wonderful, amazing cement. She clenched her bag of treasures with both hands. It was an experience oddly similar to the darker attacks she'd been having when anxiety raked across her body, except today it was a raging river of elation. It was sobering to realize that both joy and pain could bring the very same tears.

She found a place to rest in an abandoned archway to revel in the moment. The American, Wes Bowers, must have thought she was stark raving mad. How could he know she'd been inconsolable at the loss not just of her photos but of her box and the letters it contained?

She felt terrible about sneaking out of the warehouse without offering a proper goodbye, but she was a whimpering mess with no other choice. She would come back to thank the American when she was more composed.

There had been a live bomb ticking away in her flat, and yet this virtual stranger had taken the time to gather her things. His compassion was hard to imagine. How could she repay such humanity?

She reflected on the items he'd chosen to save. He'd called the WVS office in Knightsbridge to leave her a message. Did that mean he'd gone through the papers in her purse? Did he notice that her passport was from Switzerland? Did he inspect it closely?

And what about the box? Anyone holding it could tell it wasn't empty, and not easy to open, thanks to such a clever design created by her father, the engineer. Had Bowers figured it out?

If he had, would the constable be calling? The letters, after all—the bundle of envelopes so secretly stored inside—were addressed to Germany . . . to her father's factory.

A war factory.

Audrey perched in the center of her room, letting the walls keep watch on the door—though it wasn't necessary. Claire was in line with their ration cards to buy sugar and would easily be gone for another two hours.

With quick presses to the box's corners—a secret sequence that she could perform in her sleep—she slid the top lid free to release her letters, which seemed ready to stretch with their newfound freedom.

It was the letter on top she treasured most, one that she held to her nose out of habit, hoping to catch the elusive scent of home. Though the paper was no longer fragrant, her memory made do. She pulled open the tattered envelope's flap, gently tugged the page inside free, helped it yawn open at the folds, and then scanned its perfectly penned prose. She no longer read it for content, its words learned by heart long ago; rather, she read it to reminisce.

November 17, 1938
Liebe Audrey,

Hallo mein Schatz.

I know that you've been apprehensive since I told you that I'll be sending you and your brothers away. It wrenches my soul, but with God's help, it will be for the best. What is my choice?

When an unexpected storm rolls over the horizon, it's prudent to board the windows, stockpile food, fill jars with water. But how does one know which storms intend destruction and which shall pass? Should one cower at every dark wisp of a cloud?

I will send for everyone when calm returns. Until then, let the storms that blow your way provide water for your seeds. Help Claire with your brothers. Practice your studies. Know that I long to be with you all, and don't forget that love is as strong as death.

Now, as I've taught you to do in all your letters, let me share with you a secret:

I don't know if my plan to save the factories from the Nazis will work. I've never admitted that aloud until now. Truthfully, how can I know? But also, how can I not try? If we quit trying, we quit living.

I have heard the babbling, that I am like Jonah running away from God and will soon be swallowed by a fish. But wasn't the fish sent from God? Could it be that Selig is the fish who will save our heritage?

We will soon both know.

As you write your letters back, remember we are separated by distance, but never in feelings of the heart. It's toilsome to be apart, but as I've often told you: Das Leben ist kein Ponyhof—life isn't a pony farm.

Until we soon meet, dear daughter, be strong, be good, say little, but do much and it will serve you well.

Yours faithfully,

Papa

It was the final letter she'd received from her father, one written only a few days before he had hastily sent her away with Claire. Unanswered questions once again flooded her thoughts. What had changed his mind about sending her brothers? Why did Jessey and Lewy get to stay in Germany?

Audrey pulled out a pen and a blank sheet of paper, coaxing the timid ink down the pen's tip as she stroked each letter with exactness, just like her father had taught her.

She could almost hear him speak. *Few acts of human expression are more intimate and profound than that of a hand-penned letter.*

September 13, 1940

Dear Papa,

The bombing in London has started in earnest, and how odd that a German bomb landed in my flat on the first night but did not explode. I whispered to it, told it my secrets, but it refused to speak back. Did you ever suppose that the war would chase me to England?

With the bombs dropping every day, my head has been scattered. It seems that suspense is the greater discomfort. The English (including Claire and me) have spent so long awaiting the time that the German bombing would begin that now we are all at a loss as to what we ought to gab about next. I guess we shall shift our despair toward Hitler's invasion.

I read that the British are bombing Germany in

reprisal. I hope that you and my brothers are safe. Mostly, Papa, I'm writing to tell you that I've been asked by Lady Reading, an extraordinarily important woman in London, actually in all of England, to accompany her as we speak to young women, to convince them to help in the war effort. Can you imagine? Claire is uneasy, but I shall do it anyway.

Please give my love to all. Tell Jessey and Lewy that I miss them terribly and look for the day when I'll get to come home.

And now, Papa, I shall share my secret: There is an American here who showed me great kindness. I shall have to look for some way to repay him. I will keep you informed.

Until we all find peace,

Your daughter,

Audrey

CHAPTER 8

The morning streets of London were more crowded than they'd been in days—a boy selling newspapers, a young couple pushing a baby carriage, a vendor setting up his cigarette cart.

As the colonel, Wes, and Hastings approached the entrance to the tearoom, a middle-aged man in a dark knitted vest, on his way out, politely held open the door. The man jolted to a stop when he saw the insignia on the team's uniforms.

"Pardon me, but are you bomb disposal?" he asked, his eyes swelling.

"Yes, we are. How may we help?" the colonel replied, glancing about as if to be steered in the direction of an errant UXB.

"I would be honored to buy you all a pint." The stranger was bouncing foot to foot like he'd stumbled by chance upon his highness the king, out taking his morning tea. His next inquiry added to the puzzle. "Do you know Lieutenant Davies, Bob Davies?"

"I know him," the colonel replied.

"Well, thank him for us all!" He was motioning with his hand, not just at the people inside sipping tea, but at all those out on the street.

It was then Colonel Moore noticed the newspaper folded under the man's arm. He gestured toward it. "Are you through reading that?"

"Yes, yes, please take it!" He handed it over so gleefully, Wes guessed the man would also have parted with his wallet, had the colonel asked politely enough.

"And no need to buy us a pint," the colonel assured. "It's a bit early."

"Yes, of course. God bless you all."

The colonel sat, unfolded the newspaper, read the headline, then began to skim the story. He caught enough in the initial paragraph that he didn't bother to read the rest. His hands shook away in disgust as he dropped the paper to the table.

"What does it say?" Wes asked.

When the colonel didn't reply straightaway, Wes snatched it up to read the article himself and then summarized it aloud for Hastings.

"It says Lieutenant Bob Davies and his BD section are heroes. Let's see . . . at 2:25 a.m., a gigantic bomb buried itself beside St Paul's Cathedral. It plunged twenty-six feet into the ground. It says they labored painstakingly all night through dirt, sand, gravel, and mud to reach it."

"They forgot to include bedrock," the colonel grumbled.

He didn't dissuade Wes, who kept reading. "It couldn't be disarmed in place and would have leveled the cathedral had it detonated. Their single option was to remove it intact. When they, at last, hoisted it out, almost eighty hours had passed. They quickly loaded it onto a truck, sped to Hackney Marshes, and blew it up, leaving a hole in the ground a hundred feet wide. It says their 'cold-blooded disregard of supreme danger saved the cathedral.' It not only calls them heroes, it's calling all BD personnel heroes. It adds that we're 'the most gallant, matter-of-fact men of the Royal Engineers.' And there's a picture of the bomb! It's eight feet long and weighs a full ton." Wes held it up for the men to see. "I have to say, sir, it is the biggest damn bomb I've seen so far."

The colonel's weak grunt turned Wes toward Hastings for help. "I'm confused. Explain the man to me. Why all the sour grapes?"

Hastings, with no answer, turned to face the colonel himself. "What's going on, sir? Is there something more?"

Colonel Moore let a breath go free. "I wasn't lying when I said I know Davies."

"And you don't care for him?" Wes asked.

"I won't detail his antics here. Let me simply say he has a few . . . character flaws. But I'm more concerned with the press. The Germans are undoubtedly reading this story right now as well, and it's nothing but an advert taunting them, daring them to build bigger bombs, better fuzes, to kill more people. Gentlemen, these are the same bombs you and I will have to dig up. You tell me—should I be celebrating?"

Wes tipped back in his seat. He was quiet for a good minute while a woman in an eyelet apron approached to leave cups, a kettle of hot tea, and an assortment of "tea-snacks," most with biscuity names that Wes could never remember. The word that came to his mind to describe the whole spread was *dainty.*

After she scurried away, while the other men poured tea into their cups, Wes turned his chair toward the colonel. "You're missing the bigger point."

The old man sipped before answering. "Which point is that?"

"I don't know this Davies character or what he's done or if he's worthy or not to be called a hero. But if he put his life on the line, that seems pretty admirable. No heroes are perfect, but that's not important."

"Well, then, what is?"

"Take a look around and tell me what you see."

The colonel set down his cup. "I beg your pardon?"

"Look at the people's faces. I haven't seen this many folks out in days, nor as many smiles. They woke up, and their cathedral remains standing. That's a pretty fine day."

Hastings bobbed his agreement. "It's true."

Wes wasn't finished, and he jabbed the folded newspaper toward the colonel to let him know. "Sir, as I look around, I finally see hope. And if that's the case, then we need to shout our successes from the rooftops. Because if the people don't regain some hope around here, the Germans won't need bigger bombs."

Wes let his words hang in the air while he took a bite from a tiny teacake topped with a spoon of cream. "There's one more thing," he added.

"There always is with you."

Wes browsed the room. "This is the same place you came to get tea when we arrived in London."

"So?"

"There are a thousand tea shops in London. Why this one?"

"Is your little pep talk over?" the colonel asked.

Wes wouldn't concede. "Well, Colonel?"

The man sighed, surrendered, lifted up his hands while his chin lowered. "The truth is, Margaret used to love this place. She adored their teacakes. I can't stand 'em myself, but she sure loved 'em."

Wes set aside the newspaper he'd been using to point at the

colonel. It was no longer needed. Instead, he grasped his teacup like a goblet of ale. "To Margaret!" he said, but before either Hastings or Colonel Moore could respond, Wes stood reaching to the ceiling, his cup held high. This time he bellowed out to the room so all could hear.

"To Margaret!"

Nobody surrounding them knew who this Margaret woman was that the uniformed American was toasting, but if she were related in any way to bomb disposal and the men who'd saved their beloved cathedral, they would surely join in. A confident chorus of voices combined in the toast to fill up the graceful room with much-needed pride.

"TO MARGARET!" they cheered. "TO MARGARET!"

The colonel's mustache tiptoed into a smile, his eyes turning bright as if a fairy had swooped in and sprinkled the man with glitter. Hope was apparently contagious.

Hastings's lips also wired into a grin as he slapped Wes on the shoulder. "I don't care what Badger says about you. I like you, Yank. You're a bit of all right in my book!"

Café Cozier greeted patrons from Liverpool Road, a brisk quarter-hour walk for Wes from the warehouse. He'd spotted the place, or rather its "Open" sign, on his first day in the city, but he hadn't had time to inspect their fare until today, and it was anything but dainty.

The colonel had been called away to an emergency meeting of BD commanders, giving Wes and the men the morning off—and not a minute too soon. Driver was making one of his mum's recipes, using a single pan and a hot plate, an English dish called Toad in the Hole, and, based on the smell, the "toad" was getting the best of the boy.

Other than a precisely painted placard that read, *Welcome! We Are Open, Hitler Will Never Win,* the exterior of the café left little to behold. What must once have been an elegant entry was now completely concealed by a ceiling-high wall of sandbags, several feet thick, leaving only a narrow passage to a single door. The sullen, sand-castled structure protecting the café's exterior—while impressive for its sheer size and function—held no semblance of congenial English charm.

The interior of the café was a different story; what the setting lacked in allure at arm's length from the sidewalk merely served to accentuate its richness after guests ventured inside. Clearly, the woods had staged a mutiny, and mahogany had reigned victorious. It was everywhere: tables, chairs, shelves, columns, and the ornate polished bar that reclined along the far wall.

In any other environment, such lumbered abundance would be too much, but at Café Cozier, expertly accented with cloth napkins, crystal glasses, sparkling flatware, and impressionist landscape paintings gracing the walls, the surroundings swirled together to make one forget that a war was going on just outside the doors.

Winston Churchill himself had toured the area, pausing on the café's sidewalk out front, wielding his cigar like a weapon that could take out Hitler on its own. He came to visit damaged buildings two streets north, knowing that the newspapers would publish his message for all the people of London, but one that he trusted would also be carried back to Hitler: *WE CAN TAKE IT! In London, life is business as usual.*

And Café Cozier complied.

Wes had staked out a table along the north side, away from the entrance but in view of the door, where he could easily be seen if someone from his section came calling. He was finishing up some rather delicious biscuits—not really biscuits at all, but cookies—washing them down with a drink called a Warm Grapefruit Squash. Judging by its name, it sounded atrocious, but, although a pitcher of ice wouldn't have hurt, its mildly fruity flavor was oddly satisfying.

The café's owners—Jordy and Jorrell Prewett, two brothers from Leeds—seemed thrilled to have an American soldier patronizing their establishment and had been hovering close to see that all his needs were met.

"More biscuits, sir?"

"Yes, and please, call me Wes." He'd seen enough of the place to know that he'd be back, so they should start with first names. "It's Jordy, correct?"

"Yes, sir . . . *Wes.* Thank you!"

Wes returned his attention to the morning edition of the *Daily Express*; he was three paragraphs into an article entitled "Dive Bombers Try to Kill the King and Queen" when Jordy touched him on the shoulder . . . only it wasn't Jordy at all.

"Forgive me for disturbing you. Lieutenant Hastings told me I'd find you here."

He hadn't seen her slip in—the blonde-haired, blue-eyed girl whose flat he'd blown up. "Good morning," Wes said as he stood, extended his hand, then paused awkwardly like he'd forgotten her name—which he hadn't, but her hair was down, and she was dressed in a fitted blue blouse instead of her uniform, and he was so taken aback by her appearance that her name, which waited patiently on his tongue for its turn to come out, had decided it was content to simply let him stare.

Wes would be the first to admit that he knew nothing about fashion. What he did know was that the girl standing in front of him with her arm extended in his direction—Miss Audrey Stocking—was wearing it well.

"Audrey," she prodded to help him out.

Wes took her hand. "Yes, yes, I remember." He waved any conjecture otherwise aside with a brush of his wrist that bade her to sit. "It's just that you look . . ." *Was it out of place to say?* " . . . very lovely in that outfit."

It was her turn to blush and catch a smile, slightly embarrassed but also looking pleased. "Oh, this isn't mine," she said. "I mean, it *is* mine, but as you know, Claire and I lost all of our belongings, and this is a donation that came from Cora Holden at WVS."

"Well, whoever donated it would be sad they gave it away if they could see how spectacular you look in it." Wes reached for the nearby plate, held it out toward her. "Biscuit?"

"No, thank you. I'm here to apologize for running off the other day. I felt that I needed to formally thank you for saving my things. The box especially is very dear to me. My father made it, and when I thought it was lost . . . well, saving it was incredibly honorable and something you didn't need to do under the circumstances."

"You mean in light of the bomb in the room?" he asked, his eyes warming.

"Precisely," she answered, allowing an ease to enter and hold her smile. But then she caught sight of a pen and paper sitting opposite the man. "Are you writing home?"

"Not successfully." Wes had intended to compose a letter to his girl, Nathelle, but hadn't managed to write more than her name. "It seems the war makes it hard to know what to say."

While her head wagged up and down in polite agreement, her

eyes shifted sideways, but they were also beaming. "I can help you," she added.

"You can help my writing?" His brows drew together.

Hers was a bashful nod. "My father loved letter writing. He gave me guidance, taught me some suggestions. I could share them if it would help."

"I appreciate the offer." Wes paused for a skeptical swallow. "But you don't know who you're dealing with here. When I pick up the pen, my thoughts run for cover. I can't even get through a sentence."

She eased back into her chair. "Let me give you one tiny technique to start." Her voice dropped, forcing him closer. "When writing a letter to a person you care about, take the time to share a secret."

"A secret?"

"Yes. One of life's greatest gifts is that of trust. Sharing a secret is a gift to the reader since you're sharing a normally guarded part of yourself, but it's also a gift to the writer because, by sharing, you are placing trust in yourself."

She waited. He waited. "Or it may all be silliness," she said. "I'll let you decide."

"No, no, I was thinking it through, and you may be on to something. Do you have any other tips?"

Her eyes searched his, making sure he was serious. "Well, yes. Write the type of letter that a reader will long to read twice. Also, don't rush the writing. Remember that the pen, your fingers, the side of your hand, all touch the paper, and that means it carries a part of you. So, use words that carry a part of you as well."

"You have a passion for this, don't you?"

"My father often said that a well-written letter is a rare and cherished thing." She used his hesitation to add something more. "You said that the war makes it hard to know what to say, but it should be the opposite. War, with its constant threat of death, gives us permission to share things we normally wouldn't. War fosters valor in matters besides killing."

If he was staring back, it was unintentional. "I suppose that it does," he said, hoping to sound earnest. "I'll give my letter writing one more try."

She stood, shook his hand for the second time, readied to leave. "This has been pleasant. It reminds me of what life was like before the start of this dreadful conflict."

"Indeed." It had been easy conversation, pleasant company.

"Well, then," she said as she turned toward the door. "I guess we must all do our best to survive the middle game."

He could no longer see her face, only the slender back of her blouse and the catch of a twinkle from the silver buttons that still showed on each sleeve, but his mouth had veered upwards.

"Audrey!"

She turned.

"Did you just say 'survive the middle game'?"

Her shuffling feet apologized. "I'm sorry. It's an old childhood expression, a phrase of my father's. He would say that most of the action takes place in the middle game. I was comparing that to the war, and . . ."

"Audrey, I know what *middle game* means." Wes's eyes were instantly ablaze. "It means that you play chess!" He may not have realized that he was bouncing.

"I take it you play," she mused, not answering his question.

He would never lie about chess. "Only because it's the greatest strategic war game ever devised. I'm surprised you play."

"Because I'm a woman, and it's considered a man's game?" she asked, her tone giving him a pinch.

Sensing a trap, his head commanded he not answer, but his chin was already flapping. "It's a game my father taught me," he added as if that would make it okay.

"And one that my father taught me," she replied.

"Then we must play, for our fathers' sakes." He was beckoning the nearest Prewett brother over. "Jorrell?"

"Yes, sir. How may I help?"

"Do you have a chessboard?" Wes mimicked chess movements with his hands, as if it would deliver his question more quickly.

Jorrell looked to his brother Jordy, who was close enough to hear but also frowning. "I'm afraid not. But I can have one for the next time."

"That will be perfect." Wes faced Audrey. If he'd had dueling pistols, he would have held one out for her to take. "It shall be a challenge of fathers. What do you say?"

Audrey straightened and then held up her words like they were flashing. "To be clear, I'm a quiet person, not a giggle girl. So if that's what you're looking for here . . ."

Wes chased away his grin and then bent in to clarify. "I asked if you'd like to play chess, not *chest*. That's a completely different game altogether."

She mulled over his reply, then answered with a smirk. "Fine. But I should tell you, I'm not very good—at chess, I mean."

"Is that a yes?" Wes's eyes pleaded. His lips pleaded. His crinkled forehead pleaded.

Audrey's weight shifted to her back leg as she forcefully folded her arms. She looked him over as she spoke. "I'll be gone for a couple of days taking children to Watford, but you send word when you're available after I return, and we shall indeed play chess—*and may the best father win.*"

Wes had just finished helping Driver load a dozen cans of petrol into the back of the Hippo when the kid nudged his shoulder. "Why are you so chuffed?" he asked, his palms upright.

Chuffed? Did it mean fit, drowsy, annoyed? Was Driver referring to something Wes had done earlier in the day?

Wes replayed the morning's events in his head, trying to put the kid's question into context. The section had scouted out a UXB near Mayfair, determined that it posed no immediate threat, and then roped it off to let it sit for another two days before digging it up, in case it was armed with a timed fuze. But there had been no contention whatsoever; even Badger had been civil. They were headed next to Kensington, but the colonel had decided they should first drop back to the warehouse to get more fuel and take a quick spot of tea.

"Why wouldn't I be *chuffed*?" Wes finally asked, having concluded that repeating back odd phrases was generally his safest bet.

Driver shook his head. "It's jus' that stupid grin 'as been stuck to your chops all mornin', and it's makin' us all peevish."

Another pause, then a shrug. "Sure, why wouldn't it make you *peevish*?"

Air-raid sirens came to his rescue, while also reeling the colonel and Hastings outside to peer at the skyline.

"It's barely noon," Hastings hollered over the din. "It's too early. It has to be a false alarm."

Wes cocked his head to hear better while motioning the others to be silent. This was no false alarm. He could hear a faint hum above the sirens, but something about the sound was off—and it wasn't good.

To save money for college, Wes had worked for a summer at Happy Wrench, a car-repair shop owned by Jaylend Brodrick, Nathelle's father. It was there Wes learned under Jaylend's tutelage that by closing his eyes and listening cautiously, he could tell a Ford "flatty" from a Duesenberg, a Cadillac Roadster from a Pontiac Straight-8, and a healthy engine from one about to break down. "Listen closely," his former boss would say, "and the engine will tell you its story."

It was a skill set Wes had transferred to aircraft, and now, as the distant hums reached into his ears, he didn't like what they were saying.

"The deeper rumbling is the bombers, colonel, but they aren't alone. There are also fighters." Wes tipped his head, continued to concentrate. "But there are more than normal."

"More than normal?"

"Colonel, it sounds as if they've brought their whole damned air force."

The colonel listened again momentarily before barking out orders. "Get the vehicles covered and then get to the shelter. There's little we can do while bombs are falling. We'll hunker down until the all clear."

The colonel helped the men secure their equipment before leading them back inside. On the way, he declared, "For King and Country."

"King and Country," the men chorused back. Then, with a smile that felt out of place for the circumstance, the colonel added, "Bowers, you're also welcome to tag along."

Wes pulled the light closer while gripping his pen like a proud preschooler. It was still dark outside, but he wanted to finish the letter before the section headed out at dawn. He penned with confident strokes, pushing ink into characters that nearly pulsed with their own heartbeat. Why had he previously been so timid in writing?

Dear Nathelle,

Aside from the war taking my words hostage, I have no excuse for not writing sooner. The work is dangerous, and the gloom of what might happen led me to suppose that writing was useless, until I was reminded that to let fear rule is to surrender. After what I've witnessed, I can't let that happen.

There was an astonishing air battle that took place over London yesterday that I can scarcely describe. I'm certain you'll read about it in the papers. When you do, know that I observed it firsthand.

The Germans came in two immense waves, late morning and afternoon, their bombers protected by swarms of fighters on a mission to destroy London. Our planes were trying to shoot theirs down, while theirs were trying to reciprocate. The result was a twisting, turning cloud of aircraft, weaving intertwined trails of smoke, dropping bombs, shooting bullets, etching a picture so vivid into my head that I will carry it with me until I die.

The Nazis have overrun so many European countries—Czechoslovakia, Poland, Denmark, Norway, France,

Belgium, Luxembourg, the Netherlands—that only Britain remains. Many feared this was Hitler's final invasion, spelling the end of their freedoms and way of life.

We were hunkered down as a team in the basement, taking an occasional peek out the window, yearning to take part, but having to wait and see with the rest of the nervous people in London.

Nathelle, there were so many RAF fighters in the sky that the colonel supposes Britain's Fighter Command sent all of its squadrons into action—a daring move, because if the British were defeated, the war would be over. Without an air defense, Hitler could march into London at his pleasure.

But the RAF kept attacking, again and again, relentless, getting knocked down but returning to the battle, and when it was over, we heard rumors that 175 German planes had been shot down. Some British planes and pilots were also downed, but they were a fraction of Germany's losses.

I would gladly give a week's pay to have been in the room when Hitler learned of the outcome. While more determined attacks undoubtedly lie ahead, the British have secured their island home once again from invasion. A member of my team, Gunner, said it best when he stood and declared, "We have not lost!" And truer words were never spoken. The road to victory (both here and in life) is long, with much work ahead, but as of today, we have not lost!

Nathelle, I also have a secret that I'd like to share: I'm a large man, strong and proud, and though I've barely landed in this country and hardly know these people, when I saw their relief as we all realized that the RAF had withstood the Nazis during this tremendous trial, I found a place to be alone, and I wept for them.

With such dire odds, the naysayers had proclaimed there was little England could do, yet this small, isolated country stood up to tyrants. I want to live with equal determination.

Lastly, on the night I left, when you asked about our relationship and where I imagined it might go, I admit I was tentative. While I don't pretend to know what the future holds, whatever it is, I'd like us to face it together, head-on, and with resolve.

That is my plan.

Truly,

Wes

CHAPTER 9

The morning was still yawning when Colonel Moore and his men arrived at the Bryant and May Match Factory in the Bow neighborhood of London. Lieutenant G. Pringle of 15BD was there to flag down the colonel.

He was a short man wearing thin features, his spouting words rapid and clipped. His fingers swung from a quick salute to pointing at the factory. "Colonel, the place has been hit by a stick of four 250-kilogram bombs, and the factory is full of phosphorus. It'll be a sight if she blows. My team is handling the one in front on the southeast corner, as there's more room; five of my men are currently digging. Since you have a smaller team, you'll take the entry hole that's in the back where the space is narrower. Both are A1s."

Wes's eyes must have arched because Hastings took notice and bent close to explain. "Category A1 means *immediate disposal essential, detonation in situ not acceptable.* In other words, we go in and remove them at all costs."

Wes had assumed as much and leaned in to hear the remainder of Pringle's directions.

"The factory and surrounding area have been evacuated, but we're sitting on a bloody powder keg—literally."

"You said it was a stick of four?" the colonel asked. "Have you found the other two?"

The man pointed. "One is in the road a street west, the other in the car park two hundred yards behind us. They'll both cause havoc if they blow, but we don't think they will damage the factory. We've got to get the two close ones out first. I've called 17 Section, and they'll try to get here to handle the other two, but they're pretty tied up with a mess at the wharf."

Colonel Moore began to call out orders until Pringle raised a hand. "Colonel, the bomb in the car park is visible. The Home Guard is sandbagging it, but you need to know that I put ears to it, and it's ticking. We suspect that all of these are armed with (17)s. It's the reason that none of them have exploded—well, not yet."

The colonel checked his watch. "When did they land?"

"They've been ticking for seven hours and ten minutes."

The colonel was older than all the men under his command, and there had been moments previously when Wes had noticed the man's age showing, his movement slower than the others—but not today. After thanking the lieutenant, Moore quickstepped toward the back of the factory, wagging at Hastings and Wes to follow. They were just beyond the north wall when they found the burrow. It sat dead center in the narrow alley as if its entry had been meticulously measured between the company's main building and an adjacent storage facility.

The location was tricky for two reasons. First, the space was tight, with bricked walls on both sides, limiting the size of the dig and the number of sappers who could work at one time. Second, and the more pestering problem for Colonel Moore, was the water table. The soil looked wet, and if the hole started to fill with groundwater, it would slow down the effort. It would mean that to keep the excavation from caving in, the opening would need to be lined with timber and constantly pumped—and timber was in short supply.

"We can't dillydally," the colonel reminded them. "We'll work in teams of two, digging for fifteen minutes. That will reduce how long we are each exposed. Officers will dig along with the men. Pike, you and Driver start. Take picks and shovels from the Hippo. The water level may pose a problem so Hastings and Bowers, see if you can find some planks, anything to shore up the walls. I'll make a call and get us a pump, in case it's needed. Those not digging should rest at the Hippo. Everyone needs to be fresh. Let's get cracking!"

Before Pike and Driver had finished their turn, the colonel had arranged for a pump, and Wes and Hastings had coordinated the delivery of timber. They'd enlisted the help of the plant manager, who they found pacing behind the barrier and who was more than happy to accommodate their needs if it would save his factory.

At the fifteen-minute mark, the colonel, who had moved close to the hole to supervise the digging, called out the next rotations. "Gunner and Hastings, go! Bowers, you and Badger will follow."

Wes's gaze found Badger, and he was scowling, but neither man said a word. When their turn came, Wes jumped down first into the waist-deep hole and started in with his shovel. The narrow opening wasn't big enough for two men anyway, especially of Wes's size, so Badger remained on top to bucket away the dirt with an attached rope.

Although the hole was both dank and muddy, Wes actually found the digging tolerable. He'd never been afraid of hard work, and despite the pressure of the circumstance—or precisely because of it—there was a rhythm to his shoveling that soothed.

Schlup, jamming the shovel into the saturated soil; *glop,* wrenching the shortened handle back to free the scoop; then *splat,* the sound as the shoveled mud was dropped into the bucket. It was almost melodic: *schlup, glop, splat . . . schlup, glop, splat . . . schlup, glop, splat.*

"My turn," Badger called down after a few minutes had passed, the first thing he'd said to Wes that day. As Wes took a final shovelful of dirt to fill the bucket, the man's second smattering of words for the day followed . . . and they were filled with venom. "I SAID IT WAS MY TURN."

Oddly, it wasn't the time working beside Badger digging in the hole that Wes found to be most uncomfortable, since each man could stay busy with his own duty. It was their time together at the Hippo waiting for their turn to dig.

Three rotations later, just before their turn was again to start, Wes could take the silence no longer. "I've got something I want to say," Wes announced to Badger, as if the man might smile and then invite him over to a café table where they could pleasantly chat over drinks. "I've been thinking about the tension between us, and I'd like to better understand . . ."

Badger hunched, bared his teeth like a rabid dog. Wes looked to the colonel, but he was too far away to referee. Every uttered word from the man seethed with disdain. "I don't give a dog's bollocks if—"

Before either man could flinch, an explosion mushroomed across the ground, rocking everything in its violent path. As Wes stumbled back, he watched the colonel tumble to the ground. Both men were still breathing, so it wasn't *their* bomb; judging from the direction of the blast, it had to be the one in the car park.

The colonel scrambled to his feet, his head clearly trying to shake off the panic from the visible rising smoke. He checked his watch as he shifted into combat mode, his experience in the first war screaming that it was time. His voice was firm and direct. "Gather round! I'll go and check if there are casualties. Bowers, you and Badger spell off Gunner and Hastings. We've got no choice but to keep going. Can you do it?"

"Yes, sir," Wes answered as every muscle tensed—if the bomb blew while he was digging, there wouldn't be even small pieces left to collect for a coffin.

"Come on, let's move!" Wes barked to Badger, and the men rushed toward the hole. As he waited for Badger to climb down into the dark and start to dig, Wes's breathing thickened, his toes flexed tight in his boots, his mind blared the obvious: he didn't want to die today. Worse, he didn't want to die angry.

Schlup, glop, splat.

If Badger would only take a minute and listen. That's all that Wes was asking. What was wrong with that? If today was their day to die, he needed to leave this world in peace.

Schlup, glop, splat.

Wes squatted down and hollered into the hole, not intending to stop until he concluded what he had to say. "Badger, don't quit digging, but I need you to listen. I get that you're pissed at me . . . or, er, *miffed,* but I've got to say my piece, and then I'll shut up."

Schlup, glop, splat.

"I don't know what I did to you to make you so mad, but I apologize that we started off poorly."

Schlup, glop, splat.

"The colonel told me about your girl running off with the Canadian, and I'd be fuming at 'em both as well—and anyone else who reminded me of the guy."

Schlup, glop, splat.

"But Badger, we could both die any time, and dying this angry isn't right—not for me or for you. I'm okay if we don't become friends, but let's not be enemies." Wes was about to shut up, except another thought had jumped from his head to his tongue and then bolted just before he could clench his jaw. "I also think you should cut your girl some slack, especially if she'd never been out of the village. She was probably overwhelmed and then overreacted, and she's too embarrassed to admit to it."

Schlup, glop, splat.

"I'm suggesting that you talk to her, and soon. In fact, write her a letter and tell her how you honestly feel. If it were me, I'd tell her that I missed her, that my heart ached without her, that I'd do anything to get her back."

Schlup, glop, splat.

"Look, do that, and then if she chooses to stay with the Canadian, wish her the best. Tell her that she made your life better while you two were together, and thank her. I know it will be mighty painful to swallow that much pride in one gulp—it would be for me—but you have to ask yourself, how much are you willing to risk?"

Schlup, glop, splat.

"As I consider that you're digging out a live bomb with never an ounce of cowardice in your bones, I'd say you're okay with risk, which makes you a better man than me. Badger, I . . ."

Schlup . . .

The sound stopped. Badger's head rose from the hole like a

demon, his eyes blazing red, his nostrils flaring wide. He was clenching the handle of his shovel so securely that his bulging fingers looked like plump, ripened tomatoes. He didn't yell, but his demand gurgled out with such resentment, Wes slid backward in the mud.

"SHUT! THE! BLOODY! HELL! UP!" he screamed. "AND PULL UP THE BUCKET!"

He didn't swing the shovel at Wes, as he was positioned too low, but it was evident that he longed to. Wes surrendered with both hands and then reached down to lug up the bucket and dump it on the nearby pile.

Ten weeks. He hadn't been here even close to ten weeks.

Ankle deep in the sludge, he silently promised to never speak again to the man who had already disappeared into the burrow like a worm into the earth, where the squishy sound rising again from the ground no longer comforted.

Schlup, glop, splat.

Schlup, glop, splat.

Schlup, . . . The digging ceased. When Badger's voice peeked out, anger had washed away to reveal exhilaration, as if he'd struck a chest of buried treasure. "Get me a smaller shovel," he commanded Wes. "I've reached it!"

It took Badger twenty-two more minutes to clear out enough dirt around the bomb for a man to work. Like an animal hoarding its kill, he refused to abandon the space or share the task with anyone else, which the colonel allowed since Badger was still the best at this part of the job. And he was all but finished until one side of the dirt wall sloughed off to rebury the bomb's lower half.

As if death were smiling, almost giggling at such entertainment, seventeen more minutes ticked by while Wes and Hastings took turns hauling lumber to the hole, handing it down to Badger, checking to see what else he needed.

Throughout the dig, the colonel had been adamant that unless it was your turn, you stayed back a safe distance to *minimize the risk should she blow.* Of course, said reasoning never stopped him from parking near to supervise.

"I'm almost there, Colonel," Badger called out. "Almost there."

Wes obeyed as the colonel instructed him and Hastings to join the other men at the Hippo. They were out of the blast area but still had a visual. Their concerns almost chorused out loud. *Hurry, Badger. Work faster!*

As the bomb continued to tick, Wes noticed that the colonel couldn't quit glancing at his watch.

Once Badger had finished digging and moved back, the colonel sized up the hole and then shimmied down. It was bad enough that they'd had to line the walls with wood to keep the sides from caving in. Fortunately, they hadn't needed the water pump, which would have slowed down the digging even more, as there was no telling how much time was left.

The space was tighter than Colonel Moore had anticipated, perhaps on account of the last-minute lumber addition. He lowered himself feetfirst, found there wasn't enough room to bend down, and had to climb back out and start over.

On his second try, he went in headfirst, arms up, as if squirming into a sewer drain, doing his best to secure both his flashlight and his tools. He wouldn't be able to work in this position for long, already feeling the blood rushing to his head.

He directed his light's beam to the bomb, brushed away dirt from the casing, then made a quick assessment of his situation. While groundwater wasn't yet pooling, the soil in the shaft was soggy, and if he wasn't mistaken, the bomb was slowly sinking, like it was lodged in the throat of a giant who was doing his best to swallow.

A distinctive ticking startled the colonel but disappeared as quickly, causing the man to almost smile when he realized it was the sound of his own wristwatch as it moved past his ear.

As he shined his light at the side of the bomb where the fuze pocket would be, his own heart also sank in the mire. The bomb was badly damaged, the fuze face torn off, and the bomb casing cracked, so there was no way to extract the fuze. Out of hope or habit, he held his key up to where he would normally unscrew the locking ring, but it was too marred to move.

Think, think!

He placed an old stethoscope to the bomb to listen for a heartbeat, held his watch as far away as he could, and prayed. The answer that came was both audible and distinct, though not the one he'd wanted—*tick, tick, tick, tick.*

The bomb was damaged but functional and ready to blow him to kingdom come. Then, an odd idea struck.

He was just starting to shimmy back out of the hole when a voice called down. "Colonel, can I help?" It was Hastings.

"Get me a thin trowel from the Hippo, fast!"

Hastings had just turned when the ground shook as a second blast scorched the sky.

The colonel couldn't see it from the hole. "Where was that?" he called up.

Hastings shot a glance past the factory, took his bearings. "It wasn't Pringle. We got word that they've removed their fuze and are loading up their bomb. That blast was from the street. Sir, let me get that trowel!" And then, as if the explosion had been a delayed starting pistol, Hastings sprinted full speed toward the Hippo.

The colonel's plan was simple. Bombs are filled with explosives through a hole in the base. While the cone of his bomb was buried, the base plate was fractured. If he couldn't extract the fuze, maybe he could remove enough of the explosive that it wouldn't destroy the factory.

By the time Hastings had returned and handed down the trowel, the colonel had untwisted the base plate.

"Are you doing what I think you're doing?"

The colonel didn't bother with a direct answer. "Thank you for the trowel; now get out of here," he directed.

"Colonel, I want to—"

"GET THE BLOODY HELL OUT OF HERE, NOW! THAT'S AN ORDER!"

He didn't wait to see if Hastings obeyed, but wrestled the base plate to one side, hardly believing what he was seeing: the explosive was in powdered form.

His muttered prayer was the most sincere one of his life. "Thank you, dear God."

Then, wasting no time, and looking like a crazed child digging for clams at the beach, he began to wildly scoop away as much of the explosive powder as he could. As it accumulated on the floor of the dirt shaft around the outside of the bomb, he wondered if it would still explode when the bomb detonated. Was he even doing any good? The answer didn't matter. There wasn't time to haul it away, and he wouldn't further risk the life of his men.

Half an hour later, with the bomb still ticking and the colonel still scooping, his trowel tapped the fuze pocket, the tube that spread across the inner body of the bomb. With much of the explosive gone, he could see that it had sheared loose on one side. It was then that a second idea struck.

Not knowing if it was inspiration or if his brain was growing cloudy from his hanging upside down like a bat for so long, he reached in, seized the cylinder, and began to rock it—back and forth, back and forth, back and forth. The weld on the closest side finally gave way, breaking the fuze pocket completely free, allowing him to withdraw the entire device from the back end of the bomb.

He crawled out of the hole in a bit of disbelief, then stood and held his prize overhead like a fighter brandishing a championship belt after his bout. He had won. The danger was over—other than the fact that the fuze in his hands was still ticking.

He staggered through his first few steps, allowing time for the blood to return to his legs and feet. As he reached the Hippo, he motioned for a pair of pliers from his surprised section who were congregating. When he gripped the now-visible fuze and began to tug, a flash and a crack followed inside the tube at the opposite end. Puzzled, he finished pulling out the (17), unscrewed its gaine to render it safe, and then shined his light inside.

"What is it?" Driver asked.

"It appears to be a new type of secondary fuze," he answered. "But whatever it is, we've got to get it to Dr. Gough right away."

CHAPTER 10

September 20, 1940

Dear Papa,

I awoke last night to thunderous cracking as if the heavens over London were breaking into pieces. A storm had been blowing in the previous evening, and as I lay in the dark, I found myself musing over a peculiar choice for a young German girl trapped in England. Was it the sound of bombs or thunder?

As the words bounced in my head, a rhyme emerged, and so I've written it here, though mostly for my sole amusement.

Inky night, brilliant light, cracking boom, souls affright.
Wicked bomb or nature's thunder? Awe in heaven or tool of plunder?
Thunder or bombs? Bombs or thunder? I make my choice, but yet I wonder.

Should I die before the dawn, then know this truth: my choice was wrong.

When I heard rain follow, I decided it was thunder, and I gathered the covers about my head and went back to sleep.

Papa, spy rumors abound. Claire said a transmitting station was discovered in the tower of an old church and that a parishioner has been arrested. When I hear such stories, I marvel: just how many Germans are hiding out in London?

Now for my secret: Sometimes I'm so fretful. What if the British bomb your factory? What if the English army can't stand alone against Hitler, and he overruns this country? What if the Nazis win and then find out that we are of Jewish heritage?

Often, as I lie in bed at night and listen to the sirens begin their scream, these fears loiter until I hear the all clear. Will there ever be a time, Papa, when there are no more sirens in our lives? Will there ever be a time when every day is an all-clear day?

Papa, I know that a war is on, but I miss you so, and I need to come home. Is that possible? Please consider it.

One last secret: I've agreed to play chess against the American for your honor. I pray you taught me well and that I don't let you down.

Until we all find peace,

Your daughter,

Audrey

Audrey had expected to feel nervous, especially after Cora Holden had dropped in to ask if she would join Lady Reading at the Dorchester hotel the following Monday to speak to the Young Women's Christian Association.

"Be yourself," Cora had offered. "Talk about your background, how you ended up in London at WVS."

"Say nothing of the sort," Claire later cautioned. "Keep it short and tell them only about your desire to help the children."

Audrey was indeed careful, never mentioning to either Cora or Claire that the American, Wes Bowers, had invited her for a chess match on that same morning—their *challenge of the fathers,* which she, of course, had accepted.

She'd told Claire that she was taking a long early walk to loosen her nerves, leaving out the detail that her route would swing right past Café Cozier. What would it hurt to play a quick game?

Now, two doors away, she retrieved a silver compact from her purse to check her makeup. *Keep your Beauty on Duty,* the propaganda posters pasted about London declared. Even the Ministry of Supply agreed, noting, "Cosmetics are as essential to a woman as a reasonable supply of tobacco is to a man." And the government must have believed it because makeup hadn't been rationed.

She'd heard that it was a directive from Churchill, an effort to boost the morale of the boys fighting on the front line—and she would have trusted the rumor, except that the boys were . . . well, *fighting on the front line* with no women in sight. She suspected instead it was to raise the women's morale, let them closely cradle a tiny piece of their prewar lives to convince them, and those around them, that everything was fine, that life would soon get back to normal, that everyone would make it through this despicable war in one piece.

As she studied her reflection, she combed back a curl, pressed her lips together to even their crimson color, and then hand-smoothed unseen wrinkles from her blouse.

Was it even necessary? It's just a friendly game of chess.

Still, she hadn't been out by herself with a man in any capacity since arriving in England, and she needed practice, though, admittedly, that wasn't easy to come by working with women. WVS was hardly prime fishing ground. It would be like dropping a hook into your own bathtub and then wondering why there were no bites.

If she *had* hooked a man in her own bathtub—though she was now a little uncomfortable with her analogy—Claire wouldn't have allowed her to fraternize with him anyway, not while she and Claire were stowed away in a foreign land draped in war. And Audrey had never cared, until lately.

WVS was giving her life purpose, time was dampening the pains of family separation, and the rhythm of routine was repeating a truth that was growing tough to ignore: even war won't abate the longings of a lonely heart.

Audrey wasn't looking for love with the American. She fully understood that Wes Bowers had a girl he cared about back home. What she longed for instead was a patient poke when she was wrong, a pint of praise when she was right, and someone loyal enough to stay around and help her navigate between them. Someone to make her laugh on occasion would also be nice.

Audrey needed a friend.

It was such a kind act by Bowers to save her things and then invite her to play chess. It had been so long since she'd had any sociable interaction with the opposite sex that the decision on whether to show up this morning easily made itself.

Chess. What a curious start: a strategic skirmish played to the death—metaphorically speaking—and she'd been taught by a master of the game. It was true that she hadn't played in over two years, since leaving Germany, but according to her father, its lessons were lived every day of one's life.

The bigger question at hand—as she dropped the compact back into her purse and then slid along the stacked sandbag walls leading to the entrance of the café—was more complicated. It was not whether she'd win or lose. Rather, could she and the American become friends?

She had told Bowers that she wasn't very good at chess, but that wasn't technically true. She'd been taught to play without mercy and was about to humiliate a foreign challenger at her father's favorite game to make him proud. Chess was war, and you took no prisoners.

The American was waiting. *Let the battle begin.*

Café Cozier welcomed Audrey with the scent of freshly baked bread, hand-squeezed lemonade, and laughter. A gleam of artificial light pranced across polished tables with such ease one might have assumed it to be sunlight that had escaped the dawn, slid around the sandbags, and was relaxing inside with the guests.

Wes was seated at a table to Audrey's left, the chessboard centered, the pieces placed. He was fixated on the thing as if moves were already underway.

"I'm here," she said, her words tapping him on the shoulder to attract his attention.

He spun to face her, his eyes focusing directly on her ruby lips. "Hello. I'm glad you made it."

She hoped he would fancy it: the outfit, the makeup, the lipstick, all for *the boys on the front lines*—since, technically, given that the bombing had started, London was his front line. And fancied it he must have, because the man was beaming.

"My, oh, my," he declared, his voice gently lowering. "Apparently, you think you can distract me by getting all prettied up."

"Buggers," she answered dryly. "You can see right through me." She swept away the flattery as if every female chess player dressed this fashionably.

"Does your boyfriend know that you're here?" he asked next, an inquiry that garnered a giggle.

She deflected with a grin. "I've been waiting for my prince, but sadly it seems he's been detained at the castle."

He cushioned his stare with a wink. "What can I get you to drink?" he asked, gesturing toward the opposite chair. "I swear by this grapefruit drink, but it's up to you."

"Sure," she answered, taking her seat. "I'll live dangerously."

While Wes cornered Jorrell to place the order, Audrey studied the board. It was a marbled set, strikingly similar to hers back home, which caused an odd twinge in her heart—so many memories.

Ponder what each piece is worth and establish your plan.

The pawns, standing in their perfect sacrificial rows; the knights, antsy to ride into combat but so unlikely to survive; the bishops, two for each opponent but always staying on opposite-colored squares; the rooks, faithfully anchoring each corner of the board; and then the royalty, the king and queen, hiding behind their subjects as if a parade should start in their honor—but there would never be a parade. There was only war.

Pawns are the soul of the game, but remember that most will die.

She turned and sniffed, certain that she'd caught the cedar scent of her father's shaving powder. She reached for a napkin. The place had warmed, causing the tiniest beads of sweat to mix and mingle on her brow.

Open with the endgame in mind.

"Are we wagering on the game?" Wes asked, disrupting her thoughts.

Below the layers of her blouse, her chest was rising, dropping, rising.

"What did you have in mind?"

"Normally, I'd suggest the loser buys drinks, but here in England that will mean tea, so how about the loser will buy dinner?"

Watch for weaknesses and look for the chance to strike.

"Audrey?" he asked again. "How does that sound?"

She clutched her chair, then glanced back to the pieces.

Anticipate your opponent's moves, and don't leave yourself unprotected.

Her breathing had turned tedious and labored as the room's lights dimmed, and her vision narrowed.

"Are you okay?" Wes asked. "You look a little pale."

"I'm fine," she replied. "I just need some air." But she wasn't fine, and she knew it. The feeling was familiar—she was having another attack.

Not here. Not now.

Her petition for relief was futile. Experience had taught her well that such pleas were pointless. Deciding to flee, she leaned forward to stand, but her foot was tapping pitifully at the floor, and so she pushed her palm against her knee to make it stop.

"I . . . learned to play chess from my father," she mumbled, before realizing it was information she'd shared at their last meeting and had little to do with the discussion at hand.

Control the center and keep your king safe.

Wes had stepped closer and was kneeling beside her chair.

"I'm having a hard time breathing," she whispered, her mouth dry, her torso tightening. She flailed at the table, sending the chess pieces scattering. "I'm sorry, something's wrong."

"I'll call a doctor," she heard him say, his words mixing with the sound of blood pulsing through her ears.

She reached for his arm, but her fingers slipped away. "No, a doctor can't help. Please . . . call . . ." It felt like she was being held underwater with no way of coming up for air.

"Audrey, what is it? What should I do?" His voice was so small, so faint, so far away. If he could only understand.

"I'm sorry!" she gurgled. "Please call . . ."

In the end, even your king may need to join the battle.

Panting. Shivering. Nausea. Pain. Worst of all, surrounded by others, she was utterly alone.

She tried again. "Go to the Dorchester," she whispered. "Please, go to the Dorchester and tell Lady Reading."

CHAPTER 11

Audrey was nudged awake by the morning's early rays licking at her cheeks. If she believed what her body was telling her, she'd been asleep for hours, in a bed that wasn't familiar, wearing a nightdress that wasn't hers. She was surrounded by elegant furnishings looking down with a measure of pity at the poor girl who was lying helpless in their sheets.

Though her grief was gone, a tiredness hung stubbornly around her neck, and would for another day or so.

She closed her eyes to remember how she'd arrived here—for it wasn't as if she would completely black out when an attack occurred. Rather, it would take all of the concentration she could muster to fight away sadness, making it challenging to pay much attention to anything else.

There was a taxi ride . . . she had struggled for air . . . had Wes been sitting by her side? There was crying, lots of crying—that much she remembered—and voices . . . oh, and a doctor had come to visit, though she recalled little about him.

The door swung open, framing a familiar face. "I was in earlier, and you were stirring, so I presumed you'd soon be awake." Lady Reading scooted over to the bed's side. "Your color looks good. How are you feeling?"

"Better," Audrey answered sheepishly. "But, where am I?"

"You're in a suite at the Dorchester."

"How long have I been . . . ?"

She didn't need to finish. Lady Reading reached over and clasped Audrey's hand. "A day, child. You've been here just a day, but it's been time well spent for needed rest."

The hand-holding didn't help. Embarrassment had marched into the room behind the woman and was also sitting on the bed. Audrey jerked up. "No! I missed the speech, then, didn't I?" She didn't wait for the obvious answer. "I feel terrible."

"Truthfully, we both missed the speech," Lady Reading replied, too cheerfully. "But don't you worry yourself about that."

But Audrey did worry, so much that her words stumbled. "Why, you must think I'm . . . stark raving mad."

Lady Reading's kind eyes blinked with almost delight, and then the woman laughed. "You know nothing of my history, do you?" Her question preceded a pause.

Audrey knew that Lady Reading was more than capable of running a large country, that she was adored by everyone at WVS, that she walked in extremely important circles and had friends in the highest places of government, but of the woman's past . . . no . . . Audrey knew nothing. She slowly shook her head from side to side.

Lady Reading crouched closer, held Audrey's hand more firmly this time. "I don't share it with many people, but in your case, I think it could help."

The woman was plain but regal, the type of person who could

read your secrets when she looked in your eyes, but with such empathy that you'd never consider looking away. Audrey's nod offered permission to continue.

"You do know that I became Lady Reading when I married Viceroy Rufus Isaacs, First Earl of Reading, after his dear wife died, correct?"

"Yes, that much I do know."

"And then you must also know that he died just four years later."

"Yes."

"Despite our age difference, I loved the man, so much so that after he was gone, I wrestled mightily with an overwhelming grief." It was Audrey's turn to finger-squeeze, encouraging her to continue. "It was a period in my life that I can only describe as shock and disorientation, but I know you are one of the few who comprehend exactly what I'm saying."

Audrey had locked eyes with the woman and wasn't about to let go.

"After Rufus died," she continued, "I felt the need to travel to the United States. You see, Rufus was a visionary. As a former ambassador to the US, he realized very early that the future of democracy might depend upon the British gaining a greater appreciation of Americans. After he passed away, I couldn't get that notion out of my head. Now, I'll admit that I wasn't myself, that I wasn't thinking clearly—or perhaps it was the clearest my mind had been in a very long time. Either way, I left immediately for the States, without so much as a plan."

"I traveled by motorcar across the country, visiting state after state, staying in dollar-a-night lodgings." She paused to admire the immaculately furnished room. "Audrey, I even worked as a dishwasher."

Audrey bit back her doubt. "A dishwasher?"

"Not for the money, of course, but because I was so completely lost and lonely, searching for answers, and I did want to understand ordinary Americans, to know how they think. It seemed at the time like the proper way to do it." Her glance turned heavenward. "I'm sure Rufus was turning over in his grave, but I didn't know what else to do."

Audrey was like a child at story time. "What happened next?"

Lady Reading gave her another comforting smile. "It's comical, actually. My antics in the States had apparently caused something of a fuss back home in England about . . . how shall I say it? . . . my *well-being.* Enough so that one day, as I was traveling down the road on my way to another cheap hotel, a perplexed state trooper pulled me over."

"Why?"

"I shuddered to find out, afraid that I'd done something wrong or unknowingly committed some crime. He approached the car, took off his hat, and said, 'Ma'am, are you Lady Reading?' Well, I assured him that I was, and then, with a wisp of confusion rising in his voice, he said, 'I just received a call, ma'am, from the president of the United States. He . . . well, he asked if you would call him.'"

Audrey offered wide eyes and a skeptical laugh.

"I'm not making that up," Lady Reading confirmed. "I went to Washington, D.C., met with FDR, and became dear friends with Eleanor Roosevelt—we write each other fortnightly to this day. You see, I fled to America to hide from my past, but ended up finding it. I gained strength, returned to England, and here I am today."

Audrey's eyes had started to shimmer. "Then you do know what I'm going through."

There was no hesitation. "Yes, child, I think I do. It's why I came to see you. It's why I'm here today. You needn't be ashamed for having missed the speech. The soul is a tender and complicated thing, and it can bruise easily, but I've learned it's after fighting through our deepest moments of distress that our greatest strengths are found. Do you believe that?"

"I want to," Audrey whispered, before a pause. "But what about the children?"

"What about them?"

"Will you ever again trust me to be able to take them to the country? What if I were to have an episode along the way?"

"Oh, I see." Lady Reading was nodding, thinking, planning. "Well, you are always with Claire, and sometimes another aid worker or mother will travel along with you, correct?"

"Yes."

"Then, if you feel an attack coming on, they can help you get to safety and call for help. But I believe it will do you and the children more good if we continue."

Audrey's question back was simple. "What if I disappoint you?"

"Then you don't know me well enough. For me, there is no disappointment, only concern—and, speaking of concern . . ."

"Yes?"

"There was a handsome American sitting in the lobby for hours, worried that he was somehow at fault for your condition and wondering if you were all right."

Audrey's voice stood. "He was?"

"Indeed. He finally had to leave to meet his section, but I promised we'd let him know how you were doing. Shall I handle that, or will you?"

"I will."

"I imagined as much. Now, before I go, I have one last matter. When I asked you previously about your accent, you told me that you were from Switzerland. But after chatting with you longer, my ear tells me that's not true."

Audrey could lie to the woman no longer. "No, ma'am, not originally."

"It would appear there's a bit of history that *you* need to share, and I'd like to hear it, but I'm late presently for a meeting with the Home Secretary, so—in due time, child. All in due time."

When the colonel entered Dr. Gough's office at the Ministry of Supply, the man slipped around from behind his desk to meet his friend. He didn't bother with a formal greeting. "Russell, which would you prefer first: the good news or the bad?"

"That sounds like the makings of a terrible joke." Moore handed back the choice to Gough with a shrug.

"The good news, my friend, is that you're damned lucky to be alive. The fuze pocket that you wriggled out of the bomb should have killed you."

"What was it?"

Dr. Gough grimaced. "This is where the bad news will make its entrance. While your bomb's main fuze was ticking merrily away, waiting patiently to kill you, it brought along help."

"What does that mean?"

"As if the (17) wasn't bad enough, the Germans have devised a way to add an auxiliary fuze to protect it. It's called a *Zussatzünder* 40. We've dubbed it the ZUS for short."

"What does a ZUS do?"

"It's an antiwithdrawal device. Think of it as a big, ugly German bodyguard. The second fuze, the ZUS, sits behind the ticking (17) so that if you try to remove it, the ZUS triggers the bomb and instantly blows you up. It has one purpose and one purpose only: to kill bomb disposal personnel."

"ZUS isn't very friendly," the colonel replied, sarcasm seeping.

"You need to thank God that the fuze pocket was damaged. Had you managed to pull out the (17) from your bomb while it was in the ground, you would be a dead man."

"No, not friendly at all," the colonel repeated.

Dr. Gough's countenance craned. "You also should know that you had six minutes left on your (17). Had the bomb been a foot deeper . . ." He didn't need to expound. "We've been expecting the Germans would do this, just not so soon."

The colonel arched forward, pleading. "Herbert, please tell me that you have some sort of answer."

"That's why I called. We're working on several alternatives. Although we can no longer remove the ticking clock, we hope to stop it from ticking. The most promising approach seemed to be the use of magnets, but the Germans took great care to fit their clocks with a nonmagnetic balance wheel."

"I hope that's not the end of your story."

Gough turned to face the colonel more directly. "The Royal Aircraft Establishment found a weak spot. The bearings on the third and fourth wheel have steel spindles and brushes."

"And that's a good thing, correct?"

"It means that with enough magnetic force pulling on those spindles, it applies friction to counter the motion transmitted to the wheel by the mainspring."

"I love it when you speak that way, but what does that mean for the BD teams?"

The doctor looked up at the wall as if wishing he had chalk and a blackboard but pressed on without them. "It's not easy producing a magnetic field in a hollow cylinder, but using a vulcanized coil about the size of your arm, then passing 200 amps of current through it, we've been able to stop the clock—from the outside."

"At last, the boffin offers some good news."

Gough continued unfazed. "You can't extract the fuze, but with the clock stopped, you can transport the bomb to the marshes where you can then safely blow it up."

"It's bloody brilliant," the colonel declared.

"It's not without its problems," Gough clarified. "It takes fourteen 12-volt batteries, carried in three large cases, and it's not been thoroughly tested in the field. Employing typical British creativity, we've named it . . . *the clock stopper.* If you're willing to give it a go, I can have an early version for you this week."

"Do I *want* an early version?"

The man's mouth opened but then closed. It was a credible question without a convincing answer. "You want to be careful," he finally said. "No more heroics. I don't know if you've heard, but 17 Section lost two sappers yesterday—Private Van Vuren and a Scottish chap named Buchanan."

"I heard, but I didn't know them."

The two shared a moment of mutual silence for those lost before the doctor spoke again. "By the way, how's the American working out?"

The colonel gleamed like a proud papa. "Better than expected, other than he won't drink our tea. He said he tried it back home, but he didn't care for it, said it was *iced.*"

Gough's contempt nearly popped its own gasket. "Iced tea? That's barbaric! Why would the Yanks put ice in their tea?" His eyes welcomed no answer. "I must say," he continued, "I was hoping by now you'd have convinced him to call Roosevelt and have him send more soldiers over to give us a proper hand . . . but iced tea? Perhaps we should just rely on Stalin!"

The colonel smiled, raised his own cup. "Drastic times, my friend."

Dr. Gough's face brightened as he turned to a box on his desk. "Oh, I do have one more tool for you. This one you can take today."

"What is it?" Moore wondered.

"It's an electric stethoscope. It attaches to the bomb with a magnet. It has a crystal microphone that we've amplified so that you can listen to a bomb's fuze through a headset while at a distance."

The colonel was already fondling the thing. "It's ingenious, I'll give you that. But is it necessary?"

His friend's words were tentative. "Well, once we stop the clock, the mechanism in the fuze doesn't appear strong enough to start again on its own—unless the clock is jolted."

"There's always a catch. You're saying that the fuze can start ticking again?"

"I told you, the clock stopper is not without its problems. That's why, when the bomb is being moved, you'll want someone to be listening."

The colonel held up the stethoscope. "And you promise this thing will work?"

Gough lobbed back a wicked smile, the type shared between true friends, and, as a scientist, he gave a precise answer.

"Over your dead body."

"Snatch 'is arm!" demanded a chuckling Driver, prodding Wes to grab hold of Pike, who was stretched out, bum down, on the warehouse floor. The remainder of the section had rallied around the lad, and at Driver's directions were taking hold of Pike's other extended extremities. It was the first time Wes had watched the kid truly laugh.

"What's this called again?" Wes asked.

Gunner grunted, then repeated his explanation from earlier. "We're giving him his birthday bumps. It's what we do here for someone on their special day. On my command, we throw him up in the air as high as we can, and then, when he comes down, we let his bum bump the floor. It's one throw for each year and then one for luck. Here we go. Driver, count us all the way to nineteen."

Pike was heaved off the ground while Driver counted each lunge. "One . . . Two . . . Three . . ."

"Don't you mean stop at sixteen?" Wes said, pulling Pike's arm tight on the down-bounce so he didn't bump the ground as hard this time.

"Four . . . Five . . . Six . . ." they chorused.

"Shut up and bump, mate," Badger added, but he hadn't used his typical cantankerous tone, and Pike had started chuckling, and Wes didn't intend to shut up regardless.

"It would be easier if we just sang to him," Wes added.

"Seven . . . Eight . . . Nine . . ."

"I don't know, mate." It was Hastings's turn to butt in. "You haven't heard Gunner sing."

By now, Pike was giggling uncontrollably, and it was so out of character for the normally speechless kid that Driver, Gunner, and even the colonel erupted in peals of laughter. "Ten . . . Eleven . . . Twelve . . ."

The whole lot were acting like a troop of drunken monkeys. "Thirteen . . . Fourteen . . . Fifteen . . . Sixteen."

When they hit sixteen, with Pike's backside still on the floor,

Wes let go. When the rest of the men then tried in rhythm to pick up the kid, only one side lifted, causing the unbalanced group to topple into a snickering heap on the floor.

Wes helped the colonel stand, initially alarmed that the old man might have strained his back. Then their leader steered everyone into a circle around the table so they could present Pike with some gifts.

Eager to go first, Driver retrieved his messtin, covered with a cloth, from where it sat beside their communal hot plate. He handed it over proudly, letting Pike pull off the cloth to reveal a plum cake of sorts.

"I found a recipe in a magazine, but I 'ad to improvise 'cause we've got no oven, and wi'h sugar and butter being rationed, I 'ad to make do."

As the group collectively circled the cake, Hastings stepped up as the mouthpiece. "The horrors of war!"

More laughter. More camaraderie. An outsider peering in would have assumed the men had been passing the bottle.

Wes handed over his gift next, a small rectangle wrapped in toilet tissue. "Happy birthday, kid."

Pike tore away the paper, studied the cubed metal can, read the odd name printed on the label. "SPAM?" he asked, and he wasn't the only baffled one—a ring of eyebrows bunched in unison.

Wes was quick to explain. "It's new in the US. They're sending it out to a lot of the servicemen. It's rather difficult to describe, like a type of . . . ham, I guess." He was shepherding a suspicious smile. "I will say that after eating your food here for the last few weeks, I have the honest sense that you Brits will absolutely love it."

A shallow knock at the entrance door interrupted the celebration.

"I'll answer it," Gunner volunteered, he being the closest. As he opened the door, a woman's voice trickled across the room. "I'm looking for Croydon. Is he here?"

Gunner turned to the group for help. "Croydon?"

He didn't have to wait long.

Private Croydon Snee, also known as Badger, hurdled a chair, crossed the room, and thrust Gunner aside. He spoke, but not to Gunner—his focus was squarely on the girl at the door.

"Etty?"

The group watched wordlessly as Badger scooted outside while closing the door behind him. It was as if a bomb had exploded in the room, leaving everyone so shaken that they couldn't move.

Muted voices wormed in from outside, first Badger's, then Etty's, except the sounds were too garbled for the puzzled listeners inside to understand. The colonel piped up first. "That's Etty, his girl," he said, stating the obvious.

As the section commander, the colonel was too professional to suggest the group do anything further, but that didn't stop Gunner from hissing out the order like he was the one in charge. "Everyone to the windows, but don't let 'em see you!"

Wes and Driver headed east; Hastings and the colonel hustled west. Gunner, in turn, pressed his ear to the door, while Pike peeked out the opening to one side. Battlefield-style communication at its finest followed.

"She's holding a paper, but I can't tell what it is," Hastings announced.

"It's the letter he wrote her," Pike added. "The one he sent last week, that day we finished early."

"He wrote her a letter?" Wes asked, every syllable stunned.

Hastings followed. "I can't see her face. Did she go to jelly?"

"I think she's crying, if that's what you're asking," Wes replied. "Now she's reaching for his hand!"

Gunner moved away from the door and edged in beside Pike. "He's going in for a hug."

"Quiet!" commanded the colonel. "We don't want him to hear us!"

"Hugging," Gunner added. " . . . still hugging. Buggers! Now they're pulling back, and . . . wait . . . YES! They're touching lips!"

Wes took another turn at the narrative. "He's grasping her hands . . . still kissing. . . . wait, she's turned and is leaving. He's waving. She's waving . . . nope, she's coming back. They're kissing again!"

This was the best entertainment the section had had in weeks.

"They've pulled apart," Pike added. "She's leaving for certain this time. QUICK, HE'S COMING BACK!"

Wes dashed over to his cot, picked up a book, and pretended to examine its pages—which made no sense since, before the knock at the door, the group had been giving Pike his birthday presents. The colonel and Hastings lunged to the table and calmly pretended to discuss the plum cake and its edibility, while Pike studied his newly gifted can of SPAM. Driver was the only member of the group not to move away from the window. "What are we trying to 'ide?" he asked with a shrug.

When Badger stepped through the door, he was drawing full bursting breaths, and from the look in his eyes, it was the freshest air that ever existed on God's good planet. He seemed to take in exactly what had been happening in the room, not fooled for a moment. He honed in on Wes, sitting frozen on his cot, then marched right over to his nemesis.

Wes gazed up, pretending to barely notice that he had a visitor, and while Badger wasn't smiling, he wasn't frowning either. In the silent, hanging moment, Wes studied the lines on the man's face, trying to read the emotion written there, and the closest he could come to describing it would be to call it . . . gratitude.

Badger didn't speak but straightened up so rigid one would have thought Churchill himself had strolled into the room, cigar in hand. Then, without further delay, he offered Wes a razor-sharp, perfectly executed salute.

Badger had never saluted Wes. In fact, he'd likely never saluted anyone. It was fresh territory, and, not sure what to do, Wes followed protocol: he stood up, stared into the man's eyes, and then smartly saluted back.

No words were spoken because, between men, no words were necessary.

Next, Badger raised his fist as if reaching for the room's rafters, and then he jumped as high as his short-legged, bulky frame would allow, all while letting out a most glorious and satisfying cheer.

It was Pike's voice Wes heard next, only he wasn't speaking. The boy who had muttered less than a dozen full words before today had turned to Badger and was singing.

"*For he's a jolly good fellow, for he's a jolly good fellow . . .*"

By the second stanza, the entire section had joined in, and whether they were singing to Badger because he had his girl back, or to Pike because it was his birthday, or because one more day in the miserable war had passed and they were all still alive, it was all the same.

" *. . . for he's a jolly good fellow, and so say all of us!*"

When the song ended, Badger hurried to his own cot. He began rifling through his duffel bag. When he couldn't find what he needed, he turned to Driver for help.

"Hurry, find me a piece of paper. I'm going to write her another letter!"

CHAPTER 12

"Lieutenant, do you, um . . . have a moment?" Pike asked, edging close to Wes as he sat on his bunk reading.

Wes glanced across his own shoulder, as if on his way out. "I was actually going to run home for a . . . oh, that's right, I'm in England. Yes, I have all the time in the world. How may I help?"

Pike blushed. Wes should have known better than to joke with the kid, the politest in all of London, albeit a bit of a misfit. "I'm kidding. What's up?"

Pike was speaking to the ground, glancing up only on occasion to see if Wes was still there. "Lieutenant . . . I wanted to say . . . thank you for the SPAM."

They were words Wes would surely never hear uttered again in his lifetime, and he insisted his face not smile. "It was your birthday. It was the least I could do—quite literally. How was it? Did you enjoy it?"

Pike shifted his feet, drummed fingers against his pant leg. "Well, my mum's alone, sir. We don't have much, and I thought she'd fancy seeing what Yanks eat, so I sent the can to her. I hope you're not mad."

Fighting a smile quit being a problem. "No, that's very kind of you, Pike. How's your mum doing?"

"Well enough . . . and . . ." More shifting of his feet.

"What is it?"

"I wanted to say, I like that you talk to us . . . that we matter to you."

"Talk to who?" Wes asked.

"The sappers. You know, the men who aren't officers. I have a friend from Whitehaven in 87 Section, and it's not the same for him. Usually, in England, the officers and soldiers don't . . . well, they don't entertain together. But here, with you and the team, it's different. I guess in that way, the war has been good."

Wes tried not to let his head shake. "The war *good?* How so?"

Pike turned a timid chin. "In my mum's last letter, she told me she sat beside a university professor in the bomb shelter, a refined and educated woman. She said they had a jolly good chat and . . . well, that's never happened to her before. It turns out that in the bomb shelters, we're all the same, just people wanting to live another day. That's the part of the war that's nice."

Wes let the thought simmer. "I'd like to meet your mum someday. When you write to her, tell her that your Yank friend says he wishes her well."

It was the first time that Pike's eyes didn't turn away—and he was all smiles.

"I will, sir. I will."

"Audrey, I'm going to see if the market has cheese. I'll be back in a jiffy," Claire promised, except it was a blatant lie. The market hadn't had cheese for days and wouldn't tonight. Out of the view of Audrey, who was sitting in the kitchen listening to news on the wireless, Claire swiftly sheathed her letter, sealed the envelope, and addressed the front.

Claire couldn't send her letter through regular post, not with censors reading everything, and certainly not a letter addressed to Kaden Froe, a German pilot—so she'd made other arrangements. She would be paying a man who was traveling to Ireland to carry it there, where it could reach Germany without being reviewed by prying eyes.

What she was doing was illegal; if caught, she would be promptly arrested, but she would take that chance. She gathered her purse, slid the letter and several folded bills inside, and then rushed out the door.

Major Balder Leemon was a short, blocky man with a small face, slippery hair, and pallid skin. He'd been diagnosed as a child with nystagmus, a condition of involuntary eye movements, which meant that he'd been saddled with thick, rimless glasses that, due to their weight, tended to sag down to the very tip of his vigilant nose. As a result, his view of the world often arrived magnified and particularly focused on things nearby that he could dissect, analyze, and ponder, leaving life's broader observations to those with a more prolonged perspective.

He'd never accepted his condition as a negative; it wasn't how he'd prismed his existence. To him, the affairs of life were neither happy nor sad, bitter nor sweet, lucky nor unlucky. Life simply *was*. It started with birth. It ended with death. And only facts should fill the space in between. Full stop. End of line. Engaging in emotions had continually proved a colossal waste of time.

His love for numbers—which were trustworthy and tangible—landed him an early career at DMI, the Directorate of Military Intelligence, a department of the British War Office. While he'd started as a low-ranking officer in Topography and Statistics, his unfaltering loyalty to the work, coupled with the ebb and flow of government bureaucracy, eventually lifted him in the rising tide in both rank and responsibility, until it dropped him with little fanfare as a liaison to the Aliens Department of the Home Office.

Since England's declaration of war in September a year earlier, the Aliens Department had been tasked with holding tribunals to classify some 75,000 foreign residents in the UK—generally from Germany and Austria—into one of three assigned categories.

Those classified as Category A were a high security risk and would be immediately sent to internment camps across the country, the largest being located on the Isle of Man. Those classified as Category B were deemed doubtful cases and would be released, but with assigned supervision and restrictions. And lastly, those classified as Category C were considered no security risk whatsoever and would be exempt from both internment and restrictions, free to live among the populace unhindered.

Major Leemon's desk sat in a dimly lit basement room of the Foreign and Commonwealth Office. He'd never thought of the space as undesirable. On the contrary: anyone with half a pea for a brain would know that in government, all of the important work is done downstairs in shadowy, windowless offices.

It had been several months since most of the tribunals had been completed, shifting the bulk of his workload to following up. As Leemon now surveyed the papers covering his desk, a rather portly, cheerful woman entered his office, holding a teletype message in one hand and tea in the other. "Good morning, Major. I have the passport information that you requested from yesterday."

He ignored the tea and instead snatched the dispatch with eager fingers, holding it side by side against another sheet that had been spread patiently on his desk. His amplified eyes, glossy through the thick glass, first narrowed and then blinked, awash with smugness.

"Yes, I knew it. It's just as I had suspected."

"What is it, sir?"

"A discrepancy that I found in my cross-checking, with regards to two women who entered the UK last September, at the beginning of the war."

"What is the problem?" She set his tea on the only open spot left on his desk.

"Their passport information doesn't match."

"Meaning?"

"It means their papers are forgeries—very good forgeries, but forgeries nonetheless. But there's something else: while the women claimed to be from Switzerland, and it appears they did live there for a time, the Swiss paperwork indicates that they crossed in from Germany. Of course, many Germans were trying to escape the Nazis by asking for refugee status, but these women didn't."

"Curious. Do you think they're dangerous?"

"We can't know until we investigate further, but the facts point to a likely outcome."

"What's that?"

"These two women are spies."

CHAPTER 13

Wes propped himself against the tire of the truck. "Hey, Gunner, can I ask you something?"

"Don't know, can you?"

The team had just pulled an SC500 from a backyard garden in Stratford, removed its impact fuze, and then hauled the bomb to the Hackney marshes to blow it up. While the colonel was busy attaching the guncotton, Wes had parked beside Gunner at the Hippo.

"Have you ever thought of wearing a patch over your bad eye?"

There was no hesitation. "Yeh, but then women won't notice me."

The boy was expressionless, making it impossible to tell if he was joking. Still, since nothing seemed to offend him, Wes delved deeper. "What was it like when your plane was hit, and you took shrapnel to your eye? Were you scared?"

Gunner crossed his arms, replied matter-of-factly as if everyone had been hit with shrapnel at some point in their lives: "There was a boom, mate. I was knocked back. When I sat up, I was missing an eye. Didn't have a bloody choice, did I?"

"Did facing death frighten you?"

Gunner spat before answering. "I had already made my peace with death. I want to think that I traded my eye for a little more time."

Wes scrunched. "You're joking, right?"

If so, Gunner had already kicked Wes's smirk to the ground and was standing on it. "Never joke with death," he whispered. "She doesn't have a good sense of humor."

And then Wes learned an unusual truth: it's hard to win a staring contest against a one-eyed opponent.

"My turn," Gunner announced, wading into the personal questions pool. "Even with two eyes, how'd you end up in the armed forces? I can't believe they let you in."

Wes stooped closer. "Careful—I'd hate to see you lose your other eye. But if you're sincere, the answer is duty."

"Duty?"

"My two grandfathers both served; my father served; I also felt the need to do my part. One day a buddy and I headed over to Phoenix to test for the Navy Air Corps since we'd heard they would let us finish out our college year before reporting. But after they listened to my heart, they said I wasn't eligible—said it was beating too slow, that I was at risk for heart problems in battle. I got snappy and told 'em they were wrong, that, as an athlete, I was in the best shape of my life. But they wouldn't listen."

"Buggers never do. What then?"

"I stormed out, drove straight to the recruiting office for the Marines. When I walked in, the man sized me up, then asked if I was there to join. When I said yes, he asked if I was healthy and ready to serve. When I answered yes again, he stood and said, 'Raise your right hand!' He swore me in right then and there. That's the absolute truth."

"You're sayin' the Marines had lower standards?"

"Something like that." He hated it when the kid was right.

"But, mate, why ship you off so fast to England?"

Wes chewed on the question. He might as well be honest. "When they send you to bomb disposal, it's for one of two reasons: they think you're smart and have a chance of surviving, or they don't like you at all and presume you'll end up dead."

Gunner patted Wes on the back. "Well, then, do your best to disappoint them. Now, I don't know about you, but once the colonel comes back and we blow this thing up, we should find a pub. It's the one truth about war: it always makes you thirsty."

Dear Wesley,

I pray this finds you healthy, safe, and happy. I so enjoyed your last letter and the intimate feelings that you shared that I had to write back straightaway.

I stood behind a woman in the market last week who spoke to the cashier with an English accent and found myself inching close to listen. It turned out she was from Australia, not England, but it still caused a flood of familiar thoughts.

My parents often ask about you and how you're doing. I know you carry greater aspirations in life than working for my father, but once you come home, he would love to have you return to the shop, even if it's just to earn money to finish out college. It seems that he adores you more than I do.

As I listen to the radio and read the papers, I look for mention of the United States entering the war but find that sentiment is split. Some want us to help England, saying it's our duty to ensure freedom, even if it means joining the war. Many others, though, feel the conflict is too far away, that the prospect of war is so terrible, we should keep our distance.

Now, you shared a secret in your letter, and so shall I: at night, as I lie snug in my welcome bed in our safe and free country, I worry about you. I worry that you'll get injured, or worse, that you'll not return home. I tell you this because I want you to know that a girl far away is thinking about you.

My deeper secret, something I have never told you, is that I also didn't believe in the war. I didn't want our country to get involved. Who would cheer for war? But lately, I've been listening to the news reports of Edward R. Murrow. He has been broadcasting from London, right there in the middle of the Blitz. I could hear the bombs falling during his newscast. Imagine that! And I thought to myself, you may be hearing and seeing those very same bombs.

Mr. Murrow says that if the United States does nothing, bombs will ultimately reach our shores, and I'm now convinced that he's right. I don't seek war. I seek peace and forever will, but sometimes seeking peace means that soldiers must pick up their weapons and fight. That is the price of freedom. That is the price you are paying so that

I can miss you from my warm bed—and both my bed and I thank you, Wesley, for doing your part.

With Mr. Murrow's help, hopefully, many more in his massive audience will follow, and sentiment will change.

Until then, stay safe.

Love,

Nathelle

Wes was looking down, reading his paper, when she slipped in, so Audrey safely sheltered behind the coatrack guarding the door to both brush her hair and garner her gumption. When her confidence was convinced that it was ready, she walked over to where Wes was sitting.

"Are there no buildings to blow up today?" she asked, drawing his gaze away from the London news.

Wes stood from the table, tossed his paper aside. "Audrey, how are you?" He reached for her chair, but she had already pulled it out and was taking a seat beside him. "I've been worried," he added. "I'm glad you're okay. May I order you some tea?"

She welcomed his kindness but hated that it was weighed down with such concern, such pity. "No, thank you. I'm here because I owe you an explanation."

"No, you don't owe—"

She let her confession plow right into his objection, cut it short before he could even get started. "For some time now, I've been having occasional . . . I don't know what to call them, other than episodes of despair that sometimes paralyze me. That's what happened the other day."

As he straightened in his seat, she waited for him to ask how he could help, so she could kindly convey that there was nothing he could do. Or, he may suggest that she see a doctor, after which she would describe how they'd had no real solutions. Perhaps he would change the subject, like most people did, and she wouldn't blame him one bit. Instead, he reached over and lightly squeezed her shoulder. "I'm sorry that's happening. You have a lot of courage."

She had many things—angst, emotional damage, secrets—nothing that she would call courage, but before she could protest, he continued. "I like that you've followed your own advice on letter writing, and you've shared something personal here. It's an approach that's been quite helpful to me, to be honest, so thank you."

Audrey's ears twitched. Every word was heard but not properly processed. "I don't think I can play chess with you," she blurted out as if that was his greatest misgiving. "The doctor who saw me said that it's a trigger, though he doesn't know why."

Wes's hands shifted to his hips. "I've heard many excuses before from panicked opponents, but I'll say this much: yours is the most creative." A smug look was replacing his previous sympathy, doing its best to disarm her.

She lowered her jaw to speak, but no words seemed willing. All she could manage was a modest, muttered request. "I think I'd like some tea after all."

It came quickly, and as she stirred, she relaxed. It was comforting the way he layered his humor, like slices of sponge cake placed perfectly between the berries and the cream. "Is that how you do it?"

"Do what?" he asked.

"Bomb disposal. I guess humor is the only way not to go batty under such pressure. Are you aware that the newspapers are calling your teams 'suicide squads'?"

"I've read that, but it's not true. I don't want to die. I want to live. Isn't that the opposite?"

She let her arms fold. "I suppose so, but what you do is still awfully dangerous." Then her eyes grew solemn. "Does death scare you?"

"I'm not excited about the possibility, if that's what you're asking."

She rolled the thought over in her mouth like she was savoring a piece of candy. "In my view, I think we place too much importance on death. And why? People have been getting maimed and killed for thousands of years, haven't they? Doesn't life end as easily as it begins? We should keep a sense of proportion about it."

His stare back was dubious, as if she'd grown a six-inch nose. "Well, that feels a little crass, but I guess it's one way to look at it. I take it, then, you're not fearful of death?"

She rested her chin in her hands. "I . . . I used to think I was ready to die, but after helping the children, I just don't know. I suppose we should simply make the most of our lives, no matter our situation, rather than wasting time quivering. Do you agree?"

"I agree that we should pick a happier topic," he replied. "I should tell you that Badger is back with his girl because of you."

Her chin lowered. "Me? What did I do?"

"I passed along your suggestions for letter writing, recommended he pour out his heart to her, and share a secret, and it worked—too well."

"Too well?" Her eyebrows squished together. "How so?"

Wes battled a new smile. "He told me the other day that he finally understands love. I asked what he meant, and he said, 'Men are just like bombs, simple creatures, but while a bomb needs someone to kill, a man needs someone to save.'"

Audrey smiled with him. “It’s oddly profound, in a dreary sort of way.”

“Worse than that. I’ve created a monster.”

She nudged forward. “Oh, did you also follow my advice?”

“What do you mean?”

Her gaze had settled on an envelope peering out of his uniform pocket. “Is that a letter you’re writing?”

Wes pulled it out. “No, this is one I received.”

“From your girl?” Her eyes danced with new light. She reached for the letter, but he jerked it away.

“Aren’t you getting a tad nosy?”

“It’s all this talk of dying; it makes me daring. What does she say?” she playfully teased.

“Would you care to read it?”

She could tell that he was trying to be funny, but he *had* invited. “May I?” She reached again for it, snatched it before he could further object, and then tugged the letter from its envelope. “Let’s see what she writes . . .”

She watched him shift his weight as if suddenly sitting on gravel, and as she read the greeting aloud with exaggerated emotion, “*Dear Wesley,*” she giggled.

“Hey, that’s enough.”

Every muscle in her face was turning up as she continued to read silently, her eyes darting back and forth until she paused midpage. “She adores you. That’s a good thing.”

“True,” he agreed, “but keep going. She says later that her father adores me even more, and yet he used to throw greasy rags at me at the shop when I’d mess up. That should tell you something.”

“Do you have a picture of her?” Her eyes had grown round as plums.

"I do, but . . ."

"Let me see," she said, like a teacher demanding her student hand over a passed note.

Wes let out a surrendering breath, yanked out his wallet, and then parted with his only photo.

Audrey studied Nathelle's features: delicate but defined, thin brows, a mild chin, with brown hair peeking out from behind her silk scarf.

"She's pretty," Audrey noted, a declaration obvious to anyone glancing at the photo. "Do you need help writing back to her?" she asked through her grin.

"Honestly, I prefer our conversation about death. Can we go back to that?"

Audrey eased back in her chair, a stiff wooden thing that somehow felt like a relaxing chaise longue, because for the next two and three-quarter hours, she and Wes chatted about everything from Hitler's absurd little mustache to whether lemon or banana curd made a better substitute for rationed butter.

When Audrey finally looked at her watch, she jumped to her feet. "I have to go! Claire will be on tenterhooks! Thank you, Wes Bowers, for making me forget there is a war on. It was divine." She snatched up her purse, bowed her goodbye, and then steered around the table toward the entrance.

A dozen steps away, she turned. "It would be lovely to do this again."

Wes stood, raised his glass, and then in a booming voice that mimicked English royalty, he declared, "Yes, that would be absolutely *jammy!*" Of course, he had no idea what it meant or how it should be correctly used, causing both to steal a smile.

Once outside, Audrey was grateful to see that the storm that had camped over London had moved on. At least, it must have, because as she pranced down the sidewalk, it was the first time she'd felt warm in days.

She was taking long, sure strides in an effort to reach home before the sirens started, but at the corner, she realized she'd been stepping in tempo. It was that silly "Private Payton" song by Arthur Askey that had been playing on the wireless in the café and was now stuck humming in her head. Instead of fighting the mildly annoying melody, she admitted defeat and began to sing along.

Come a little closer, Private Payton,
Whisper sweet affections in my ear.
Kiss me on the cheek, Private Payton . . .

She couldn't remember the last stanza, so she filled it in with her own nonsensical lyrics, singing them loudly, which brought both looks and laughter from an elderly couple passing on the street—and oddly, she relished it all.

You're heading off to war, Private Payton,
Our time is short before you'll soon be gone.
So kiss me on the lips, Private Payton,
Let's hold each other 'til the break of dawn.

Yes, despite the war, it was an incredibly pleasant evening indeed.

Urged forward by the colonel, Wes crept toward the bomb, looking back at his commander the same way one might glare into the eyes of a horse just before climbing on to ride for the first time.

"You've watched me do it before," the colonel assured. "There's no reason to be nervy. Not with this one. Not after what you've been through."

To Wes, it seemed obvious. "That's why I *am* nervy."

Badger and Gunner had exposed the ordnance, just four feet down, and then attached the electric stethoscope, now being monitored by Badger from a good three hundred feet away. It was merely for practice since, if the fuze markings were to be believed, this small, fifty-kilogram bomb was armed with a simple (15) impact fuze. Unless the Germans had unexpectedly started to mismark their bombs, this was one of the easiest of all ordnances to defuse.

Wes caught himself swaying. "I'm nervous," he told the colonel, "because this time, the outcome is on me. If I'd have died while *you* were disarming the fuze, that's one thing. But if I become a gold star in my mom's window because of my own stupid mistakes, why, she'll never forgive me."

The colonel's arms unfolded. "Let me go over it one more time," he said, his voice fatherly. "Place the Crabtree Diffuser over the fuzehead and tighten the side screw. Let the charge drain from the condensers for at least thirty seconds, and then use the key wrench to unscrew the locking ring. Carefully extract the fuze, then unscrew the gaine. Put the gaine in one pocket, the fuze in the other—and you're done."

"And there can't be a (50) or a ZUS to booby-trap this one, right?"

"Not if we trust the number stamped into the fuze, and plus, the fuze pocket is too small."

Wes exhaled. "And you'll be right by my side?"

The colonel coughed like an almond was stuck in his throat. "Do you think I'm daft? No, I won't be by your side, but I'll be close enough that you can shout—and call out what you do each step of the way. If you blow yourself up, I want to know why." There was no grin hitched to his statement, no humor tagging along whatsoever.

Wes knelt reluctantly beside the bomb, unbuttoned his shirt collar, took out his tools, and set them in the dirt to wait their turn. Most important was the Crabtree Diffuser. It was a shallow-rimmed brass disc about the size of a pocket watch whose insides had been taken out and replaced with two parallel prongs used to depress the bomb's plungers. According to the colonel, it was the earliest innovation of the Backroom Boys, developed during the war's first days once bombing of the port cities had started. The boys in the lab reasoned that if Germany could charge their fuzes by leaking electricity into firing capacitors after their bombs had left the plane, then the British could probably discharge them in the selfsame way—and they proved to be right.

Wes slowly pressed the device against the fuze, screwed in the thumb bolt, and then waited for the second hand on his watch to circle once—allowing ample time for the charge to drain.

Next, he unscrewed the locking ring and gripped the Crabtree still attached to the fuze. "Fire in the hole," he muttered, chuckling once because it was funny, and then again because he was the only one there to appreciate his humor. Then, without further fanfare, he gave it a pull.

There was no fire. No explosion. No drama whatsoever. In fact, the fuze slid out so easily it would have fallen into the dirt on its own had the bomb been rolled over.

"That wasn't so bad."

Wes unscrewed the gaine, separated it from the fuze, slipped it into his pocket, and then hollered toward the colonel, "All done."

His tone was tranquil, as if he'd just cooked breakfast for the team and was inviting them to gather.

The colonel moved in close to inspect. "You forgot to call out your steps."

Wes held out the fuze. "Sorry, I was caught up in the delicate nature of my work. So again, just to confirm, with the fuze and gaine removed, there's no way for the bomb to explode, correct?"

"That's true. I've watched soldiers use the high explosive as a fuel, and it burns nicely. Without a fuze, the explosive material inside is as safe as sand."

Wes wiped his face for the last time. "All right, now what?"

The colonel kicked mud from his boots, then turned back toward the men. "Unless you have a better idea, we'll have the sappers carry the bomb to the Hippo, and then we'll drive it to the marshes."

Wes's shining eyes let the colonel know that he did have a better idea. "Badger likes me now, right? You saw him salute me the other day, didn't you?"

"You're wearing an evil grin," Colonel Moore noted. "What are you thinking?"

Wes was squinting toward the team. "I think," he replied slowly, still formulating his plan, "that we all deserve to have a good laugh."

Badger repositioned the headphones of the electric stethoscope, continuing to marvel at the innovation. This instrument was ace, pure genius. Without it, the team would be forced to use a doctor's stethoscope, usually borrowed from a local hospital, and that meant crouching right beside whatever devil bomb they were defusing just to make sure it stayed dead. With this contraption, he could safely listen at a fair distance away, and as teams across London began to use it, this marvel was going to save countless lives, perhaps even his own.

His thoughts were interrupted, first by a bit of static, but then by the distinct sound of terror.

Tick, tick, tick, tick, tick . . .

Badger sat up and adjusted the headphones.

This couldn't be right.

He snugged them tight against his ears to keep out all other noise. The rhythm, barely audible, was deafening: *tick, tick, tick, tick, tick . . .*

It was difficult to tell which body part sprang into action first: hands flapping, feet jumping, or mouth swearing. As he turned toward where the bomb had been resting, his eyes grew to the size of overwatered fall grapes.

Bowers had hoisted the bomb onto his shoulders, restarting its jammed fuze, and was walking right toward the section as they waited at the Hippo.

It could blow at any moment. The stupid Yank was going to kill everybody!

Badger jerked off his headphones. "PUT IT DOWN!" he hollered at Wes. "IT'S TICKING! THE BOMB IS TICKING!"

Hastings stood, stretched, stared. He didn't appear to fathom yet what was taking place, but he could see enough of Badger's fear to know something was very wrong. Gunner, Pike, and Driver, who'd all been sleeping in the dirt beside the Hippo, sat, then stood, then also readied to run for cover.

Wes kept coming, dragging the stethoscope cord behind him.

The idiot American, oblivious and misunderstanding of the

danger, met the frenzied reception with nothing but a dopey grin—as if he was being welcomed to a beach party where he'd been charged with carting in a tub of cider.

Badger screamed louder, waved faster, jumped higher. "PUT IT DOWN, YOU BLOODY FOOL! IT'S TICKING!"

Wes cupped his free hand to his ear, as if too deaf or stupid to understand.

Badger pivoted, gauged the open space between himself and the Hippo, and then readied to sprint away. But the cord to the headphones had managed to entwine behind his shoulder, and by the time he'd wrenched it free, the bat-crazy Yank had already plopped the bomb down in the dirt with a thud.

There was no explosion, only delight dancing across Wes's face as he raised his arm, leading everyone's focus to the now-visible wristwatch that he'd positioned against the stethoscope's microphone.

Wes plucked the ticking timepiece free and then, in the worst British accent anyone had ever heard, declared, "I see that it's almost three. Shall we all go for a spot of tea?"

Gunner was the first to giggle. Pike shortly followed, then Hastings and Colonel Moore.

Badger, who hadn't budged, still looked a bit bewildered until Wes extended his hand and exclaimed, "I got you, my friend! I got you!" Badger's sour frown sweetened so quickly into laughter that once he started, he couldn't stop. When he extended an arm so that Wes could draw him in close, the two hugged like long-lost brothers.

Wes turned to the entire group. "Now, unless we've got another bomb to defuse, I believe a little merriment is warranted, and the first round is on me!"

It was later, on the drive to the closest pub, that the colonel confided to Wes, "I haven't seen the men this relaxed in days. I think the laughter reminds us that we're still alive." He slapped Wes again on his shoulder, continued his praise. "That was good, Bowers. That was very good. You're fitting in fine after all."

October 8, 1940
Dear Papa,

This week I sat behind two young lads on the bus who spoke excitedly about the day they'd join the British army, ship off to war, and kill Germans. I wanted to whisper that a German was sitting right behind them, watching and listening, but I didn't.

While they were just children and I paid them little mind, I see hatred once aimed solely against the Nazis spreading to include all Germans, and it troubles me.

I devour two or three newspapers daily and then listen to the wireless every evening—waiting for news, waiting for news—both of the attacks on London and of England's reprisals. Unfortunately, when we do hear reports, we can never be sure what to believe. The news is so heavily censored that I've heard it said the Ministry of Information should be renamed the Ministry of Misinformation. But we continue to listen.

In general, while people here do look sleepy and often strained, on the whole, I find them going about their work as usual, cheerful enough, considering our circumstances.

Oh, and guess what? The sirens screeched again last

night, but my secret is that I didn't hear them. Instead, I slept like a fed puppy and only found out about them after Claire told me in the morning. It does give me pause. On one hand, if I grow apathetic to the sirens, it may put me in danger. On the other hand, to finally sleep through the night was blissful. Could it mean that I'm shedding despair and accepting my situation? What I do know is that Claire was up brooding and is now in the most fitful of moods.

Speaking of sirens, it's odd that I can walk down Oxford Street, try on a hat at Selfridges, eat lunch at the Criterion, all while sirens wail. I fear we're becoming true Londoners.

Until we all find peace,

Your daughter,

Audrey

CHAPTER 14

"Claire, have you found the boys? Check in the back of the coach!" The panic in Audrey's voice was rising like high tide.

They'd been outside the school near Langbourn—their first stop of the morning—for less than half an hour, and they'd already managed to lose three children. The brothers—ages six, seven, and eight—had been a handful from the time their mum had dropped them off. She had approached Audrey uneasy about their billeting and was kindly assured that everything possible would be done to keep the little mites together.

"You don't understand, miss," the haggled mum with one waving arm and a shawl-wrapped baby shot back. "I don't want 'em billeted together. They fight like stray cats. I want you to keep 'em far apart!"

A teacher helping nearby voiced her utter disgust, not as much with the children as with their mother. "It's a simple but sad fact," she declared to Audrey as the mum walked away, "that some parents are quite delighted to have their obligations hauled away. I have seen it often!" Audrey didn't argue the point.

But now all that mattered was to find the boys. She flagged down two passing strangers—an ill-tempered man in an old raincoat and a middle-aged dockworker—and begged them to join the search. To Audrey's great relief, the dockworker eventually discovered the delinquent threesome playing in an adjacent park, and by the time the children were loaded into the waiting vehicles, it was almost noon.

The caravan—one ambulance, two Austins, and a coach—headed to Andover, but twice had to backtrack after the lead driver made a wrong turn. Few blamed him. With Hitler's invasion of England still likely, all street signs had been taken down to make it more toilsome for the attackers to find their way once they'd landed. Of course, this also made those who struggled with navigation secretly wish that Hitler would hurry things up.

If getting lost had been the only problem, life would have been dandy. But, in addition, an eight-year-old lodged his thumb in a hole on the frame of the metal seat and couldn't get it free; a girl of ten tossed her gas mask out the window, despite her timid denials; and the youngest of the lost delinquent boys, when told by Claire not to fret about his sticky hands as he'd get a nice hot bath on arrival, immediately began to bawl. Apparently, he'd never been in a bath and was terrified that he would drown.

Then, as the children seemed to settle down at last, a few began to complain that they weren't feeling well, and a tot two rows up from Claire puked all over the boy beside him. Apparently, the little ones had never traveled in a moving vehicle so far across the country, and they battled carsickness for the balance of the ride.

As a final straw, just before exiting the bus late that afternoon,

Audrey noticed that the dear thing who had snuggled up against her, a five-year-old girl, had a head full of lice.

"I pray for the house where they'll be billeted," Claire whispered, referring to no child in particular, and Audrey was tending to agree.

After paperwork had been filled out and the children suitably distributed to their host families, Claire and Audrey headed next on foot toward the bus station. While most of the assisting teachers had decided to stay over, Audrey and Claire had opted for the last bus to London so they could sleep in their own beds.

Twice, as they walked down the street, Claire turned to peek behind them.

"What is it, Claire?" Audrey asked.

"Nothing, I suppose."

If it was nothing, why was Claire picking up her step?

After another quick turn of her head, Claire affirmed, "Audrey, there's a man back there. I think he's the same one who was at the school when we started this morning."

Audrey twisted around, scanned the street, could see no one looking suspicious. "The same man? Where? What does that mean?"

Claire clinched her purse. "Hurry! It means that we're being followed!"

It was ten minutes past nine when Wes and the team arrived at the intersection of Garfield Road and Columbia to check out what an elderly air-raid warden had described as a direct hit on an Anderson Shelter. A newly married couple had taken cover there and hadn't been seen since the raid.

The small, arching, shedlike structures fabricated out of

corrugated metal were named after Sir John Anderson, a British politician who had spearheaded prewar air-raid preparations. Anderson Shelters were designed to be easily assembled and then partially buried in a yard or garden before the outer roof was covered with a foot or two of dirt. An opening in front—half the size of a normal door and usually shielded with wood, canvas, or metal—stepped down to a 6.5-foot-long by 4.5-foot-wide room that would provide snug protection against most bomb blasts for a family of up to six.

The kits for these shelters were given out free by the government to poorer residents and made available for a small fee to those of means. More than two million had been constructed in yards across the city by the time London was first bombed. Some neighborhoods had even held competitions for the "prettiest shelter" for anyone choosing to doll theirs up to make it more inviting.

The colonel stepped up beside Wes. "Are you ready?" he asked.

For the past week, the colonel had been teaching Wes how to determine a UXB's size based on its entry hole. An eight-inch hole was probably a fifty-kilogram bomb, while an eighteen-inch opening belonged to a bomb weighing ten times as much.

The method wasn't foolproof, as the nature of the soil and the density of material the bomb had penetrated could sometimes skew the results, but it was a fair guide. Nor was the exercise carried out merely for curiosity's sake. It was crucial to know what they were dealing with in order to determine safe evacuation distances for the surrounding populace, not to mention other members of the section who were not digging.

Today would be a test. It had been decided at breakfast that Wes would go in initially and make a quick assessment, followed by the colonel, who would confirm how he'd done.

"It will be a doddle," the colonel insisted, prodding Wes forward toward the shelter, leaving him to assume the man meant *easy.*

"A doddle it is." Wes courtesy saluted before marching to the shelter's roof, first to study the dead-center hole and then around the opposite side to gain a better angle—but this one was tricky to gauge. Dirt around the hole had caved into the opening, obscuring it, and while it didn't look larger than eight to ten inches—meaning it should be a smaller bomb—he couldn't be certain.

"Let it be true," he mumbled, having recently learned that the (17) fuze, the ticking time bomb the section was growing to dread, was seldom used in smaller ordnances. By examining the hole in the ground on the inside of the shelter's floor, he could confirm what risk he was dealing with.

Wes approached the entrance, kicked away a metal sheet that had been pushed up against the opening from the inside, and then stepped down the two visible stairs.

An engulfing stench speedily swathed him, creeping up his pant legs, inside the open gaps of his uniform, around his collar, and into his nostrils. It clung stubbornly to any surface it crossed, refusing to let go. He staggered back, bumped into the bottom step, reached out to keep from falling, but pressed his hand into a sticky crimson stain splattered with pieces of skin. When the beam of his frantic flashlight finally came to rest on the floor, chaos was staring back: a wooden bed once in the room's center had been splintered into fragments, its ragged edges mingling with broken bones, wet with thickened blood.

Amongst the rubble, Wes could see no complete bodies, only shredded pieces that no longer fit together as a whole: a forearm, two fingers, part of a knee, a misshapen foot. He was hyperventilating now, as he tried to place the back of his boot onto the stair, but it was catching on something that his light soon revealed to be a rib cage.

The room was turning, twirling, cold, and hazy. He longed to flee, but his legs, like the flesh around him, would no longer move—until a strong grip seized his collar, hefted him up, and helped him exit away from the gruesome sight.

"It's all right, Bowers. Take long, deep breaths," the colonel commanded.

Wes had seen dead bodies before. They'd even passed several on their preliminary ride into London, but never so violently dismembered, never such ghoulishness up close.

"Bend down, son. You need to get your head between your legs and breathe deeply, or you'll faint."

Wes didn't need a mirror to know that his own skin had also turned a waxy gray, his blood beneath the surface still too stunned to flow. Instead of passing out, he stumbled a dozen steps forward, fell to his knees in what once was a family garden, and vomited.

He coughed, choked, then vomited again.

The colonel waited until he'd finished, then offered a lesson likely vastly different from the one planned. "You'll get used to disarming the bombs," he said, "and the fact that you might be blown to smithereens at the tick of a clock."

He paused, let Wes pull in more air. "You'll grow calloused to the sirens, to the destruction of buildings, to watching families lose a lifetime of belongings in a single evening."

One more moment as Wes filled his lungs.

"You'll soon hardly raise an eyebrow when sitting beside a live bomb to extract its ticking fuze; but Bowers, in all my years of war, I've never gotten used to the sickly scene of unrecognizable pieces of flesh and bones that hours ago were living, loving, laughing human beings—their lives instantly ended without reason."

The colonel reached down to help hoist Wes to his feet. "No, son. Don't even try. You'll never get used to that."

Wes was quiet after returning to the warehouse, informing the section that he wouldn't be available to play Scabby Queen with them, as he needed to write home.

It was partly true.

He sat on his cot, took out a piece a paper, and addressed it to Nathelle. He then scribbled two simple sentences in the body of his letter, a message that he never intended to mail.

It was a thought that had entered his head in the Anderson Shelter a few hours before when he'd helped place pieces of a couple he'd never met into a sack. The words sickened him, but there they were: standing at attention, written out in his own hand, demanding deeper reflection.

Dear Nathelle,

I'm growing to truly hate the Germans. There are times I want to bash in their filthy faces.

Love,

Wes

He stared, waited, stared longer, before crumpling up the paper into a tight ball and flinging it into the nearby garbage can. It was an introspection that he would grapple with another day—any other day, as today he feared it might consume him. Hate would keep the war alive for him forever, even after he returned home, and he wanted no part of that prolonged battle.

He called out to Driver, who was across the room with the other men. "I've changed my mind. Do you have room for one more?"

Wes had ordered biscuits and tea for Audrey, as always, but today the lighthearted banter he usually served alongside had been silenced by the sober certainties of war.

"I find that with each day, I'm losing my sense of time. A few minutes sometimes feels like an hour. A few hours may feel like an entire day. Is that happening to you as well?"

Audrey had been patiently listening, offering the slightest of head movements, her eyes tracking his, hoping to convey that she understood. "I'm sorry for what you had to do, for the people who died. It's sad that we as humans spend so much of our time and energy scheming for better methods to blow each other up. If we could only put that effort into helping one another . . . but I suppose that's a lesson we need Hitler to learn."

There was a rise in his volume. "That's the irony: we'll have to use guns and bombs to teach it to him." Then an ache edged into his voice, as if what he had to say next might cut his mouth. "I will admit, while I was placing another person's body parts into a bag, I found myself . . . hating the Germans."

Her words flew out swiftly. "You mean the Nazis."

"Yes, but aren't the German people following along? I've seen the newsreels, and people there line the streets, wave their swastika flags, and cheer wildly for their Führer. How does that make sense?"

An ache pressed against Audrey's heart, pushing for a proper reply. "Some German citizens cheer blindly in the name of national pride," she suggested. "Others perhaps applaud out of ignorance, not recognizing what he is about. But Wes, not all Germans are evil."

Anguish was scrunching his eyes. "I know. I just don't understand how one man can cause so much hatred—hatred against Jews, hatred against England, even hatred against Germany." Wes sat tall. "It all sort of makes me hate the man." It was clear that he wanted to smile, but his lips wouldn't play along.

Audrey took his hand, hoping to pass along a measure of comfort. "You're not alone. When we took a group of children to Beaconsfield, an argument broke out about what they would do to Hitler should the man ever set foot on England's shores. I can tell you it will not go well. Beatings and beratings were mentioned, but then one little fellow described in gruesome detail how, with his knife, he would flay Hitler open like a mackerel, and then rub him down with tanning salt. It made me ask myself, what's become of the commandment to love thy neighbor? I didn't know what to say to the lad, but found myself going along with the crowd, raising my arm in praise and insisting that his idea was absolutely smashing."

"I would recommend *coarse* tanning salt as a better alternative," Wes added, inviting the taut lines in his face to finally relax.

"I will pass that along," she replied.

Although the moment had warmed, the levity didn't linger. "Audrey, will we make it through this war?" he asked, every pleading wrinkle begging for bravery to see past the scenes that death had painted in his head.

She lifted her arms, yearning to wrap them around him and promise that it was going to be all right, but could she be sure? She settled for a squeeze to his fingers. "Yes, I should think so."

Wes's voice was still lumpy. "Some days, I don't see how. As I look around, there is so much death and pain and misery. I know that there are pockets of joy, I get that. I imagine you see it on the faces of the children and their mothers who you take to the country. But honestly, some days, I wonder if the good will ever balance out the bad. Audrey, if we take all the joy in the world, all the goodness, all the beauty, and weigh it against all of the heartache, all of the evil, and all of the agony, are we tipping the scales even slightly? Are any of us really making a difference?"

She watched worry spill from weary eyes, search the surrounding space to find no answer, and then return to rest on her.

She inched closer. "When Claire and I were returning home from Battersea last week in the rain, we walked past the rubble of the once stately buildings that stood along Burns Road, those hit by the earliest of Germany's raids. To my surprise, in between a mound of stone fragments sitting just off the street, I saw the most beautiful English primrose, full of warm yellow flowers."

"Primrose? In the rubble?"

"It must have come from a flower box once perched in a window bay, and despite its fall from loftier heights, landing in the most untenable of circumstances, the blessed plant was thriving."

"But it's been so cold and rainy."

"That's why it was striking. Claire said there are varieties that will bloom even in winter when everything around them is gray and miserable. I couldn't help but pick a petal to press in a book. Wes, the war brings heartache and despair, but that English primrose refused to give up."

When the moment hung, he drew a breath. "I think you're saying we should do the same."

She offered a slender nod. And then neither Wes nor Audrey

whispered a word for a long stretch of time until Jorrell approached to ask if they desired more tea.

By the time he stepped away, Wes had softened. "I don't mean to dump my burdens on you. Yesterday was . . . well, overwhelming."

"I've had those days myself." Then a curiosity popped into her head, a topic that they had yet to discuss but that suddenly seemed relevant.

"Are you religious?" she asked.

"I would say most days I'm a Christian."

"Most days?"

"Unless God makes a poor choice—then, for a day or two, I'm an atheist." A smile had entered his voice. "How about you?"

She could think of no good reason to lie. "Most days, I'm Jewish."

"And the others?"

Her retort would not be as easy. "I should explain. As a child, before my mother died, we attended shul, followed typical Jewish traditions. But after she passed, well . . . we stopped."

Wes connected the obvious dots. "Was your father angry at God?"

"One might assume so, but we stepped away slowly, over the course of a few years, and . . ."

"You suspect it was something else?"

"My father is a resourceful man, Wes, and politically insightful. I've often wondered if he didn't distance himself willfully as he watched the Nazis rise to power, thinking it would protect us. If that's true, was he being cowardly or wise?"

Wes pushed out a shrug. "Could it be both?" He searched her eyes. "Do you miss it? The traditions, the community, the faith?"

She lifted her chin to look up as if her answer was printed on the ceiling. "I suppose," she said slowly, "but do you know what I miss even more? And don't laugh!"

"No. Please tell me."

"I miss the stories."

"The stories?"

"Yes. We Jews are storytellers, and it's through story that the core of our lives can be understood. Take the Torah, for example. It's a collection of books about the beginnings of the Jewish people and their relationship with God. Mostly, though, I miss the personal stories."

"I'm not sure I understand."

She sat silent for a second, thinking. "I remember, for example, my father telling me a story about a rabbi named David whom he knew in Hamburg, a man facing what felt like an avalanche of miseries, including the death of his youngest son, debilitating arthritis, and potential financial ruin.

"One night, in the midst of his hardships, after a long and complaining prayer to God, the man had a dream in which he was taken to *olam ha-ba,* the world-to-come, and placed amongst a mass of belligerent people who were complaining loudly, both individually and as a group, that their lives on earth had not been fair.

"The rabbi listened, considered the injustices he himself was confronting, and then, with righteous indignation, lurched toward the throng to join them. But as he edged closer and listened more intently, the truth became plain.

"As the crowd complained, they were shouting that their lives on earth had been blessed with *too much* abundance, wealth, and ease, without sufficient suffering like so many *fortunate others* whose trials had given them wisdom and strength in preparation for their next life—and in that instant, the rabbi awoke."

Audrey half smiled as if waiting for his reaction before she would let out anything more. "Those are the types of stories I miss," she said.

Wes was fidgeting, blinking, like he wanted to believe. "Do you think it's true, or is it simply a story to help those of us who struggle to feel better?"

Before she could answer, an air-raid siren howled in from outside and slithered in between them. Audrey pushed out her chair while Wes checked his watch. "Do you need to get back?" she asked, her apprehension mounting.

He shook his head. "No, we won't go out until morning. We should get down to the shelter. There's one in the building here."

She followed behind him as they trailed other patrons down a flight of stairs to an elongated cement cellar. They sat beside one another on a planked bench that stretched across the longest wall of a simple but sturdy room.

It was awkward to talk with others listening, so they mostly sat together in silence, eavesdropping on the whispers of strangers, sharing occasional glances, all beneath a single illuminating bulb hung in the room's center.

A distant explosion sent the walls—and many of those sheltered within—trembling. Specks of mortar and dust that had latched to the ceiling jarred loose, sprinkling down in a cloud on those below.

Seconds later, at the rumble of a closer bomb, the room's solitary light flickered and died, causing Audrey to startle. Out of fear, or perhaps seeking comfort for more deeply flowing emotions, she reached down and clutched Wes's fingers.

He not only squeezed back but also draped his free arm around her shoulders and protected her gently in the dark. How could he know that it was the first time in years—since she'd left her father—that she'd been held so tenderly and so close?

Then, until the bombing had stopped and the all clear had sounded—though neither could say for how long it lasted—they clung to each other closely, contentedly, caringly in the dark.

October 26, 1940
Dear Papa,

Do you remember how on Sundays in Stuttgart we'd listen to the bells from the St. Maria Church? Here in England, church bells are being used to warn of the arrival of enemy paratroopers, and members of the Home Guard have been trained to shoot them before they reach the ground. When I heard the bells ring out last Sunday, I found myself looking heavenward, though not for the reason the original creator of the bells intended.

Papa, I had a discussion yesterday with the American about the war—not the one between Germany and England, but the one between despair and hope. He'd had a terribly bad day, and I didn't know what to say to console him. I know that he'll feel better tomorrow, but in the moment, I could do nothing but hold him and let him hold me. And as we held each other quietly, I thought of you and mama.

When I finally got home, Claire said that the air-raid warden had left a warning note on our door. Apparently, a sliver of light could be seen escaping from our window, even though it was covered. I am growing so dreary of the darkness and London's imposed blackouts. We humans are creatures of light. Subsisting in constant darkness scratches at my soul, and I know a London bus driver who might agree. Last week, when coming home, the driver could hardly see the road, and he hit the car in front of him. There were no harsh words exchanged, as people seem to have accepted our murky state, but Claire and I had to walk the final distance in darkness, and we stumbled like drunks.

Now for my secret: On the especially dark nights, when there is no moon, I find myself almost longing for the fires, since they provide the only light the city will see. It's just that, when they burn on Parliament Hill, they are so beautiful.

I miss you, Papa, and Jessey and Lewy. Cuddle them for me. May you continue to be well and watched over.

Until we all find peace,

Your daughter,

Audrey

CHAPTER 15

"Is it ready? Is the fuze exposed?" Colonel Moore asked.

"Yes, sir, but . . ." Badger scratched his feet in the dirt, possibly to steady himself before he delivered the bad news.

"Speak up! What is it?"

"It's not German. It's one of ours."

Wes raised a hand like a new student in school. "How can it be one of *ours?*"

Badger let the colonel run with it. "It's rare. A returning bomber, if going down or damaged, will sometimes jettison its load." He twisted to Hastings. "Find out if the RAF lost any planes, probably 57 Squadron at Upper Heyford or RAF Mildenhall."

The team all turned toward the Hippo as if their work was done.

"Don't we diffuse it?" Wes asked.

The colonel's answer was scarcely a mumble. "We'll report it to the RAF, who will send a team."

Wes's feet remained planted. "Why?"

His one-word question would take several dozen to answer. The colonel stepped up. "That's a bit of a hornet's nest. It seems that . . ."

Badger shoved in at the first pause. "The RAF bastards won't tell us how."

Wes turned an ear. "Your *own* military won't tell its *own* BD personnel how to diffuse its *own* bombs that they drop accidentally near their *own* cities?"

It apparently made no sense to the colonel either because his jaw had lowered, but he spat nothing out.

Hastings marshaled a proper reply for him. "The official term is *bureaucratic codswallop.* Of course, we have no choice in the matter."

The colonel grumbled as if to frighten the topic away. "It's late. We're through for today." He shooed everyone toward the Hippo, like a disgruntled child packing up his sandbox toys to head home. "And we'll be off tomorrow. I have a meeting with the Unexploded Bomb Committee."

The topic changed, but not the chatter. "Is that really what it's called?" Wes asked.

The colonel's eyes squinted. "Can you think of a better name?"

"In my sleep," Wes replied. "In the USA we'd call it . . . I don't know . . . the National Bureau of Risk Detonation."

Gunner chimed in next. "How about the Boom-Boom Group?"

While the team chuckled, the colonel cringed. "I say that sounds like a Latin brothel."

"Rumble Command?" asked Pike, unexpectedly joining in the fun.

And for the next half an hour, the section brainstormed ridiculous committee names, while the colonel derided them all as preposterous, and by all accounts—since nobody had come close to dying—it was regarded by all to be a reasonably successful day.

"I will admit it looks quite impressive. But does it work?"

Colonel Moore had already circled the contraption twice, like a teenager buying his first car. He'd heard rumors, had seen drawings, but he'd never been under the hood, at least with this updated model—and it was not what he was expecting.

The steam sterilizer, as it was being called, was a densely packed metal mash of cogs and gears, pipes and levers, that looked like the doings of an eccentric inventor who'd been locked in his lab too long.

"Explain exactly how it operates," Moore invited.

Dr. Gough was equally eager to oblige. "Did you ever poke holes in eggs as a child and then blow out the insides? Well, in similar fashion, this machine drills a hole in the bomb's casing and then inserts a pipe to pump in a mixture of steam and soap that will dissolve the explosive. It's all driven by the pressure of a boiler. Think of it as a more efficient method of scooping out the explosive, much more so than your antics with the UXB at the match factory."

"You said I was lucky that I didn't die with that one."

"Precisely. The steam sterilizer does all its work remotely, so there is no need for you to be sitting beside the bomb. The main risk is attaching it. As you know, the idea has been out there for some time, and different groups have been tinkering with it, trying to refine it, but it's this latest implementation that is showing some real promise. Why, even Churchill is up on it, asking we increase production and get them into the field right away."

The colonel had bent over to probe the mechanics of the drill bit. "We live in a truly remarkable age, Herbert, and you're doing unequaled work. But I must ask, why do I need to steam out the bomb if I have a clock stopper? Isn't it safer to stop the ticking clock and then merely cart the bomb away to a secluded location for detonation? Why take the time to drain the explosive when the bomb could blow at any moment?"

Dr. Gough slouched. His gaze, which had been fastened solely on the colonel to read his reaction to the steamer, now dropped like a German bomb at his own feet. "I was getting to that part." After mustering his nerve, he looked up. "Russell, we lost three men from 4 Section last week defusing a UXB that shouldn't have detonated. The sapper who was listening swears the clock never restarted. That's when we suspected . . ."

"I don't care for where this is going."

Gough reached behind his desk and hauled out an unusual new fuze, held it out for Moore to see. "Then, six hours later, 12 Section withdrew this from a UXB in Fulham. I'm only holding it now because it was damaged. Otherwise, two more sappers would be dead. The Germans have stamped it with a (50). I wanted you to see it here before you encounter one in the field."

The mechanism had three sets of trembler contacts, two with spiral springs, all surrounded by a metal tube. "It looks like a motion fuze," the colonel chimed in, a fact obvious to both.

Gough nodded. "When the Germans backed up their timed fuze, the (17), with the ZUS, it made it all but impossible to take out the ticking timer. But we could still use the clock stopper and then carry the bomb away where it could do no harm."

The colonel glared at the thing, wishing he could send it instantly to hell with looks alone.

"With this fuze," Gough continued, "those days are over. It arms after the clock has started, and if the bomb is moved at all, even slightly, the switch triggers an explosion."

The colonel tugged at his mustache, distorting his face. "This will bring our work to its knees." He was visibly gritting his teeth. "When is the madness going to end? Please tell me you have an answer for it."

Gough cleared his throat. "Our test shows that the fuze's electrical charge drains away after about 60 hours. You can't touch it before then, but it soon becomes inert . . ."

Moore couldn't help but intrude. "But it's still ticking, and we can't move it for almost three days!"

Gough placed a warm hand on his friend's shoulder. "We're working through possible solutions. The collective thought right now is that we create a vacuum within the fuze to pump liquid inside to gum things up. I'll keep you updated."

There was only one way for the colonel to say it. "Herbert, this is a disaster!"

Gough's eyes didn't buy it. "No, it's just a snag. We'll figure it out." He set the new fuze back down on his desk, pointed toward two empty chairs, suggested they sit. "I know this feels dire from your perspective, being the one in the field disarming the bombs. However, when I take a longer view of the war, when I look past these infuriating fuzes that the Germans keep developing, I see possibilities that were not there a few weeks ago."

"Well, Sunshine Susie," the colonel mocked, "I'd love to hear more, but right now, I need a pint."

Gough was unfazed. "Think back to when London was first bombed before the Blitz had started."

"That was when? Late August?"

"The twenty-fourth, and a few military leaders with a higher rank than mine believe that the bombs that fell on London that night were a mistake. They surmise that the German planes were supposed to hit military targets outside of London, but they strayed off course, striking the capital itself. Regardless, we bombed Berlin the next day in reprisal, our first attack on the German capital, and our intelligence reported back that Hitler was incensed."

"Please, do tell how a maddened maniacal dictator in command of one of the world's most vicious armies is a good thing."

"Because revenge is a canker that clouds clear thinking. Until that night, the Germans were specifically bombing military targets, trying to wipe out our defenses as they readied for their ground invasion. Hitler had forbidden the Luftwaffe from targeting civilians—but after we bombed Berlin, all that changed. Hitler shifted his attacks from military targets to the innocent civilians of London."

The colonel's arms were out, his hands upturned. "Let me ask again—for the good people of London—how is that a good thing?"

"Our military targets had been bludgeoned to near destruction. Case in point: the massive air attack over London on September fifteenth. We threw everything we had at the Luftwaffe and limped home victorious—barely. We had no reserves left. None! Had they hit us again, we'd have been in trouble. This strategy shift of Hitler's means that while he's exacting revenge from civilians, our factories are producing more planes, our runways are being repaired, more pilots are being trained. Russell, while Hitler mindlessly attacks folks who can't fight back, we're rebuilding our armed forces that can—and soon will. It all makes me wonder . . ."

"Yes?"

"What if, in the grand scheme of things, as the universe balances out good and evil, the first accidental bombing of London wasn't an accident at all? What if it was fate turning the tides of war?"

"You always were the more optimistic one, constantly looking for light in every dark night."

"I may be naïve, and I've been accused of worse, but what if it's true? What if life's worst disasters—our greatest defeats—are the beginnings of our greatest victories?"

"What are you saying?"

Gough spoke directly, assuredly. "I'm saying that, as hard as it is to endure Hitler's vengeful bombing of London, if our people hold firm, it may just win us this war!"

Major Leemon's foot tapped out an impatient rhythm on the tiled floor while he waited for the kneeling man to pick the flat's lock. He'd brought two others along as well, army specialists, and could have demanded they abruptly break down the door and enter with force, as he certainly had the authority.

Soon, but not today.

"Leave no trace," Leemon instructed, as the lock clicked its surrender and the door pushed ajar.

Drawers were slid silently open. Contents were scrutinized. Papers were read, photographed, and replaced. Even the women's clothes found inside were rifled, checked, and then refolded—every complete inch of the place noiselessly violated.

The major pensively peered through the thickest part of his glasses, supervising it all.

"Did you take a picture of this?" he asked, picking up a photograph that had been hidden beneath a box.

"Yes, sir. We did."

The major yanked it closer, studied the faces. When he turned it over and read the names scrawled on the back, his eyes squeezed together as slits. "Interesting."

Next, he picked up the polished ebony box itself. It felt heavy. He passed it off to the soldier standing beside him. "Can you open it?"

The man turned it slowly, examined every side, pressed at the corners, felt how they gave ever so slightly, all triggering a rare smile.

"It will take me a couple of minutes, but I can open it."

Six minutes later, after a multitude of corner combinations had been tried, the top of the box raised its arms, yielded, and slid away. The major gazed inside and then plucked the letter from on top. He sneered at the address.

"I knew it," he declared, victorious. "Take a picture of them all—every last one."

Audrey shuffled her papers and then peered out the car's window, looking for Paradise Street. As they approached, it was anything but. A policeman at the corner was signaling traffic past.

"The road is blocked," their driver explained. "You'll have to walk from here."

They were to meet Mrs. Lilla Burkhardt, a very pregnant mum with two girls, ages seven and eleven, and accompany her children to the hamlet of Chigwell Row. The woman was a teacher and had agreed to help out at the village school as soon as her baby was born and fit to travel. Until then, her daughters would stay in Chigwell with a family there who lived in a cozy basement flat below the library—but only until the bombings in London subsided.

A hundred feet down the street, it was apparent why no cars

were getting through. A two-story building had been directly hit during the night and reduced to pebbles. The wreckage had spilled out into the road and was hindering the way. A good dozen men from Rescue Services were studiously clearing the remains while probing for survivors, and, from the looks of the men, they had been working through the night.

Dread pumped down Audrey's arms to her fingertips that still clutched the woman's address. She didn't need to double-check to know that she was gazing at the same building.

"Excuse me, sir," she said to a man walking past with a shovel. "Are there survivors?"

She followed his eyes to a lumpy tarp spread across the sidewalk. "Just an arm and a foot," he confirmed. "The poor bloke."

He had already turned when Audrey called after him, probing, pleading. "Sir, are you saying the remains were a man? No women, no children?"

He aimed the nose of his shovel toward the tarp's corner, inviting her to check for herself. Then a voice carried past them both. It was coming from a worker near the back of the demolished building. "I've got something!"

"Audrey, stay here!" The command came from Claire, who had scooted up behind Audrey. Rather than heed her order, Audrey trailed the men to where the brick had been cleaned away from what looked to have once been a bedroom. She scrambled up a nearby pile of stones to get a better view. As the workers formed a line to cautiously weed away the remaining debris that had buried a bed, the outline of three bodies emerged.

The building had crumbled in around them so rapidly, they looked to still be sleeping. Indeed, as the brick fragments were brushed away, all could see that the girls were wearing only knickers and slips. The older man in the group commented that it was unusual to see the deceased looking so peaceful. Usually, the bodies they discovered in bombed-out buildings were scattered parts, or at least so bloody and mutilated, they were tricky to identify.

Two men beside him, no doubt drained from working all night, moved near to cart away the bodies. The first, standing beside the girl's head, hesitated, unclear on where to grab. The second man, opposite, reached down toward the girl's feet.

"STOP!" Audrey commanded before the pair could even flinch. "Not like that! They deserve respect."

She had come here to accompany the girls. Was she not still responsible? Either way, she wouldn't allow their bodies to be lugged off by their limbs so casually, wearing only their night clothing and in full view of the ogling horde.

The men halted, turned, looked back down at the young ones. The gentleman closest to Audrey, a man of about forty, conceded with a nod, as if he'd known all along but his cloudy head had needed fresh reminding.

He called to others out front. "Get me blankets and stretchers!" Then, once they had been delivered, he carefully slid one arm beneath the first child's head to offer support, then placed his other arm under her knees, and he cradled her up so tenderly, it looked like he was caring for his own daughter. As he set the girl gently into the arms of the stretcher and then kindly pulled the blanket over her head, Audrey heard him say, "There you go, dear. You'll be all right now."

He repeated the procedure with the second child, speaking the same words, and for a moment, the workers all quit what they were doing to bend their heads as Isabel, Jennifer, and Lilla Burkhardt were carried reverently to the ambulance that would take them to the morgue.

Audrey's legs jellied, causing her to slump down onto the pile of dirty and tumbled stones, but a hand rested on her back. Claire had climbed up from behind to help and was sitting beside Audrey in the dust.

"I should have come yesterday," Audrey whispered.

"And if you had," Claire answered back, her consoling support draping around Audrey like a quilt, "today two grieving orphans would be sobbing for a mother's final hug that would never come."

Audrey spun free as her voice stood. "Are we helping as we scurry these children away from their families and this wretched war, Claire? Or are we creating deeper scars from the separation? At times I'm not certain."

Claire let the thought settle, let it get comfortable with her in the dirt. When she was ready to answer, she coaxed Audrey back to her side. "Are you asking for the children who you've helped, or does this question stem from your own experience?"

Audrey's breath turned thin, skirting just along the surface. "I do miss them, Claire. I miss Papa, Jessey, and Lewy. I miss them terribly. I even miss Mother, a woman I barely remember. How can that be?"

Claire's face softened. "In our lives, we weep for our own separation—and that is okay. You didn't cause the bomb to hit the building, Audrey. You've only been trying to help. Give Providence a bit of credence. Know that sometimes life metes out pleasure and other times it metes out pain. We're destined to experience both."

"You sound like Father."

Claire let both the thought and the sun warm her. "I'll take that as a compliment."

"Miss?" The worker who'd carried the girls to the stretcher was calling. "The ambulance is ready. Would you care to ride along?"

CHAPTER 16

In a single motion, Major Balder Leemon wiped his sniffling nose with the back of his hand and poked his drooping glasses into their proper place.

"How long did you work at the factory in Stuttgart?" he grunted, taking a drag from his cigarette and then blowing the smoke intently into the witness's face.

The man being interrogated—mid-fifties, with thinning hair, a long neck, and tense eyes—had a right to panic. He'd been pulled off the line at his job in Surrey in front of his coworkers, escorted out by two armed soldiers, and then driven without explanation to a heavily armed building where he'd been locked alone in a tiny, lifeless room for hours.

When he answered, his German accent flowed with fear. "Six years in Hamburg and three in Stuttgart. I worked at both factories. What is this about?"

Leemon ignored the man's question. "When did you leave?"

The confining room left no place for the man to rest his gaze.

"On Kristallnacht, the Night of Broken Glass, when so many Jewish businesses were looted. We packed that night and were gone by morning. We had no choice if we were to survive."

"How did you get into England?" Leemon demanded, smashing the end of his cigarette into the desk.

"I had a brother here, sir. He helped me."

The major nodded knowingly. "Were you acquainted with the factory owner?"

"Yes, naturally."

The grilling gained speed, leaving no time for the man to tinker with his responses. "What was his name? How many children did he have? Was he also Jewish?"

The man gulped at the stifling air, labored to draw in ample courage. "His name was Walther . . . Walther Strumpf. He had three children, and yes, he was . . . and still is . . . Jewish."

"Was his factory damaged?"

"No."

"Did he attend synagogue?"

"No. He no longer associated with the Jewish community."

"But he did at one time?"

"Many years ago."

"Why did he stop being a Jew? Was it to save his factory?"

The man stumbled over the question, his words falling to the floor.

"Answer me!" the major bellowed, having no patience for gray.

The man quickly gathered them. "Sir, you can't *stop* being a Jew. Strumpf will always be Jewish, even if he chooses not to observe the Jewish faith."

Leemon gawked through his thick rims at the man, then shifted direction. "You say his name is *Strumpf* and not *Stocking?*"

"Stocking?"

"Yes."

The man's eyes stiffened. "Strumpf *means* stocking, sir . . . in German. Is that what you're asking?"

The major scribbled on a page. "Three children, you said. Who was the oldest?"

"Her name was Audrey, a pretty girl."

"Did she work at the factory?"

"No, but she was there on occasion."

"What did you make at the factory?"

"Condensers—electrical condensers—used in radios. Mr. Strumpf was an electrical engineer. Quite intelligent."

Major Leemon dropped a photo in the man's lap. "How about this man? Did you ever see him at the factory?"

"I . . . he looks familiar, but I . . . I don't know."

"Look again!"

The man obeyed, focused on the face. "I can't be certain, but perhaps I saw him with Mr. Strumpf's partner, Selig, at the factory a few weeks before I left."

"His name is Herbert Rühlemann. Does that help?"

The man stared again. He was almost shivering.

The major's voice blared. "He designs German bomb fuzes!"

"I'm sorry . . . I don't know him."

The major then threw down a second photo onto the man's quivering legs, one covertly taken a few days before of Audrey and Claire entering their flat. "How about this one? Do you know these two women?"

This time his eyelids elevated. He tapped the photo with his fingertip. "Yes, this one is Strumpf's oldest daughter, Audrey."

Leemon leaned in tight. “And how about the other woman, the girl’s aunt, did you know her as well?”

The man’s eyes coiled into a question. “Her aunt?”

The major snatched up the photo, held it directly in front of the man, pointed, so there was no confusion. “Yes, isn’t this woman her aunt, Claire Bergmann?”

A swell of trepidation sloshed into the room as the man stretched his neck, trying to keep his head high enough not to drown. His eyes pleaded for mercy.

“ANSWER ME!” Leemon commanded.

“I’ve met the girl’s aunt,” he stammered. “She has just one—Claire Bergmann. She came to the factory on a handful of occasions. Mr. Strumpf introduced me to her himself.”

“What are you saying?”

“Sir, that woman in the picture is not Claire Bergmann.”

Audrey had her hand up, ready to knock, when Driver pushed past her out the warehouse door with Wes trailing behind. Never missing a beat, the boy called back. “Luv, I can’t see you now. We’re jus’ leavin’.”

Wes paused beside Audrey while shooing Driver forward toward the Hippo. “Ignore the child. He’s delirious.”

Driver took aim next at Wes. “She’s different than the other girls you ’ad ’ere las’ night, yeah?”

“You must admit,” Wes said, his eyes never leaving hers, “he’s impressive. The kid can deliver lines with the best of ’em, and without smiling.”

Audrey offered a bow of her head to agree. "I guess we should all cultivate our talents."

"How may I help?" Wes asked, changing the subject.

"I'm just glad I caught you. We'll be leaving an hour earlier on Friday. Can you still make it?"

It was an easy answer. "Sure. I'm excited to see a new part of the country. Remind me the name of the place?"

"Weeley. Is the colonel okay with you leaving?"

"The timing is perfect. Hastings's oldest boy is receiving his First Communion, and the colonel is a godparent. He served with Hastings's father in World War I, and so the two are traveling up to Grimsby. It means the rest of us get two glorious days of leave."

"Well, I thank you for spending that time with me, but please wear your civvies."

"My what?"

"Your civilian clothes. It scares the children if they think a soldier is taking them somewhere. Is that all right?"

"Of course. I understand." Wes nudged her shoulder. "You never told me what Claire's reaction was. Sometimes she seems a little tense when I'm around. Is she fine with me coming?"

"She . . . well . . . I . . ." Audrey shuffled back. She was trying to answer, but the words were sticking to her tongue.

"You haven't told her, have you?"

"Yes . . . I mean no, not yet, but . . ." She licked her lips. "I will. I will."

Major Balder Leemon hunched over his desk, groping at the storied evidence laid out before him, shoveling his facts and photos back and forth into disparate piles to fill in the remaining holes.

"Here you go, Major." His secretary entered and set down his tea. "To clarify your earlier directive, shall I make arrangements with the Metropolitan Police?"

Leemon never looked up—that would be too polite—his eyes instead skating from pile to pile. "Have them ready, but wait for my call," he instructed. "There is one more person with whom I need to speak—the American."

His secretary's head turned. "Should I inform his commanding officer? He'll be unhappy if you don't." She was speaking to a man who proudly wore the disdain of others as a badge of honor.

"No, not yet."

"Do you think the American knows anything?" she asked, pinching at her jaw.

Leemon's head tipped up, his magnified eyes meeting those of the woman for the first time that morning. It was unusual for him to lay out his plan to anyone beforehand, but a rare smile shadowed the man's mouth.

"I shall smack this ugly little hornet's nest with a stick, and soon enough, we will all find out."

Wes was on his way out of Café Cozier, heading back to the warehouse, when a uniformed British officer loitering by the door stepped in front of him.

"Lieutenant Wesley Bowers," the man said as if stating a fact.

Wes saluted the officer, a major, as he visibly frisked Wes from head to toe through the lenses of weighty glasses. "Yes, sir. May I help you?" Wes asked.

"Please, let's sit down."

Wes agreed, led the man back to his usual table, watched him open his attaché case and extract a photo.

"I'm Major Balder Leemon," he said, looking up to see if perhaps Wes might recognize his name. "I am with the Directorate of Military Intelligence, working as a liaison to the Aliens Department of the Home Office."

"That's a very long title," Wes replied. "How may I be of assistance, Major?"

The man passed Wes a photo of Audrey. "Do you know this woman?"

"Yes, that's Audrey . . . Audrey Stocking. Is she all right? What is this about?"

"What do you know about this woman?"

"What do I know?" Wes repeated as he collected his thoughts. "Well, Audrey is from Switzerland. She came to London to attend school, but when the war started, she joined WVS to help children—oh, and I blew up her flat."

Leemon peered at him, unamused. "Do you care if I smoke?" the major asked evenly, not waiting for Wes to reply before lighting up.

"Lieutenant Bowers," he said, after drawing a prolonged puff and then letting the smoke clear, "this woman's real name is Audrey Strumpf. She is from Germany, not Switzerland—and the papers she used to get into Switzerland and then England were forged."

They were heavy words that struck Wes across the face. "You must be making a mistake."

The man was ready. "Is this her handwriting?" He tossed across a photo showing one of Audrey's letters.

Wes pulled it close, noticed the familiar penmanship, the same stationery she'd used when they'd sat together in the café. When he spoke, the sound was subdued. "It looks similar. Yes, I . . . I think it's hers."

The major's puff was blue and pungent. "She's sending her letters to a factory in Stuttgart—a factory that makes parts for German bombs."

Wes said nothing, his reply strangled by surprise.

"Has she asked you about your work, the skills you're learning in bomb disposal?"

Had she? Wes shifted in his chair, arranging his reply. "I . . . I don't think so." But his hesitation cut off his answer at the knees. "She helps children. She takes them to the country for safety," he added, as if this tidbit of information would change the major's mind and save the woman.

The man was bobbing his head. It was information he already knew. "Yes, who would suspect someone working so closely with our children? It would be such an easy way to gather intelligence."

Wes pushed back his chair, needed more room, more air.

"I presume that you've also met the woman she calls her aunt?" the major asked while inspecting Wes's eyes. "She has been asking for the locations of our antiaircraft batteries scattered about London."

"Yes, Claire. It's because if they take children and the sirens start, they need to know . . ." His words halted on their own.

"Claire, you say?" the major asked.

"Yes. Claire . . . I don't believe I know her last name."

The major tapped on the first photo. "This woman, Audrey, from Germany, indeed, has an Aunt Claire." It was information he stated with surety. "But the woman she is with here in England . . . is not her."

It made no sense. How could this be? "Then who is she?"

The major inhaled yet another self-satisfied puff. "I don't yet know, but I intend to find out."

Wes leaned through the smoke to confess. "I'm to go with her . . . with them . . . tomorrow to Weeley."

Every smug line in the shorter man's face seemed to look down at Wes. "Then it's good that we had this talk today. I would suggest that, for now, you go and quietly watch and listen. Let me know if you see anything out of the ordinary."

Was there anything about Wes's life in London that had been *ordinary*? "You want me to *spy* on them?"

The major squinted. "You do know, Lieutenant Bowers, that I am meeting with you out of professional courtesy? You may consider this a caution in order to spare you or your government any unnecessary embarrassment."

When Wes took a breath, his chest hurt. "Thank you," he muttered. "Do you plan to arrest them?"

"Lieutenant, you ask a lot of questions," Leemon noted, his own words paced, planned, prodding. "The one that should frighten you most about this woman with whom you've been—what shall we call it?—romantically involved . . ."

"But, I'm not . . ."

"The question, Lieutenant Bowers, that should keep you up at night is simple." He took his final puff.

"What's that?"

"Who is Audrey Stocking?"

CHAPTER 17

It had always been confusing to Audrey why the Ministry of Health sent ambulances and not more typical transport to evacuate the children from London. While many of the younger boys seemed to find them thrilling, constantly asking if they could run the siren, for the little girls, an ambulance only raised alarm.

Last week, for example, a strong-headed urchin of four refused to climb inside, emphatically declaring, "I not sick!" And the wee thing *wasn't* ill until the driver began to pull away from the curb, leaving the child's mum sobbing in the street, afraid that she'd made the wrong choice, and the youngster holding forcefully to Audrey's arms, kicking and crying, demanding that they stop instantly so she could run back home. In a flicker, it became powerfully clear to Audrey why an ambulance—a vehicle made to carry those who are deeply injured—was an inspired choice.

She trusted that today's ride would prove less dramatic. They would be heading to Weeley, near Colchester, to bring back a mother and her son—personal friends of Cora Holden—to be reunited with the woman's husband, who was returning on leave from his duties with the war.

Audrey was out front when the ambulance arrived, and just the sight of it brought along a grimace. Many of the vehicles placed into service by the government for London's evacuation efforts were leftover ambulances from the Great War, and on a good day, the majority would be called *dodgy*. By all appearances, today's ride had no intention of lifting expectations.

It was one of the old Ford Model T-based vehicles that had been popular with the Red Cross: more truck than car, sporting a padded bench seat in the front for the driver and passenger, with a covered, boxy compartment in the rear, painted thick in camouflage green and then adorned on each side with a crimson cross in a white circle—an emblem that let everyone know an ambulance was passing and to pray for whoever happened to be riding inside.

"I called up the best for you, knowing you'd be coming along," Audrey quipped as Wes approached with a small bag of his gear. "It won't win an award for comfort, but it has four tires and comes with a driver, so there will be no complaining."

Wes barely smiled, opened the back, and heaved his things inside.

She thought little of the fact that he said almost nothing and hadn't looked her in the eyes.

"Are we ready?" asked the driver, a stoic Scottish woman of forty named Mrs. McGruder, who was wearing a full-length blue coat with a lancer front, complete with two rows of white metal buttons that fastened to the collar, a common outfit for members of ARP, the Air Raid Precautions.

Today, Claire would sit up front to keep Mrs. McGruder company while Audrey and Wes rode in the back. After Wes had taken his place on one of two parallel bench seats, Audrey sat opposite so she could see his face.

"You look quite posh in your civilian clothes." She pushed a smile in his direction, waited for its return. Instead, he cast the compliment aside with a curt toss of his head.

Stillness strolled in, and though silence had never been uncomfortable to either of them, today, it felt scratchy.

Audrey touched his knee. "What's going on? Have I upset you?" she asked, certain that she must have said something terribly improper at their last meeting.

He insisted there was nothing amiss, that he just had a tremendous amount on his mind and needed some time to think through a few things.

"Let me help. I'm good at figuring out problems."

He told her no, said that he was fine, but she could see his eyes were smoldering, as if the slightest breeze would set him alight, and anyone standing nearby would get singed.

A dozen minutes later, she tried again with declarations about the woeful weather, how the newspapers were no longer allowed to print forecasts, the scandalous scarcity of butter (a topic that had been preempting chatter all across London), and even a report that affirmed only 50 percent of Londoners still carried their gas masks.

He grumbled through all of it, finally announcing that he wasn't feeling well and that for the balance of the ride, he was going to close his eyes and get some sleep. Except Audrey could tell he wasn't really sleeping, and so she sat silent, confused, watching, and wondering.

An hour later, when the driver stopped for petrol and to visit the toilet, Wes sat up to announce that he was going to take a quick walk to get some air.

"What's wrong?" Claire asked Audrey as she came around the back to see how the two were doing, only to find the girl sitting alone.

For a moment, Audrey said nothing. She hunched on the bench, rocking softly, with her head close to her knees, her eyes glued to her feet.

Worry levered Claire's chin. "Are you having an attack?"

Audrey shook her head. If only it were that easy.

"What, then?" Claire asked, her brow wrinkling like old fruit. "Did Wes say something to upset you?"

That was the problem. He'd scarcely spoken a sentence, sharing little and admitting nothing—but the truth had been trickling from his eyes so freely, she ought to have handed the man a hankie.

She should have listened to Claire from the beginning, but she had been so taken by the thought of having a regular friendship—if that was the relationship she and Wes had—she'd forgotten from where she'd come.

Audrey coiled around to face Claire with wide eyes, a drawn mouth, and wringing fingers. She shared a suspicion that was all but certain.

"Wes knows!"

It was late afternoon when Claire slid open the window that separated the ambulance cab from the rear and called back, "It's right up ahead."

The village of Weeley in Tendring, off the eastern coast of England, was considered charming by almost anyone's standards, boasting all the desired traits of a respectable parish: a railway station; bus routes (to both Clacton-on-Sea and Colchester); a village hall; two local parks; and of course, St. Andrew's, the parish church (though it shared its priest with neighboring Little Clacton).

Its name was derived from the Old English *Wēo-lēah,* signifying "temple clearing," since it was believed that, prior to the Christian era, there had once been a heathen temple nearby, though not a single resident could say where.

Although the village was situated in the path of enemy bombers flying across the channel from Germany to bomb London, it would never be deemed a tactical target, unless the Germans developed a vengeance toward sheep. But perhaps they had—because as the ambulance slowed to a stop in front of the village hall, the citizens of Weeley were out in force and running in scattered directions.

Audrey squeezed Wes on the shoulder. "Wake up. Something's happening!"

When she thrust open the back door, a man was there, and he was holding a gun. His eyes drooped with disappointment when Audrey stepped out. "My regrets," he said. "I thought you were from the RAF."

"No. I'm with WVS. We're here to escort a mother and her child back to London. Can you tell me what's going on?"

The man pointed to a distant grove of trees where a line of smoke was rising. "A German bomber fell out of formation. We could hear that it was having engine trouble. It went down in Weeleyhall Wood. We've called the RAF, but Farabee couldn't wait and went to have a look."

"Farabee?" Wes pushed past Audrey. "Who's Farabee?"

"Our constable." The man trained his finger toward the woods as if they could see for themselves. "He's a member of the Home Guard."

"How long ago did the plane go down?" Wes asked, his words marching in military cadence.

"Five, ten minutes."

Audrey watched Wes. His eyes darted from the man to the trees and then to the neighboring farms spread out in between. He tracked the fence lines, surveyed the ditches, searched for places an enemy could hide.

"I'm Lieutenant Wes Bowers, with 5BD London, 37 Section. I'm out of uniform because . . ." he motioned toward Audrey, " . . . we're picking up children." His voice quickened. "Is Farabee alone?"

"He is."

Wes reached around to his back waist and withdrew his service pistol. He was already turning. "I'm going to see if he's safe."

"Before you go, you should know that Chas Kantor—a member of the Observer Corps who spots German bombers and calls the counts into London—he saw a parachute come out before the plane crashed."

Wes wrestled a nervous breath, then addressed those huddled close. "Stay near the vehicle and be careful." And then, before anyone could object, he sprinted, gun in hand, toward the outcropping of trees called Weeleyhall Wood, its silhouette now framed by a smoke-sullied sky.

Wes crouched as he ran. If a German crew member had bailed out and soldiers were hiding nearby, the last thing he wanted was to advertise his own arrival. As he ran, he continued to study his surroundings: the woods were not quite a mile away, the ground sloping gently down toward them. Between the trees and the village hall where they'd parked were fenced farms with stretching fields, almost looking like a runway. That may have been where the pilot was trying to land his plane.

Wes desperately wished that he'd been watching out the window on the ride in and not pretending to be asleep. They'd driven in from the direction of the woods, and if he had been paying attention, he would now have a better knowledge of the terrain that lay beyond.

The problem was that he'd never been a good liar—not that it was a trait to which one should aspire. It was just impossible for him to lie to people close to him, those he cared about. Had he looked Audrey in the eyes, her glare would have sliced him like butter for an English crumpet—and she would have known something was amiss.

Major Leemon had requested that he *keep an eye out for anything unusual,* but hiding problems wasn't his nature; he preferred solving them. He had half a mind to ignore the major's directive and confront Audrey, get out in the open who she really was and what she was doing in England. He made up his mind that he would do just that, as soon as he knew that the downed German soldier wasn't going to kill someone first.

As he drew close to where the plane went down, he spotted two, perhaps three separate farmhouses that could provide cover, with ditch lines that extended toward the trees. Were they deep enough for a man to hide in? Was he being watched even now?

Wes slowed as he entered the trees, stepping cautiously through the brush and around saplings to avoid making any sound. He could see the damaged fuselage ahead; its wings were torn off, cockpit smoking. The constable, Farabee, was standing close—too close—and out in the open. Surely if a German soldier was hiding nearby, looking for an opportunity to attack, he would have already taken a shot at the man.

Wes took another glance around, a second careful listen, one more read and assessment of the situation. The constable was armed, and since being shot accidentally by friendly fire would kill you just as dead as purposeful German fire, Wes held up his gun to no longer look threatening and then called out to him. "Farabee!" The man lurched around. "Don't shoot! I'm Lieutenant Wes Bowers of 5BD in London. I'm here to help."

He watched Farabee exhale, then beckon him closer to share what little information he'd been able to discover. "I counted four dead crew members inside, but I didn't see any ordnance. It was probably jettisoned over the ocean."

Wes examined the wreckage more closely. "This is an Fw 200 Condor." He pointed to the fuselage. "They were probably dropping shipping mines along the coast and then turned toward land when they developed engine trouble. This plane typically flies with a crew of five. You said you counted four dead?"

"Yes."

"That means either they were flying shorthanded or, if the man in the village really did see a parachute, there's one more out here. What's beyond these woods?"

The constable squatted, making himself a smaller target. "Farms, empty fields, Colchester Road, and then, eventually, the ocean. I'll bet he bolted off in that direction to steal a boat." The man let his uneasy gaze dangle, snagging up in the far-off trees.

Wes was rightfully fixated instead on the circling woods. "If there's a German soldier out there, he could be scared, wounded, and hiding."

"And when people are frightened, they're irrational and unpredictable," Farabee added.

Wes wouldn't argue. "I could see two farmhouses on my way in. Have you checked either of them?"

"No. I was waiting for the RAF to arrive."

Wes wiped his free hand on his pants, switched his gun, and then wiped his other hand. Even in the cold, his palms were sweating. He then shared information that the man may not have wanted to hear. "We can't wait. By the time the RAF gets here, it will be too late. Follow me!"

The men had just reached the boundary of the trees where the farm fence crossed when something on the ground ahead caught Wes's eye.

"Here!" he called out, signaling Farabee over to a mound of branches and rocks covering what appeared to be a pile of dirty laundry. Except when Wes jerked on the cords that wrapped around the bundle, a German parachute unrolled.

Inside the village hall, Audrey and Claire learned that the man to whom they'd been speaking was Squire Lander Weeley, a man whose family had owned land in the area for generations. He proudly detailed how four of Weeley's villagers were members of the Home Guard, including Farabee (the constable) and himself, and how, just before the ambulance had arrived, Lander had sent the other two Home Guard members to ready a few of the local men, should the RAF need assistance.

"Here's William now," Lander exclaimed, gesturing to the man scooting through the door.

William, a bit elderly, was gasping and holding his stomach with both hands, and it took a minute for his breath to catch up. He had apparently come dashing back from the crash site.

Once he'd settled down enough to speak, he delivered his report. "I just left Farabee and the American. They counted four dead Jerries in the plane but then found an abandoned parachute—which means there's a German soldier on the loose. They're going to search the nearby farms." Another pause. More breathing. "I say we send a few men back to retrieve the bodies, but I'll take the remainder, and we'll comb the woods. That's where the bloody Nazi will be hiding."

On hearing the news, Claire feigned a cough while tugging at Audrey with her eyes. Clearly, she wanted to talk in private.

Audrey turned to Lander. "Excuse me, is there a toilet anywhere?"

"Yes." The squire politely pointed. "It's there in the back."

"And I'd better go as well," Claire added.

Once the door was closed and no one could hear, Claire let the dread she'd been secreting seep out. "What if Kaden is the one out there alive?" Her eyes carried concern. "Worse, what if he's one of the dead?"

Audrey took her by the shoulders. "Claire, there must be thousands of German pilots. The chances of Kaden being on that plane are so small. Besides, what are we supposed to do, tramp through the woods calling out his name?"

Claire's head lowered. She was a smart woman and knew that Audrey was right, but love and reason had never been known to hold hands. Yes, the chances were slim, but they weren't at zero.

"You're right," Claire admitted. "He probably wasn't on that plane, but isn't there a fair chance that one of the men on the plane knew him or served with him? What if the man who's loose has met Kaden and can tell me something—anything?" Her question begged like a prisoner for mercy. "Audrey, it's been two years, and I know nothing. I don't even know if Kaden is alive."

It was a foolish argument for Claire to throw at Audrey, and they both knew it. Audrey had been away from her father and siblings for just as long. And yet, for that very reason, it was also the perfect argument.

As Audrey's eyes met Claire's, her own heart beat in sympathy. "Let's watch when the men return with the bodies," Audrey advised, "so we'll know if Kaden is one of them. But if he's not, if there's a chance that he's the soldier still out there, I have an idea how to find him."

As the townsmen lugged in the lifeless bodies of the German soldiers, the man in front called out to Claire and Audrey, "Look away! Ladies shouldn't have to see this."

But Claire *did* want to see, and so she held the door open as the bloodied corpses were hefted past on stretchers, one by one, where she could study their bruised faces. Each glance held its own breath, and every breath exhaled appreciation. When the last soldier had passed, Claire looked to Audrey, inviting her to share in a silent second of relief.

The bodies had barely been stacked in the council chambers and covered with a single sheet when the men gathered both their hurricane lanterns and their loaded guns to join those already out searching for the missing German still on the run.

"If 'e won't surrender quickly," Claire heard one man say to another, "then we'll bring 'is body back to kip down for the night with 'is friends."

The room churned with both laughter and distress, the men supplying the bluster and Claire the worry. "They'll kill him," she whispered, but Audrey was already on her feet following the men out the door.

"We're not going with them, are we?" Claire asked as she stepped outside.

Audrey paused so the men could gain distance. "Certainly not." She motioned Claire toward the ambulance, using her chin. "Carefully climb up onto the back of the ambulance, almost to the roof. Then, look out in the direction of the woods and tell me what you see."

It was dusk, soon to be dark, but Claire did as Audrey suggested. "I see the outline of the woods. The smoke has mostly cleared. I see farms . . . fences . . . I don't understand what you're expecting me to find."

Audrey waved Claire back down, then spoke softly but distinctly. "Claire, if you were a German trying to hide in England, where would *you* hide?"

Claire's eyes circled, making sure no one else was close. "But, Audrey, we *are* Germans trying to hide . . ." Claire's objection paraded to an instant midsentence halt, the words behind bumping up against those in front. She repeated the thought again to hear it aloud, this time taking it to its finish. "We *are* Germans trying to hide . . . *and we aren't cowering in the cold, dark woods.*"

Audrey pointed toward the farmhouses. "Did you see the ditches that followed the fence lines?"

Claire answered with her voice rising. "Yes. They run toward the village. They run toward us." Her brain was quickly assembling the puzzle of possibilities. "Do you think he's hiding somewhere in the village? Is that possible?"

"There are two or three farmhouses close by, so he could easily have stolen some clothing. I don't know for certain, but aren't the woods the first place everyone is going to look? Hasn't hiding in plain sight worked for us?"

Claire's nod was fervent. It was a good plan.

"There are lanterns inside," Audrey said. "What would it hurt to borrow a couple and have a look around? The problem is that the two of us can't cover the whole village on foot, and Mrs. McGruder is . . ." Audrey tried to be nice. " . . . well, she's a bit stern and detached."

"Oh, child," Claire scolded, sounding again like her old self. "You didn't ride all the way here sitting next to the good woman. Maggie isn't stern or disagreeable at all. She's been sitting alone in the front of the ambulance all this time because the poor woman is trying to get some desperately needed sleep. She's been working three jobs to get her family through this war."

Audrey's eyes scrunched. "Maggie?" she asked.

Claire was already beside the ambulance, tapping on the window. As the door opened, Claire didn't bother with hello. "Maggie, about our little chat on the way here and the men in ARP who don't take you seriously because you're a woman with children at home . . ."

"Yes, Claire," Maggie answered. "What about it?"

"How would you like to prove the buggers wrong?"

After scouting around the village hall and finding nothing out of the ordinary, the three women squeezed into the front seat of the ambulance and drove to the most popular place in the village—for that matter, in every village across England—the local pub.

In Weeley, it was a building that had once been a coaching inn but had been converted into a public drinking house in the mid-1800s and named *The Black Boy,* after Merry King Charles II, one of the Stuart kings of England.

The three women first studied the folks outside, those both coming and going. When they discovered nobody looking or acting particularly suspicious, they ventured indoors.

Maggie voiced the obvious. "If I were going to hide, it would be in a pub. Everyone is too drunk to notice if a German is sitting beside them."

"And if they did," Audrey added, "would they even care?"

True or not, the only strangers in the building—the only ones not drinking—seemed to be the trio of sleuths themselves. "Let's go," Claire finally commanded. "The German is hiding somewhere, but he can't be so daft as to wander in here."

Their next stop was the rail station, a seemingly clever move for the German since a stranger at the station would not have looked out of place. Of course, he probably wasn't going to stroll boldly up to the ticket window and purchase a one-way fare to Berlin, but a man buying a fare to leave the village would hardly be deemed dubious. Except they found that the station was under renovation, with a new bridge being constructed over the tracks. The construction had so drastically reduced the number of scheduled trains making stops that the place was a graveyard.

There was a man passing by outside on the street in front who looked unusual, but only because he was herding three goats while leading a leashed pig. Besides, he didn't look German and weighed a good 300 pounds, making the likelihood of him piloting a plane—enemy or otherwise—a smidgen unlikely.

The village school came next, but the doors were chained and the windows locked, and not a soul was loitering outside.

The stables then provided the most promise: they were dark and a mite remote, and their stalls offered plenty of places for friend or foe to hide. When Claire stepped out of the vehicle, her shoulders tensed. "Do we dare?"

"I have a gun," Maggie assured, pulling it from beneath her seat to be greeted by four wide eyes.

With Maggie providing the protection and Claire and Audrey each holding a lantern so the three of them could see, they inspected every stall, scoured every inch in the building's loft, and even beat some of the bushes in back with a wooden pole they'd found inside. Nothing moved, no noise escaped, no frightened German fled into the night.

"Perhaps this wasn't such a good plan after all," Audrey conceded to silence.

Three more locations were searched: the post office, the rear of the bank, and an empty cabin off Clacton Road that a woman at the pub had mentioned.

"I think we should return to the village hall," Audrey whispered, her way of admitting total defeat. "If Wes comes back, he'll be wondering where we've run off to."

Maggie's assessment was far more direct. "Well, this little adventure has been completely shambolic. Short of banging the doors on village houses, I'd say we're a wee bit short on options."

Audrey remained quiet on the ride back into town, snuggling up against the door, letting the darkening sky draw away her doleful stare. "I was just so sure," she finally mumbled.

Maggie, like a good mum wanting to console a daughter, held the wheel with a single hand while stretching out the other to pat Audrey's knee—a gesture of comfort that seemed to work rather quickly, because Audrey bolted forward and then turned her head.

Her eyes, clouded at first with confusion, filled with sudden light. "Did you see that?" she asked.

"See what?" Claire answered as Maggie slowed the ambulance.

"That lane that we just passed, the one with the trees that line both sides. Quick, turn around!"

Claire nudged Audrey's side. "Why? What is it?"

Maggie slowed enough to make a wide turn, but then pulled off to the side of the road so that Audrey could explain—and she was, using both words and hand gestures.

"Claire, back at the village hall, when we climbed up the side of the ambulance, do you recall seeing the ditches? Those that followed the fence lines leading to the village?"

"Yes."

"I assumed that our German had followed one of those to the main village, stealing clothes along the way to blend in—but I was wrong."

Claire's voice straightened. "What are you saying?"

"That lane ahead runs perpendicular, and notice the long row of trees. If it keeps going, which I'm guessing it does, it will butt right into those ditches."

"So?"

"Claire, can't you see it? There's a building partway down the lane that's peeking above the trees. I only noticed when we drove past because it's faintly lit. I don't know why we didn't think of it before. It's truly the perfect place to hide."

Claire and Maggie's voices chorused together. "Where?"

"Ladies," Audrey said, her eyes bubbling in the night. "The German pilot is hiding in St. Andrew's Church."

"Stay here," Claire whispered, clasping both Audrey and Maggie by the arm before she peered in through the slightly ajar church door one last time. "We don't want to startle him—but feel free to burst in if you hear me scream."

The church was empty but for a sole parishioner offering his evening prayer. He was kneeling, with his head bowed, half a dozen rows up, in the middle pew. But, unlike most country worshippers, this man was wearing an overcoat with a hat pulled tightly down around his ears.

Claire was about to go inside when Maggie stammered back, still holding her gun, her voice stiffening. "Not yet. There's something I didn't tell you."

Audrey and Claire twisted around together, their waiting eyes facing the woman.

"I do have a gun," Maggie continued, holding it up, "but I've never fired it. I'm not exactly sure how to use it."

The scabby silence stretched.

Audrey was the first to interrupt. "That's a secret you should not share with the men in ARP," she said, taking the gun from Maggie and gripping it herself. She turned to Claire. "I honestly don't know how to use it either, but if you shout, I'll come in waving it."

With their plan set, Claire pushed through the door, purposely letting it squeak and then bang softly, wood hitting wood, as it closed. The man didn't move, didn't turn around.

Now that she was drawing closer, Claire's heart pounded like a cannon against her ribs, reminding her that this was a completely daft idea, that if the man stood and shot her dead, she would positively deserve it. But she also knew that to keep up the charade that she was living for much longer, she would need more than pipe dreams. Yes, speaking to this suspected German soldier was a terrible risk, but when she was stuck in the middle of a lousy war with no way out, it was a risk she had to take. Love was never about playing it safe—whether during war or peacetime. If you hoped to win your battles, you had to strap on your polished boots and march yourself forward.

She paused at the pew behind the man and slid in, sitting close, but still off to one side. She could see that his eyes were shut, his lips were mouthing words, and then she watched as he methodically touched fingers to his forehead, lower chest, and each shoulder, making the perfect sign of the cross.

Were they wrong? Was this man just a village farmer who had come to St. Andrew's after a hard day's work to offer gratitude? He was dressed, after all, in farm clothes. But as Claire knelt, she noticed his black boots—German military boots!

As her knees pressed against the cushioned tuffet, she whispered, but loud enough for the man to hear.

"Our Father, who art in heaven, hallowed be thy name."

Although Claire had pretended to be Jewish for these last two years, taking on the role of Audrey's aunt, beneath the *Shabbats* and *Shaloms,* she would always be Catholic at heart.

"Thy kingdom come, thy will be done on earth, as it is in heaven."

How genius of him, hiding in a church, pretending to be so committed. Who would suspect a man devoutly and deeply in prayer?

"Give us this day our daily bread, and forgive us our trespasses as we forgive those who trespass against us."

But what if he wasn't pretending? Could he be a genuinely religious man who had been pushed reluctantly into the war, as had so many others?

"And lead us not into temptation, but deliver us from evil."

Should she disturb his meditation, tap him on the shoulder and introduce herself, ask her question, and then be on her way? She crossed herself, as he had done, and then, rather than touch him to get his attention, she stood, lifted her voice, and spoke to him in fluent German, one countryman to another.

"*Bitte hab keine Angst. Ich bin auch Deutscher und frage mich, ob Sie einen Piloten namens Kaden Froe kennen? Wir sollten heiraten.*" ("Please don't be afraid. I am also German, and I am wondering if you know a pilot name Kaden Froe? We were to be married.")

The soldier's lips stopped their whisper, his eyelids cracked open, and he stood to face Claire with features so contorted, he must have reasoned that he'd stumbled into the church after the crash and died and now an angel had come to take him home.

His face crumpled as he spoke. "Kaden Froe?"

Claire's begging eyes probed the man's face for any hint of recognition, but before either could mouth another word, the doors opposite to where Claire had entered swung in with a clap as Wes and Constable Farabee surged through, their guns raised and ready.

"Stop! Don't move!" the constable screamed.

Confusion teeming in the German's eyes curdled into concern—or was it contempt? His shivering body said it all: this wasn't heaven, he was still in hell, and he would do his best to fight his way out. He yanked a gun from his jacket, grasped Claire by her blouse, dragged her over the bench to shield his body from their menacing weapons—and then he shoved the barrel of his gun into her cheek.

"*Ich werde sie töten! Ich werde sie töten!*" he screamed.

Audrey bolted into the chapel from where she and Maggie had been watching. "*Halt! Nicht schießen!* Stop! Don't shoot!" she begged. She threw Maggie's gun to the floor, so as to appear less threatening, and then turned to Wes and the man beside him. "He's saying that he'll kill her! Please don't shoot!"

"Tell him to let her go!" screamed Farabee as both he and Wes instinctively squatted down to take more careful aim.

And then, before anyone else could scream—in German or otherwise—the cornered pilot pulled the gun away from Claire's cheek and pointed it toward the most threatening man in the room: the constable wearing a uniform.

He jerked the trigger. *Boom! Boom!*

The constable crashed backward to the tiled floor, his gun skittering sideways like it was running to hide.

The German turned next toward Wes.

Boom! Boom!

The sound of two more shots filled the church, reverberating through the metal cross hung over the stained-glass window in front of the pews, except these rounds came from Wes's gun, sending the German pilot toppling backwards, Claire falling to the floor at his side.

"No, no . . ." Audrey called out, rushing forward, fear following behind.

Still holding his gun—ready, aimed, and deadly—Wes moved in beside the wounded German lying flat and twitching on the parquet floor. The man was panting—*in, out, in, out, in, out*—as if he suspected he was close to death but wanted to cling to his precious life for just a few minutes longer. His open eyes looked past Wes to the ceiling, or even beyond.

With blood oozing from wounds in his torso, the German

coughed and then turned his head to look at Claire. He gazed at her with such regard that had it not been for the blood, smeared warm and salty across his cheek, one might have believed that the two were good friends sharing a personal moment together.

He reached out for her hand, but his fingers stopped short, lacking the necessary strength. Then he mumbled a final message, a secret that life required he share if he desired to leave this world in peace.

"*Kaden Froe . . .*"

His trembling lips struggled in vain to finish, but as the light drained from his eye, the soldier fell limp to the floor, leaving the war for good.

Although the German had died, the heavy breaths continued—*in, out, in, out, in, out*—and Audrey realized the sound was coming from Wes and not from the lifeless pilot lying at their feet. Still holding his gun toward the motionless man, Wes craned his neck toward Maggie, who was sitting at the fallen constable's side, holding pressure to his shoulder.

"He was hit just once," she called out. "I think he'll be all right."

With the threat gone, Wes's hands began to quiver. Fearful that his gun might accidentally discharge, he holstered it back in place.

"I had no choice," Wes exclaimed, as if anyone in the chapel had objected to what he'd done, but he wasn't looking back at those still living. He wasn't even looking at the man on the floor whose life he'd just taken, who would also likely have agreed. Rather, he was calling to the front of the room toward the sculpture of a man with outstretched arms, hanging from a silver cross, who was about to give up his life as well.

He seemed to be looking down at Wes, or was he looking past

him at the dead man? Either way, he was wearing his own circle of thorns, and he looked to be crying.

They had stayed the night at the home of the squire in Weeley, and then, in the morning, picked up the mother and her young son and delivered them to a flat in Dagenham, a good forty minutes east of the city. There, Claire, Audrey, and Maggie watched a once forlorn father embrace his wife and child with such abounding joy, it proved that flashes of happiness remained possible, even in times of war.

Wes had missed the tender scene, choosing instead to wait in the back of the ambulance alone. His hands were no longer shaking, his breathing no longer labored. The adrenaline that had pulsed so effectively through his veins the night before had long since abated, its effects distant but clearly not forgotten.

Ten minutes later, as the vehicle rolled toward London with Maggie's firm hands clenching the wheel and Claire sitting beside her in the front seat, Audrey edged closer to Wes as they sat together in the back. "There are things I need to tell you."

She had intended to have this conversation at a later time, but the words she'd been holding captive had staged a mutiny, breaking their collective chains, rushing to set themselves free. Their escape proved futile, however: Wes didn't move, didn't respond, his thoughts once again wandering a million miles away.

"Wes?"

Only when she nudged him did he return, looking almost startled that she was there at his side, that he wasn't alone. "I'm sorry. What did you say?" he asked.

"I said, I'm glad this ordeal is almost over," she answered, heaping one more lie onto the pile of her guilt.

He stared back, his mind plainly preoccupied with a notion that had wormed into his head and refused to leave.

"The German shot the constable first," Wes blurted out, "because he was wearing his uniform. It made him look more threatening. I'm a much bigger person, a larger target. Had I been wearing my uniform, as I'd wanted to, he would have shot me first."

It was an astute observation, but to what end? "Well, I'm glad that he didn't." Audrey reached for his hand to make another observation equally evident. "Wes, you did what you had to do. You saved lives!"

He said nothing, and, for a moment, Audrey wondered if he would drift away again. When at last he spoke, his voice was barely standing, his gaze fixed back at his feet. "If that's true, then why do I keep reaching up to wipe blood away from my own chin—blood that isn't really there?"

She squeezed his fingers, but he didn't seem to feel it. "Oh, Wes," she exclaimed. "Taking a life—enemy or not—is hard on our souls, even during a war."

When he offered no nod, no acknowledgment that she was right, Audrey bent forward. "Wes, I've told you some lies and need to explain, because I want to quit hurting as well." This wasn't the right time or place, but would it ever be?

"Can we talk about it later?" he asked, looking as if one more burden dropped on his heart would surely cause it to stop beating.

"You're right. I'm so sorry," she said, scooting away to give him distance.

Little more was said until the ambulance pulled in front of

Claire and Audrey's flat, where there seemed to be a commotion on the sidewalk.

It was after Claire had stepped out of her side and walked around to the back to help Audrey gather up her things that a squatty, uniformed man scurried over to them, followed by several soldiers, letting all understand that the group was huddling for them. The man lobbed commands over his heavy, low-slung glasses.

"Miss Audrey Stocking? Or should we call you Audrey Strumpf? It's not important, because you—and this woman with you, whatever her real name—you are both under arrest."

CHAPTER 18

"Take a seat," Colonel Moore instructed, aiming Wes toward a chair. "We need to talk."

Wes sat, his head groggy, his thoughts still stumbling around in a fog. "Where are the men?" he asked, barely realizing that he and the colonel were in the warehouse alone.

"I sent them for tea."

"Have you heard back from your commander?" Wes asked. "Do we know where Audrey and . . . Claire . . . are being held, what charges are being filed against them?"

"He's getting the runaround, but I'll keep trying and let you know." While the colonel waited to make eye contact, Wes's attention wandered the room. "Wes, look at me. I've been told that you're a hero, that you saved people's lives in that church."

Wes replied with wilting words. "They would be wrong."

"Look, I know you feel bad for taking a life, but if you hadn't killed that German, he would have killed you. Worse, he would have killed people you love, and that is an almost impossible guilt to survive."

"Yes . . . but after he was dead, I pulled out his wallet."

"What?"

"Before the constable came with the Home Guard to move the body, I could see something in the German's pocket. I reached in and found his wallet, and inside was a picture of his wife and two young sons. How do I live with that?"

The colonel stretched back to organize his thoughts. "Let me ask you this: have you ever known anyone who served in the Great War—besides me?"

"I knew some men back home," Wes answered, finally meeting the colonel's gaze.

"What did they tell you about their experience?"

"That it was challenging and . . ." Wes's jaw was stuck open like it had forgotten how to close.

The colonel jumped right to his concern. "The answer, if you're being honest, is *very little.* Almost to a man, they came home and wouldn't speak about it, even men who had done heroic things—myself included. Why do you think that is?"

Wes rubbed at his eyes. "I . . . I guess they saw and did some pretty horrible things as well—like me."

The colonel gripped the edge of the table, nudged himself closer to the boy. "The answer, Wes, is *shame,* and shame brings guilt and pain and loss. We'd rather forget or pretend we can pray it all away, but life doesn't work like that. Do you hear me?"

His answer barely crawled. "I do."

"But do you believe me? Look, in the end, when the war is over, the public will want us to march in parades and hoist our flags, and they'll sing patriotic songs, and all that should sound splendid, but it's also going to ache—at least at first."

"Is that why you don't wear your medal, on account of the pain?"

The morning sun was streaming gold through the warehouse windows, and so the colonel pushed his chair into the light to let it soak into his face as if nature were there to support and confirm his assertions. "I don't wear my medal because when I got home from the war, I flung it into a bog. Oh, I regret it now, but at the time it felt right."

"Why?"

"I was distraught. Half the men in my platoon died," he added. "It didn't seem right to wear a medal for that. How in heaven's name was that heroic? Yes, I saved some, and it's true that more could have died, but it's the soldiers I lost, the men I let down—that's the grief that gnaws at my soul like a dog who's constantly chewing on his own sore leg. It's the same grief you feel for taking a man's life, even if he was the enemy."

The colonel invited Wes to slide with him into the light, but Wes's face clouded. "What do you do to cope?"

"My best. That's all I know how to do. I love my country, and I know you love yours, but this is not about patriotism. You killed a man, and whether he deserved it or not doesn't really matter if you're waking up with night sweats, if you still see him cry out to you in your sleep. The killing of another person stays with you. It changes you. Even those who argue otherwise find that out."

Wes let another troubling thought spill out. "We presumed the German fled to the church to hide because he knew everyone would be searching the woods, but I don't think that's true. I believe he actually *was* at the church to pray, that he was just as scared and confused as the rest of us."

The colonel persisted. "But he shot first. You made the right choice. Still, I know my praise won't make it any easier for you. It's not *my* respect you need, but your own—so forgive yourself. It may not happen today, or next week, or next year—but someday. Look forward to that day."

Wes's question burned hot. "How?"

"First, talk about it. Talk to a doctor, to a priest, to the man sitting next to you at the bus stop, if you think it will help and he'll take the time to listen. Second, be gentle on yourself when you've had a bad day. And third . . ." The colonel pointed to the sunlight radiating into the room. "Look up from the darkness in life toward the light, each day, every day. It's the only direction that will help. I don't have all the answers. I simply wanted you to know that you're not alone."

The door opened, and Hastings poked in his head. "Colonel, we're here and ready to leave anytime."

Colonel Moore blinked his okay and then turned back to Wes. "Are you ready, Bowers?"

Wes took a breath, feeling the man's fervor. His eyes followed the light's rays to the windowpane, and then on to the outside sky. His reply was timid, but it was tipped with hope.

"Let's do it."

Major Balder Leemon slumped over his piled papers like a wolf protecting its kill from the pack, a trait nurtured from years of government service. He was double-checking transfer details for the two spies who were to be sent to Camp 020, the interrogation center at Latchmere House in the southwestern suburbs of London, when his office door swung open.

"Major," his secretary said in a whisper, "Lady Reading is here to see you, but she doesn't have an appointment."

Indeed, the wolves were circling. "Tell her that I'm busy, that I—"

"Good morning, Major Leemon," Lady Reading said, stepping into his office. "I don't know if we've had the pleasure of meeting formally yet, but this will only take a minute of your time."

He wanted to growl back, to snarl her away, but instead he pointed toward a single chair. "Please, Lady Reading, take a seat."

She shooed his offer away. "Thank you, but I prefer to stand. I'm here to speak with the two women you have detained."

"Which women?" Leemon asked, doing a poor job of keeping his facial muscles rigid. He watched a smile hitch to the woman's lips, smug and annoying.

"I believe you know precisely to whom I refer," she replied, directing him like a servant. "I would like to speak first to Audrey. You may bring her to me, or I can go to where she is being held. Either option will work."

She stared back so firmly into his distorted glasses that he removed them. He wished only to chase this vicious she-wolf away. "You must be referring to the German spies," he replied, as if he was only now understanding. But then he spat out an inquiry that was souring in his mouth. "On whose authority have you come, if I may ask?"

When she spoke, he could see her teeth. When she lifted a finger, he stepped back. "On the authority of Lady Reading," she answered, verbally nipping at his throat. "And if that's not good enough for you . . ." She turned to his secretary, who was dawdling by the door. "What's your name, miss?"

The woman's squint at her boss didn't go unnoticed. "Yes, I'm talking to you, not the major," Lady Reading declared. "Let me ask again: what is your name?"

"My apologies, Lady Reading, it's Darcy . . . Miss Darcy Cowden."

"Thank you, Miss Cowden. Would you kindly get Home Secretary Morrison on the telephone so the major may speak with him?" While her voice lowered in volume, it raised with resolve. "And if the Home Secretary is not available, I shall have you call the Prime Minister himself." She turned to Leemon to confront any objections. "Will that be necessary?"

When the major released the air he'd held in his lungs, it caused him to slouch. "I'm sure that I can oblige you without bothering either," he muttered. He turned next to Miss Cowden, barking out instructions, though it sounded more like a yap. "Please take Lady Reading to see the two women in custody."

Lady Reading licked her lips, as if she'd just eaten something terribly delicious for breakfast, and then prepared to follow Miss Cowden down the hall. As she walked away, she called back toward the sulking man who was keeping a safe distance but following after them. "Thank you, Major Leemon, for being so accommodating."

Though he had backed away from this snapping wolf, this vile woman trying to rob him of his kill, he wouldn't stay away for long. It wasn't fright shining in his eyes, but fury. He would circle around, watch with rabid eyes, and look for a second chance to attack—only next time, he would tear the bloody she-wolf's head off!

The sparsely furnished room where Audrey was being held had brick walls, a cement floor, no windows, and a solid door that locked from the outside. Unless its captives had thought to bring a hidden hammer, saw, or hatchet—none of which Audrey had—it was sufficiently secure to hold its provisional prisoners until more permanent arrangements could be made.

Audrey was resting on a slender, metal-framed bed when the lock clicked open, and Lady Reading scooted inside. The door was left ajar beside a soldier outside guarding the opening while the two women spoke.

"Hello, child. I fancy you're doing all right," Lady Reading said, her voice ushering in the first kindness the room had likely welcomed that day. She accepted Audrey's nod and then, in her usual manner, sat down beside her and jumped right to business. "When we last spoke, you were about to tell me from where you'd come. Shall we continue that discussion, this time with more detail?"

As Audrey rocked, the old bed frame squeaked. "I haven't been telling the truth. I'm originally from Germany. I was only in Switzerland for a year before coming over to London. My father owns a factory in Germany, and when he could see the war beginning to close in, he sent me away."

"Why did you lie to me? I would have understood," Lady Reading said, as the space between them seemed to narrow.

"Have you not seen how people here gossip about Germans?" Audrey exclaimed with searching eyes. "We'd have been locked up in a detention center for sure."

"Not if your papers are in order."

Audrey's words raced out. "Our papers are *not* in order. Our papers are forged. My father feared that the Nazis wouldn't allow us to leave through the proper channels, and since he had the means, he took an alternative approach. It was more risky, but he believed more certain."

"So, is your real name Audrey Stocking?"

"Sort of . . . it's Audrey Strumpf, which means *stocking* in German."

"And is your family still living in Germany?"

"Yes, in Stuttgart."

"Have you been in contact with them?"

"Only by letter."

"And Claire—she is not your aunt, correct?"

Audrey's admission pulled her eyes to the floor, held them there. "No, my aunt is in Germany with my family. Father said that I should say we were related to reduce suspicion." She looked up, started again to speak, but cowered.

"What is it?" Lady Reading asked. "Are you afraid of her?"

"No, of course not, it's just . . ."

"Audrey, if I'm to help you, I need to know everything!"

A breath, a pause, a moment for Audrey to collect her courage. "You know that I've been having attacks of melancholy, times when I feel overcome?"

"Surely."

"I haven't had one in weeks . . . that is, until last night."

Concern carried through every crease in the woman's face. "I'm awfully sorry. I imagine that was trying, locked up all alone."

Audrey's voice withered to a whisper. "Sometimes, when I finally go to sleep . . . afterwards, I dream. And it's often the same dream, but lately, I've been seeing larger pieces of it."

"What do you mean?" Lady Reading asked.

Audrey paced her reply. "When the dreams first started, I was repeatedly ascending a mountain alone, but over time that mountain turned into a stack of wooden crates. Then, just as I would reach the top, before I could peek over the edge, someone would cover my mouth, trying to suffocate me. And at the very instant I was about to die, I would startle awake, gasping for air."

Lady Reading draped her arm around the girl. "Oh, child, that's terrible."

"Yes, but last night, before I jerked awake, I turned around in my dream in time to see the person who was trying to kill me, and . . ."

Instinctively, Lady Reading pulled her tight. "You're safe now. Go ahead."

Every word wavered. "The woman smothering me, trying to kill me was . . . it was Lilli!"

"Lilli? Who's Lilli?" Lady Reading asked, her eyes pinching.

Audrey had reached down and was clutching the bed's metal frame. "Lilli Perlen is my tutor," she exclaimed. "She's the woman I've been calling Aunt Claire."

The room where Lilli Perlen was held was nearly identical to Audrey's, and again, Lady Reading wasted no time with pleasantries, jumping right to business without any semblance of her previous sympathy. She sat in a chair across from Lilli to stare directly into her eyes.

"Tell me your name—your real name," Lady Reading demanded, sounding more like an interrogator and less like a lady.

"My name is Cla . . ." she halted mid-syllable. "Forgive me. I've been calling myself Claire for so long, it's a tad hard to shake the habit. My name is Lilli Perlen."

Lady Reading aimed her focus like a rifle. "Who are you, and what are you doing in London?"

"I'm not a spy, if that's what you're asking. I've been Audrey's tutor since the girl turned nine, the same year that her mother died."

"Her tutor?" Lady Reading asked, still skeptical.

"Yes, for Audrey, but also for Jessey and Lewy, her siblings. Mr. Strumpf spared no expense when it came to educating his children. My strengths are language and history."

"You do speak English flawlessly. Where did you learn?"

"My mother is English, originally from Leeds. My father is German. I was born in Frankfurt but attended school at Victoria University in Manchester. Check with the school—under my real name—and you will see I'm telling the truth."

Lady Reading continued to poke and prod. "I spoke with Audrey. She has been having dreams where she said you're trying to suffocate her. What do you say about that?"

Lilli answered calmly, but with a tinge of regret. "Those are not dreams. Those are memories."

"Then you admit you tried to kill her?"

"Kill her? No! Is that what you think?" The woman's eyes had flapped open. "I've been trying to save her."

"Save her? From whom?"

Lilli's eyes bounced off every corner in the room as if looking for the right way to explain. "Her life was once in danger, but now I suppose I am trying to save Audrey from herself."

"I don't understand."

Lilli beckoned Lady Reading closer, waited until she had pulled up her chair. "Audrey's father, Walther Strumpf, owned factories in Hamburg and Stuttgart. He was a gifted electrical engineer who had devised a way to build condensers for radios more efficiently.

The Strumpfs were Jewish, at least in heritage, so as the Nazis rose in power, Walther grew increasingly troubled. He spoke of his concerns often, told me so himself."

Lady Reading straightened as if the words prickled. With a rolling motion of her hand, she cued Lilli to continue.

"He had devised a plan to weather the Nazi rise by partnering with a man named Selig, a German who worked for him first in Hamburg and then in Stuttgart. Some in the factory whispered that he was partnering with the devil; others said he was hiding from God. I suspect he saw it as the only way to preserve his heritage—until Kristallnacht."

"What happened then?"

"It was the night that Jewish businesses all across the country were looted and damaged, but not his factories. It appeared that his partnering strategy had worked—until he discovered that Selig, with his new authority, was making arrangements to sell their condensers at higher prices to a man named Rühlemann—and Walther was furious."

"Why?"

It was Lilli's turn to lift her eyebrows. "Have you not heard of him?"

"No, should I have?"

"It was common knowledge in the factory. Rühlemann's company was developing and building fuzes . . . fuzes being used in German bombs."

Lady Reading's face paled. "Please continue."

"It was then that Walther moved up his previous plan for his children to leave the country with Claire—the real Aunt Claire—while he would stay behind. He was a confident man who thought that he could convince Selig of his mistake, help him understand that whatever the Nazis touched would wither."

Lilli drew in a huge breath, as if she were using up the last of the room's air. "Claire readied the younger children at home the following evening, while I went with Audrey to pick up their papers. We were to meet Claire and the other two children at the factory so they could cautiously bid their father goodbye."

"I take it that didn't pan out."

"No, there was a problem with one of the passports, and it took longer to pick up the documents than expected. When we returned, I found two strange cars parked in front of the factory, and so Audrey and I entered quietly from the back. We could hear angry voices, and I signaled that we needed to leave—but the girl didn't obey. She never does. She sneaked up the stairs and then scurried up onto a stack of crates from where she could look down into the main part of the factory. She was peeking over when the shots rang out."

It was the first time that Lady Reading had noticed Lilli trembling. "Take a minute if you need to."

Lilli nodded, but mostly to offer thanks. "I was right behind Audrey and could see that she was about to scream out, so I reached up and clasped my hand forcefully over her mouth, holding it as firmly as I dared, knowing that if she let out even a whimper, and they found us, we would both be killed."

"But they didn't hear her?"

"No, but I held her too long, and she passed out. I was frantic, not sure what to do, so I simply stayed hidden until the men had gone, hoping Audrey wouldn't wake up screaming."

"And she didn't?"

"No, not before I had dragged her to the back of the warehouse and hefted her into the car. It was odd, though: she had watched her father, brothers, and aunt all be gunned down, with Selig himself standing right there, but when she awoke in the car, she spoke as if her family were still alive. I don't pretend to comprehend how, but her brain refused to accept what her eyes had witnessed. She had stepped above it. Does that make her crazy?"

Lady Reading's tone was no longer ranting. "No, it makes her human. What did you do?"

"I did the only thing I could think to do. Claire and I have similar features and build, and Walther had explained his plan to me. They were to go to their home in Switzerland, where I'd been many times, and wait out the war. So I told Audrey that her father had asked *me* to take her instead. I told her that he had decided not to send the other children for now."

Lilli clenched her teeth, a threat to the moisture emerging in her eyes. "I couldn't tell her that her father and family were dead—not until she was ready to hear it and accept it. I just couldn't."

"No, you made the right choice. Children can be delicate. I'm curious, though, why did you leave Switzerland?"

"It was one of the few countries the Nazis didn't invade, but that doesn't mean that they weren't there. We were doing well until one day, on our way home from the market, we spied men in front of the house—Germans. I don't know what they wanted, but I couldn't risk finding out. We watched until they had gone, and then, while Audrey sat in a nearby café, I sneaked in and took our passports and what money we had left. I paid most of it to three men from France who smuggled us to the coast hidden in the bed of a delivery truck, and then on to England by boat."

Lady Reading patted Lilli's knee, but the woman had more to say. "You implied that I was a criminal, but I ask you, Lady Reading, is it a crime to try to stay alive, to hide this girl in a foreign land with the hope that we'll somehow make it through this cursed war?"

Lady Reading reached next for Lilli's hands, giving them a squeeze like a child would tug on a doll. "No, it's not. I, too, like you, have been in desperate situations." She had pinched her mouth as if sucking on a thought. "At times in our lives, we all hide, even from ourselves."

Surrounded by the room's sudden stillness, Lilli lifted her face to meet Lady Reading's gaze. "My interest is only for Audrey. As you noted, she is beginning to remember, and I fear that if she's alone when the truth floods back, it will be too much weight for her fragile soul to support, and it will crush her."

Lady Reading asked no further questions but instead turned to the open door. "Major, will you please come in?" When there was no sound, she called again. "Please, Major Leemon, I don't have all day. I know that you've been listening."

The major slid around the corner past the posted guard. "It was my duty, Lady Reading, to ensure you stayed safe."

"Yes, of course," she answered warily. "Now, do you have anything further that you'd like to ask Claire . . . I'm sorry, she's right, it's a hard habit to break. Do you have anything more for either Lilli or Audrey before I take them out of here?"

He crushed the unlit cigarette that he held in his fingers. "Lady Reading, you can't believe what she's saying!"

"Yes, frankly, I do. I'm sure you already have people checking with the university she mentioned. If you find something scandalous, let me know. Until then, the women will be in my charge."

Leemon's hands were flailing around his head, scattering bits of tobacco to the floor. "But the girl was sending information to a war factory in Germany! That's a crime!"

"No, she wasn't," Lilli added, speaking up to the man for the first time.

"But we have the letters!" the major shouted. "I can show you copies!"

"You have Audrey's letters, but she never mailed them. You see, deep inside, I think she knows. She would write them and then place them in her box, but she never actually sent them."

Lady Reading turned. "What box?"

"Have you heard of tefillin?" Lilli asked.

"No, please tell me."

"It is a set of black boxes worn by observant Jews to hold parchment inscribed with verses of the Torah, as a way to remember God. As a young child, Audrey missed her father dearly when he traveled, and so, inspired by the tefillin, he constructed a black box for Audrey large enough to hold letters. He told her that no matter the distance that separated them, if she would write to him and then place her letter in the box, he would feel the words in his heart. She believed it as a little girl, and I think she still believes it today."

Lilli faced Major Leemon with new defiance, staging her own rebellion. "Does she deserve to be imprisoned for having hope?"

Lady Reading provided reinforcement. "Yes, major. Are you going to prosecute a child trying to survive the war?"

The major let out an incoherent grunt, but it only encouraged the woman. She took a step closer. "Sir, there are no crimes here, only sadness. File formal charges, if you think you have a case, but I'm telling you, these women are walking out of here right now with me."

She turned to Lilli, leaving no room for further objection. "Pick up your things. We're going to get Audrey. We'll take her to a safe place, and then we need to tell her the truth. It's time."

CHAPTER 19

The women sat in plush chairs around a rectangular wooden table that graciously held their tea, cups filled with comfort. The walls in Lady Reading's home were papered with elegance, a blossoming floral that modeled a country garden, the scent in the room enhancing the illusion.

Lady Reading gripped Audrey's knee. "Lilli has a story that she wants to tell you, Audrey. It's about your family and how much your father loved you. It's time for you to hear the truth."

Audrey reached forward to pick up her cup. The girl should have tensed, but as the women watched her stir, she held steady, let the steaming tea bolster her composure, perhaps revealing the true reason the British so adore the drink.

Sharing the news went far more smoothly than Lady Reading or Lilli had imagined. Lilli held Audrey's hand as she listened, though it turned out that the teacher shed far more tears than her pupil she'd been protecting, a girl still clinging to a handmade wooden box. Lady Reading had a doctor waiting outside, a specialist, in case his expertise was needed, but he was never called inside, and Audrey never knew that he was there.

"I suppose inside I've known," Audrey admitted. "My heart just needs to accept what my body has been trying to tell me."

"I've been thinking," Lady Reading said, as Audrey and Lilli prepared to leave. "It may be good for you both to get out of London. I have a friend, Sister Mary Catherine, who runs a girls' school in Sheffield, and I know that she would appreciate the help. What do you say?"

Lilli glanced at Audrey as if she'd known about this plan all along. "It sounds promising. Do you agree?"

The corners of Audrey's eyes crinkled. "Tell me about the children," she said.

Lady Reading obliged. "The school is small. I don't know how many girls attend, but I do know that you'd love it, and the children would adore you."

Audrey breathed the encircling scent of safety as she weighed the possibility. The moment seemed to pause with her, let her carefully consider it before nudging her to answer.

"Yes, that would be lovely, but before we go, there's someone I need to see."

Lilli was standing in front of Café Cozier, proper and erect, against a lamppost that seemed pleased to offer needed support.

"I don't know your real name," Wes said as he approached. "I know it's not Claire."

Her reply was crisp, precise, just like the morning air. "My name is Lilli. I'm Audrey's tutor, not her aunt. I'm sorry that we both had to lie, but it was for our safety."

"The colonel told me that you'd been released. He filled me in on some of the details."

She would give credit where it was due. "All thanks goes to Lady Reading. I shudder to think where we'd be without the help of that noble woman."

Wes rocked in place, foot to foot, his uncertainty swaying with him. "How is Audrey . . . is it Strumpf? Is that correct?"

"*Stocking* is her name in English, and it's perfectly proper. She didn't lie to you about that part. In fact, that's why I'm here. There are some things you need to know."

Lilli watched Wes reach out to the post to steady himself as well. "I'm listening," he said.

Her mouth puckered as if her words had spoiled. "When you and Audrey first met, I didn't care for you, not at all," she admitted. "Audrey is young and naïve, and foreign soldiers have a reputation for leaving wounded hearts on the battlefield. But you've been different. You seem to have helped her heart heal. It's all been quite incredible." Lilli shook her head, still grappling with the idea.

Wes's eyes latched onto hers. "I appreciate that, but you could have trusted me."

"No, the risks were too great. You know that she lost her family, don't you? She was there and saw it all happen."

"Yes, I was told."

"She's fragile," Lilli explained, wiping at the worry in her eyes.

"Aren't we all?" Wes answered back.

Lilli couldn't dispute it and lowered her chin to agree. "I don't know if you realize, but Audrey's emotional attacks have been far fewer and less severe since she met you. I see a joy in her eyes that

I've not seen since she was with her family in Stuttgart. I think that deep inside, she knew they were dead, but she never reconciled her loss because, in her head, she never presumed she'd make it out of the war. But now she's facing it, and you've had something to do with that."

"Me? How?"

"You're giving her something to live for."

Wes shuffled his feet. "Will she see me? Where is she, if I may ask?"

In spite of her best effort to keep it hidden, a pleased smile surged across Lilli's face. "Audrey didn't know if you'd want to see her. I'm so very happy to hear that you do." She stood back, staring at him, watching, wondering, as if expecting him to mutter some sort of magic phrase.

He pressed impatiently at his knuckles. When he finally spoke, an irritation edged in his voice. "Is your aim to stand there all day and torture me, or will you please tell me where I can find her? Seriously, do I have to beg?"

Lilli remained unruffled. "You know, you are as impatient as the girl." But then she turned and pointed across the street. "Do you see that bookstore on the opposite side? You'll find her in the *Mystery & Crime* section. Dramatic, I know, but considering what we've been through, she said if we got this far, you'd find it amusing."

It was Wes's turn to hang on a smile. He glanced first at the store window, and then back to Lilli, as if she needed to undo a hidden leash.

"Go!" she demanded. "You're excused! Get out of here! I'm sick of looking at you."

She watched Wes sprint across the street, circle a low wall of sandbags, heave open the door, and then rush inside, all with such abounding anticipation that it ushered in sudden thoughts of Kaden Froe.

Is he alive? Will I one day have a similar reunion?

She fidgeted, trying to enjoy the moment, but she was also hesitant, knowing that she hadn't been completely honest—not with Wes, Lady Reading, the inspector, or even Audrey.

Lilli Perlen still had one last secret she hadn't shared.

Wes didn't need the London bookstore owner—an older woman who plainly adored pastels—to point toward the nervous girl with the alluring smile. He could see Audrey propped fretfully against a display of Agatha Christie novels, brushing at her despair like stains on a skirt.

"You came!" she exclaimed, seemingly stunned as he turned the corner. "I'm so glad. There are several things that I need to explain."

He gazed down watchfully, let his own wanting eyes pour into hers. "I would like to hear them because I have things to say of my own. But first, there is something I need to do."

"Yes, of course," she answered flatly. "Go ahead, whatever it is. I'll be right here."

Wes curtly nodded. "Yes, I'm counting on that much." Then he reached one hand around Audrey's waist to support the small of her back while he draped the other around her shoulders. He pulled her tight, lifting her heels from the floor before pausing for the tiniest slice of time to catch his own breath. Her eyes had arched, briefly baffled, until an understanding washed between them with such warmth, it could have coaxed tears from coal.

Then, with a distant wireless playing "If I Could Be with You

One Hour Tonight," he pressed his lips against hers, kissing her tenderly and letting her kiss him back.

A few seconds later, or much longer—again, it was hard for either to say—Wes drew back ever so slightly and inquired, "Now that we're clear on that, was there something more that you needed to tell me?"

With her arms clasped around his neck, as if her legs were shaky and letting go would drop her to the tile, she leaned in and returned the whisper to his ear. "I think you've about covered it."

And then she stretched up to kiss him again, because truly, with a war on, nobody knows how much longer one has.

"Are you two going downstairs?" the peevish store owner asked.

Wes turned toward the voice, his confusion melding with Audrey's. "Downstairs?" he asked.

"Blimey!" the befuddled woman called out. "Can you not hear the sirens?" Her tone was trumpeting disgust or admiration—it was hard to tell which.

A pause, a glance, a second to listen, and then laughter.

Of all the people across London hurrying toward shelters for protection from the imminent raid, there were likely only two who—even if just for a moment—were both entirely content and completely unafraid.

When Wes stepped out from the lavatory, still drying his clean-shaven face, he found his team circled around the table, holding one of Driver's nasty cakes, pouring tea, and ready to sing—and they were waiting for him.

"What's going on? It's not my birthday?"

"Better than your birthday, mate," Hastings answered. "It's November 16th!"

Wes countered with a slow-motion shrug. "This is England, so there's no Thanksgiving. Is it National Tea Day? I've told you that I only drink tea if it's brewed in a harbor." When nobody flinched, he tried again. "Fine, is there a sale on fish and chips? No? How about Eat-With-Your-Fork-Upside-Down Day? Am I getting close? Come on, give me a hint."

The colonel stepped forward, openly weary of dragging this out. "There's ten candles. It's been ten weeks, Bowers, and you're still alive. You made it. The men thought that deserved a celebration, and so I agreed."

"You shouldn't have," Wes answered.

"It was the men's idea, and I . . ."

"No!" Wes interrupted, his voice climbing over the colonel's. "I mean, you really *shouldn't have.* Now you've all jinxed me, which means I'll get blown to pieces . . . TODAY!"

Badger, the obvious driving force behind the merrymaking, pushed in front. "Bowers, we voted, and you get the day off, so unless you step out in front of a truck, you made it through ten full weeks!"

"But I don't need a day off."

Badger's tone sharpened. "Listen, mate, you beat the odds. Accept it. Enjoy the day. Also, know that you're likely to stumble into a friend at that café you visit. Do you understand what I'm saying?"

"Well, if you put it that way . . ."

Badger shielded his mouth so only Wes could see. "I'm getting married. I haven't told the others, but she said yes."

Wes tried to keep his voice low. "That's great, Badger. Congratulations!"

Badger pointed his stubby finger. "Take your own advice. There's a girl waiting. You may not have another chance, so go and tell her how you feel about her."

Wes ended with a whisper. "I was right. I've created a monster."

Wes sat beside Audrey at Café Cozier, no longer across the table. She was wearing a red blouse with a dark knee-length skirt, and while she offered excuses for her attire, claiming to have little to work with, she made every stitch proud and patriotic.

"I heard from a reliable source that you'd be here," he said, with glad eyes. "The team insists that I celebrate my ten weeks' survival. That or they want to be rid of me."

She took a bite of tea cake and then pushed the plate aside, apparently to make room on the table. "Well, I'm glad that you're here because I have a surprise." She retrieved a box from beneath her chair and set it in front of him, a box that rattled.

"What's this?"

She wrangled a smile. "Based on my previous experience, I can't guarantee that I'll make it through to the end, but I'm ready to try." When she drew back the cover, Wes could see chess pieces trying their best to peek out. His eyes curled with concern.

"Audrey, there's no need. I don't want playing chess to make you . . . you know."

She picked up his pillowed words and fluffed them. "If I faint, will you promise to revive me, lips to lips?"

Wes raised his palm like he was stopping traffic. "I'm serious.

How do you know that you won't be . . ." The proper phrasing again fled the room.

She coaxed it back. "Sad?" She placed her hand on his, but today didn't let go. "It seems that my body has been in mourning for two years, and it's taken me that long to accept it—but, Wes, I think I'm ready."

He said nothing, but the two had locked eyes to communicate plenty. When she gleefully dumped the contents of the box onto the table, it was the pieces themselves that seemed the most delighted to finally stretch and cheer. As she positioned them on the board, she made small talk—though it didn't feel small.

"Have you written to Nathelle lately?" she asked.

"Are you trying to distract me?"

"I'm simply curious. From the letters you've shared, I will tell you that I like her. She seems like a gallant woman—and she must be, if she's writing to you."

It was the first time he'd ever heard her genuinely giggle. "What might you be suggesting?" he asked.

"Nothing at all. I'm saying she has a good, motherly quality about her. That's all."

"But I'm not looking for a mother."

Her eyes darted toward the board. "Would you care to be white?" she asked, changing the subject. "You'll move first."

"You know that will give me a slight advantage?"

"I've heard that," she replied, but her voice lacked innocence, sounding more like she was honing her sword. She got up, sat in the seat on the opposite side of the table, and turned the board. "I think we're ready."

When he looked up, her eyes had narrowed and her cheeks had

drawn taut. She was already analyzing the readied game. "Are you sure you want to do this?" he asked again.

"I'm sure," she replied, and so Wes reached out and nudged his king's pawn steadily forward two squares.

Without pause, Audrey advanced her own king's pawn. "It's sad that so many pawns have to die," she said, possibly trying to throw him off again, but she brimmed with such sincerity he had to speak up.

"They're infantry," he told her, as if their title alone justified a quick death. He then moved his king-side knight, attacking her pawn.

She defended with her pawn, and then he developed a bishop, and their game started out as many similar contests that were being played across the world that day, except music was playing softly in the background, and the way her gaze sometimes curled around her moves, neither seemed sure if this was a game of war or a game of dancing.

"Are you enjoying yourself?" he asked as the game proceeded.

"Immensely," she answered without looking up.

While one studied the board, the other studied their opponent—and for that portion of the contest, Wes was certain that he had the better end of the deal.

In watching, he noticed that she fingered the pieces first with her eyes before ever making a move with her hands, but it wasn't with cunning. Rather, he could sense compassion, as if the fate of each soldier she sent into battle would be her own.

Pieces were pushed forward; pieces were pulled back. A turn for him, a turn for her, until, amidst their play, he could see that she was protecting her central pawn majority. In her bid to safeguard the lowliest of her chess pieces, she was making a clear mistake, leaving more valuable pieces vulnerable. But she was so intent; he wondered if he should be kind and explain.

It wasn't her innocence that finally compelled his sympathy, but her beauty. "If you move there, you'll expose your queen."

"I'm aware," she replied. Then, glancing across the board as if sitting atop a grand horse perusing a battlefield, she added, "Sometimes in life you have to sacrifice your queen in order to save your pawns."

He covered his mouth, pretended to cough, hoped she didn't see him smirk—because that was pure nonsense. The pawns were there to shield the queen and the king, not the other way around. That was how the game was designed; that was how it was played. It was a reflection of real life.

If she noticed his bemusement, she ignored him. On her turn, she advanced her knight to take his bishop, then let his queen's bishop's pawn recapture her knight. She stared expectantly and then moved her next piece.

Wes probed her eyes one last time, and then, seeing no other choice, he used his rook to capture her queen. If this was a game of war, he had taken her top general, and total defeat would be only a matter of time.

"She served nobly," was all Audrey said, and although she was playing foolishly, he had to admit that she was playing with confidence. She even seemed to be masking a smile as she then recaptured, creating a dangerous pair of passed pawns.

More staring. More studying. More maneuvering of pieces.

After she advanced a pawn, he moved back his remaining rook, but as his fingers lifted from his piece, a curious pattern of open squares caught his attention.

"Should I order more biscuits?" he asked, giving himself more time to survey the board.

"If you'd like," she answered.

He doubted that she had noticed, and he would soon close up any opportunity, but she must have, because, two moves later, she pushed her pawn unopposed to the opposite side of the board and requested that he make it a queen.

She didn't grin, didn't gloat, but instead spouted what sounded more like life advice than chess guidance. "My father often reminded me that pawns could also become queens, if you just look for opportunity and give them a proper chance."

Her newly anointed queen, sitting smugly behind enemy lines, changed things a bit, and as Wes pondered the board more prudently, his heart sank. Not only had she been able to queen her pawn, she was in a position in two or three more moves to do it again. He could stop her, but doing so would cost him his knight.

How did this happen?

He'd been too busy scrutinizing her major pieces, her game play, to attend to his own. If he were going to salvage this game, it would take some concentration. He bowed close, made mental moves in his mind, and countered them again and again. "I think I'm being played," he whispered.

He used his knight to take her bishop, knowing that his own bishop would be left undefended, but she moved her knight to deliver a check, forking his king and rook—a vulnerability he'd missed seeing.

The game's ending was beginning to draw focus, and it wasn't pretty: in six more moves, he would lose the game.

It took her only four. "Checkmate," she whispered.

"You beat me with your pawns," he muttered, trying to shake away his disbelief.

"No," she corrected. "They were never pawns. It sometimes just takes them a little while to realize."

"Well, congratulations!" he added, finally letting a smile paint broad across his face.

"I owe it to my father. He was a very persistent teacher."

"And you were undoubtedly a very perceptive learner. Should we play again?"

"Actually, I want to talk for a minute," she said. "I have some news that I need to share."

Wes scooted back beside her, met her with his eyes.

"Lady Reading thinks Lilli and I should get out of the city, away from the bombing. She knows a woman in Sheffield who runs a school. She claims that I'll be a tremendous help and that I can work directly with the children. The city has been largely spared from bombing, so it will be a much safer place to wait out the war."

Reluctance crawled out of the silence to roost at Wes's feet. "Sheffield? How far away is that?" he asked.

"It's north, five or six hours by bus. I could try to come back to London on occasion to see you—if you'd like—or we could meet in the middle."

His look of longing then melted into resolve. "If it's safer in Sheffield, then that's where you should be. When do you plan to leave?"

Audrey's conviction was trying to find its own steady ground, every questioning word still light and fragile. "Lady Reading is finalizing the details, but in a few days. Honestly, do you think I should go?"

Wes filled his lungs with air and then forced a lie. "I think you should. You'll be helping the children," he reminded. "That's who you are. We'll still see each other. We'll find a way."

"You're right," she said, letting her arms drape into his.

"Besides," Wes added, "if you don't go help the children, who will?"

CHAPTER 20

As much as Driver hated to admit it, the day hadn't been the same without Wes along. Who would have guessed a bunch of Limeys would miss the funny-talking bloke?

Driver elbowed Pike. "Hey, the Yank would 'ave luv'd this one," his sarcasm hanging humid in the air—and he was right. The bomb they'd spent the day digging out—weighing a thousand kilograms and painted with a sky-blue body and a yellow-striped tail cone—had landed beside a German hospital in Hackney, of all places.

Pike stepped behind Driver and picked up the rope, watching for the colonel to give the command. "Serves the Jerries right," he confirmed.

Short of the location, it was a textbook disposal case, lacking the drama of so many other bombs they'd defused. The greatest tension that morning had come after Badger and Gunner had excavated down to the fuze pocket to find that it was armed with both a (17) and a (50). They scampered like scared squirrels from the hole, letting Hastings and the colonel bring in the stethoscope and a clock stopper, only to realize that the bomb's clock wasn't ticking at all, as it had been damaged on impact.

The bent fuze ring wouldn't budge, meaning the fuzes inside were staying put, but it made no difference. In true scientific fashion, Dr. Gough had been tabulating statistics culled from various sections' reports and had determined that once jammed, just one percent of (17)s resumed working. As comforting as the statistic sounded, the colonel let the sappers finish and then slipped back down to attach the clock stopper for good measure. He also wanted to listen once the bomb was ready to be raised, merely a precaution to make sure any jarring didn't somehow restart the gears.

The accompanying (50) was likewise of little alarm. The bomb had landed nearly a week before, well past the necessary waiting time for the charge in the backup fuze to drain, so it would also now be inert.

The team's biggest obstacle wasn't the fuzes, but the bomb's size. There was no way to hoist it out of the hole directly, so Moore had sent for sheer legs and tackle to erect a tripod above the excavation. Once ready, the colonel threaded the pulleys and then securely roped the bomb before climbing topside to don headphones and listen.

There was apparently no ticking because he signaled Badger, who relayed the message to Pike and Driver, both ready at the end of the rope. "Pull!"

"Wish we could 'ave used the bleedin' 'ippo," Driver said to Pike as they strained to draw up the slack.

"Shut it an' pull," Pike commanded back, the most aggressive words the kid had mumbled since joining the team. Both set their feet to better grip the now-taut line.

As the bomb lifted, the tripod stiffened, and the colonel called out his encouragement. "Good! Keep pulling, keep pulling."

"Easy for 'im to bloody say," Driver grumbled through his flashing grin.

"A little more," the colonel called back as the obedient bomb rose, hanging upside down like a bagged bird in the sunlight.

Suddenly one of the tripod legs shifted.

"STOP! STOP! STOP!" the colonel hollered.

The settling leg had caused the bomb to swing, like a happy child on a playground, but with each sway, the errant tripod leg raised off the ground. The colonel rushed toward it, intending to put some weight on the thing, while Hastings grabbed the rope to counter the motion.

Gunner, who had been standing nearby, picked up on what was happening and dashed to the colonel's side to assist. With both men holding the tripod leg, they steadied the structure.

"Don't let go of the rope!" Hastings yelled toward Driver and Pike, and then, perhaps feeling the slightest bit of give, and worried the two wouldn't have enough strength to keep it stable, he ran to where they were pulling and latched on himself.

"Let me get this," Hastings said to Pike, digging in his heels. "See if you can help the colonel."

Then, with the bomb still swinging, the colonel stepped beside it and reached out to slow it with his hand.

"A little more," Driver grunted to Hastings. "Just a little bit . . ."

There was a blinding flash, and both men toppled backward as the taut rope gave way. But it couldn't have been the bomb: there was never an explosion, just silence—complete and total quiet.

Driver was on his back beside Hastings, staring heavenward, puzzling over the odd and prolonged hush that had come over them, when a storm of gravel, sand, and brick began to rain down from the sky. He instinctively rolled over and covered his head.

When the pebbled hail ended, he reached for his ear, wondering if it had become clogged, only to find that the side of his head was wet and crimson, his hand bloody. His gaze then swerved to where the members of his section—Colonel Moore, Badger, Gunner, and Pike—had stood moments ago. There was no one there. In place of where the bomb had dangled was a huge crater.

For the length of a tortured moment, his eyes continued to argue with his head about what the scene meant. When truth at last connected with reason, it came stabbing, like a hot knife plunging into his chest.

Everyone who'd been circled around the bomb was gone.

"God bless the waning moon," Audrey whispered, glancing up at the pale orb as it peeked through a break in the tenuous clouds.

Air-raid sirens continued to whine in the distance, but there had been no bombers, no explosions, no fires, and without tonight's milky moonlight, it would have been almost impossible for her to make her way to the warehouse.

The windows were dark, the main door was locked, and, like every other building in London at night, the place looked black, sad, and empty. Still, she groped her way in the dark and knocked anyway, hoping he was inside.

There was no sound, no movement, and so she tapped again at the wood a bit louder.

Rustling followed, shuffled steps, and then a click to undo the lock. The large door swung sluggishly inward to reveal the shadow of a trembling man who seemed barely able to stand.

She stepped in from the chill, kicked the door closed with her foot, let her smaller arms harbor and hold his larger fragile frame.

"Wes, I am so sorry."

His body was quivering, but he didn't feel cold; he sniffled but hadn't been crying. He stood limp, his arms dangling at his sides as if his disconnected brain had yet to divulge that he should raise them up and embrace Audrey back.

As she continued to rock him gently in the dark, neither of them speaking, she felt his hands gradually rise, his grip cautiously tighten, his frame tug desperately against hers. It seemed the warmth of a closely held body, the balm of unguarded human connection, was melting the icy emotion he'd been battling so bravely to control.

His stuttered breathing quickened; a gentle gasp curdled into a muffled moan. It was not supposed to be like this, him clinging to her for help.

Did he not understand that he was here in England to do the saving and not the other way around?

The groan of a truck passed on the street outside, chasing the incessant sirens that reminded all to seek shelter. She didn't care. Even if bombs began to fall, she wasn't about to let go. She knew well, from her own experience, that emotional wounds exposed to the air at nighttime invariably cause the sharpest of pain. His sorrows would scab over, but a cut this deep would take time to fully heal.

She held him lovingly, never loosening her grasp—rocking, rocking, rocking back and forth to settle the man's subdued sobs. She would stay with him as long as needed, so he wouldn't be alone. Because in the middle of a war, or anytime a person is hurting, being close is the surest remedy for sadness.

In the quiet of the night, with grief fluid at their feet—the whole experience being one of the most painful of Audrey's young life, yet one of the most moving—her answer came.

It was a disquiet that had been pestering her for days, a question Wes had posed earlier.

She wanted to pull back from him at that moment to explain, but it was not the right time. She would tell him about it in the morning. Better still, she would make her father proud: she would lay it all out proper on paper.

Audrey would write Wes a letter.

Botleys Park Hospital, southwest of London, had opened in 1939 as one of England's few modern hospitals for treating mental-health ailments. With the declaration of war, however, it was quickly commandeered to treat sick and wounded service personnel, particularly casualties from the air raids.

The room where Driver and Hastings rested held thirty beds, fifteen along each side, with three coke stoves down the middle doing their best to heat the ward.

A doctor had filled Wes in on their condition: Hastings had suffered a laceration to his head and a broken collarbone but was expected to make a full recovery. Driver had lost all of his hearing in one ear but still had a fair range in the other. He'd also had a concussion and was nauseated, but his symptoms had recently improved.

The men were bedded on opposite walls, so Wes approached Driver first, the kid edging himself up in the bed when he noticed Wes coming. "Hey, mate, got any smokes?" he asked as casually as if they had bumped into one another on the corner. He patted his bandaged ear. "An' speak loud!"

Wes padded his pockets. "I apologize. I don't have any."

"Buggers. The nurse takes 'em, right, but she's scrummy, and so if I put one to my lips, she'll come over."

If *scrummy* meant beautiful, the kid had the right idea. "Other than tormenting the nurse, how are you doing?"

He was watching Wes's mouth, clearly having trouble hearing. "I'll be deaf in one ear, so I'll fi' righ' in."

"Fit in?" Wes asked.

"Gunner 'ad one eye, I'll 'ave one ear, and you got 'alf a brain."

Yup, the kid was going to be just fine. Driver threw his next glance toward the door. "They're lettin' us out, you know? We'll be discharged, sent back 'ome."

"No, I didn't know. What will you do?"

"Come again?"

"I said, WHAT WILL YOU DO?"

"Don't be teasin', but me mum always talked about openin' a flower shop, an' I'd take the deliveries."

Wes didn't so much as twitch, his face never more serious. "That's great, Driver, but I have one suggestion."

"Yeah?"

"Get a real license to drive." He winked at the boy, perhaps now more of a man, then thumbed his intention to cross the room to see Hastings. Before he could, Driver swung up his arm and offered Wes a salute—so Wes saluted back.

"I didn't know that you knew how," Wes said.

"You earned it, mate."

"As did you, my friend. As did you."

As Wes stepped next to Hastings's bed, he could see that his head was bandaged, partially covering one eye. "Lieutenant," Wes said, greeting him. Hastings tossed back a nod. Of all the men in the section, he had been the closest to the colonel.

"I'm so deeply sorry," Wes added. He tugged at the buttons on his sleeve, his condolences weighing heavy, making it hard for either man to know what to say next. "I heard that you're being discharged. Are you heading home?"

"Until I heal, but then . . ." Hastings glanced around, as if the colonel might be walking in. "He thought he was so secretive," he added, shifting the topic, "but I know that he called in favors to keep me with him. The man was always trying to protect my family and me, and I can't fault him for that. But after I'm better, I have a mate in the 7th Armoured Division, fighting in Tobruk . . ."

Wes intruded with a knee-nudge to the bed. "You'll head to the front? You know they shoot at you there? Of course, that's nothing to anyone who's been blown up and lived to tell about it."

Hastings replied with a brittle laugh. "We can be taken any time. It's how life works. I can't control when I go, but I can control how I spend the time I have, and I can't go home and look my lad square in the eye while men are out there dying, while our freedom isn't secure."

"I can see what the colonel saw in you," Wes said.

Rather than humbly accept the compliment, Hastings lifted his eyes. He seemed to be looking past Wes. "What is it?" Wes asked.

Hastings's voice dropped. "Bowers, I'm telling you, he's still here."

"The colonel? Is that who you mean?"

"Look, I can't explain it, but I feel him, as if he still cares and is watching, even helping. Does that sound mad?"

Wes mulled it over, tasted the notion. "It sounds exactly like the man." Both let the admiration settle. "I'll check back on you," Wes said before saying goodbye.

"I'll do the same."

As Wes pulled open the door to leave, a man in his early fifties, wearing a dark coat, starched shirt, and striped tie, was entering. When he noticed Wes's uniform, that it wasn't British, he promptly twisted around. "Lieutenant Bowers?"

"Yes, sir."

"I'm Dr. Herbert Gough, chairman of the—"

Wes cut the cordial introduction short. "Sir, I know who you are. Colonel Moore spoke of you often."

"That's kind."

"Truthfully, he never shut up about you. He told me countless times that when England wins this war, it will largely be due to your efforts—you and your Backroom Boys. He said it was a disgrace that so few know that your group even exists."

"Well, we'd like to keep it that way." The man rocked forward. "You must know that he admired you equally, and also spoke about you often."

"Nice things, I hope."

"Oh, I'd say Russell thought of you as the smart, good-looking American son that he could never have here in England. I think his only regret was that you never took to his love of tea."

"Prodigal children," Wes replied flatly, his lips swathed with a smile. "The colonel is going to be dearly missed. Have you figured out what happened?"

Resolve settled into Gough's reply. "The bomb's (50) fuze should have been inert, since six days had passed, but it was buried in the cold ground, so we believe that the freezing temperatures slowed the drain of the charge—and recent lab tests bear that out. We've modified procedures for the teams." He shifted his feet to take the weight off his words. "What I'm trying to say is that Russell didn't die in vain. His experience will save other men." His head tipped toward the roomful of wounded. "Those two men lived because they were tugging so hard on the rope. When the bomb exploded, they fell backward, and the explosion rolled over the top of them. Had they been standing, like the others, then you would be the sole member of your team left alive."

"Dr. Gough?"

"Yes?"

Wes clasped the man's arm as if expecting him to flee. "I just want to say, don't stop. Keep testing, keep calculating, keep finding ways for us to fight back against the dirty Nazi scum. Will you tell your group that from me?"

"Yes, son. I will. By the way, have you spoken with Colonel Mackay?

"Who?"

"He'll be contacting you shortly."

"Am I being reassigned to another section?" Wes wondered.

"Lieutenant, Colonel Mackay has been in contact with your CO. The decision has been made—you're going home."

November 27, 1940

Dear Colonel Moore,

I've slept little since you were taken, wondering what might have happened had I been there. Could I have made a difference, or would I be dead along with everyone else?

Hastings says that he still feels you close. I try, and while there are times when I think he's right, mostly, I feel empty.

One of the first questions you ever asked me was if I had prepared myself for the afterlife. It seems that I never gave you a proper answer, and now I find myself wondering what an afterlife might look like. Can you see us? Can you somehow continue to make a difference in our lives?

What I must trust is that our short, seemingly insignificant lives are not insignificant at all. My hope is that the continual marching of time doesn't bury the short speck of our existence and the relationships we develop, but that it helps them to grow stronger and deeper. I trust that love endures. It's the only answer that makes any sense.

I guess it's an irony of war that love is needed among soldiers. We grew to love each other, and without that bond, we couldn't properly wage war. But love also creates the greatest of pain when one is lost.

Colonel, let me share with you a secret: They're sending me home—though I guess you know that—but I'd prefer to stay in England. At home, I'll have to break a girl's heart, and that makes my own heavy.

I plan to come back to England, as there's a girl here whose flat I blew up who has edged herself into my life, and I can't let her go.

Lastly, sir, I salute you. You are one of the finest human beings I've ever had the chance to meet, and it was an honor to serve with you.

Give my best to dear Margaret—and if it's possible, stay in touch.

Warmly,

Second Lieutenant Wesley Bowers

Wes walked into Café Cozier somberly, his gait matching his mood, every step pensive. It would be the last time that he would set foot inside the place—that is, until he returned to England.

He didn't mention that fact to Jordy and Jorrell when he ordered his biscuits and a Grapefruit Squash—a drink he would never find in the States—and a ginger tea for Audrey. He would wait to break the news to the two brothers until it was time to leave.

Audrey strolled in minutes later, her eyes also glancing around, looking like a girl taking a last look at her childhood home before heading off for boarding school. She shouldered a fabric bag, which she laid gingerly on the table.

"It's kind of sad leaving, isn't it?" she said. "We must come back here after the war."

Wes liked that she had marched right into their conversation, conceding that formal greetings between them were no longer necessary. It felt like *being together* was now their natural state, not being apart, and he loved that it was all so . . . comfortable.

"And we shall come back," he answered, before casting his eyes toward her bag. "Thank you for bringing it."

While she gently removed her carved wooden box, he pulled an envelope from his front pocket. He waited as she pressed the corners of the box to open the lid, and then held the letter toward her. "You place it inside," she told him, as though it would be more personal that way.

Wes slid the sealed letter inside, the handwritten name of the addressee, *Colonel Russell Moore,* upright and visible.

"He seemed like a good man," Audrey said as she closed the lid and then tapped the outside of the box, as if that were somehow part of the magic in sending the letter on its way. And whether Wes honestly believed or not that this box could miraculously send his letter to the colonel was irrelevant. He felt better having taken the time to consider his feelings, to express them on paper, and what would it hurt, relying on hope that the colonel could somehow know?

He leaned back in his chair and took a long drink from his glass, content to simply sit with her in comfortable silence since she'd already taught him that the space we leave around our words is sometimes as important as the words themselves.

After a moment, Audrey reached again into her bag and pulled out an envelope of her own. "If you hadn't guessed, I wrote you a letter." She passed it over to him. "And we don't even have to put it in the box. You can read it directly—but not now. It's for later, so you won't forget me."

He took it with both hands. "But I don't have one for you."

"Of course not. You must read this letter first and then answer it. That's how letter writing works."

He accepted her smile. "Thank you. I will absolutely answer you—often. Too often, I'm sure. I do wish, though, that we could also talk on the phone."

She replaced her smile with a sigh. "If only that were possible. Unfortunately, we'll be in different countries. Besides, my father used to call the telephone the worst invention of the century, said it would ruin mankind."

"Alexander Graham Bell might disagree."

"Yes, Papa was a bit dramatic, but he wasn't completely wrong. A well-thought-through letter whispers with sight, touch, smell—and, most importantly, time. You don't get any of those when chit-chatting by telephone."

She scooted her chair closer. "When do you leave?"

"Saturday. You?"

"We're driving up tomorrow."

"I'm glad you're going," he blurted. "I'll hate being apart, but you'll be safer in Sheffield."

"And I'm glad that you're also leaving. You'll be safer in . . ."

"Arizona," he added.

"That's right. You've told me."

"Of course, I don't know if I'll be sent somewhere else first." He flashed encouraging eyes. "Opinion is shifting in the United States. People are becoming less afraid. We may join your little war yet, and if we do, I may try to get assigned here, come back over with the rest of the troops. What do you think of that?"

"You should just stay safe, Wes. The fighting will eventually end. It always does. Then, if you haven't forgotten about me . . ." Audrey's head turned toward the bar as if she'd realized midsentence that music was playing from the wireless.

"We've never danced," she said, her jeweled eyes brightening.

"Well then, we should," Wes answered, extending his hand.

It brought both a grin and a giggle as she took his fingers. "Aside from the fact that it's morning and nobody else is dancing."

Wes pushed out his chair. "Then, that would make it the best time to dance." He led her to an open area between tables, took her slender fingers in his left hand, and placed his arm around her waist.

A song by British singer Vera Lynn was playing. Wes didn't know the lyrics, but Audrey did. As he drew her tight, swaying ever so softly to the music, she sang along.

Just stay strong and true, and I will think of you,
And let our love cast all my worries far away . . .

He let his eyes drift shut, allowed his body to soak in her warmth, begged his ears to record every inky inflection.

We'll be together soon, beneath a brilliant moon,
Together on that warm and welcome day.

CHAPTER 21

The St. Mary School at Sheffield, built in the early 1900s at the site of an old quarry, was reflective of the good sisters who ran it: safe, sensible, and stout.

Upstairs, above the classrooms on the main level, were offices, a sickroom, and dormitories, including a room assigned to Audrey and Lilli. Though the building didn't have a full basement, its expansive cellar system came pretty close, with a set of stone stairs that led down from the main floor to storage rooms that housed everything from coal to candelabras.

A large watchtower had also been built at the structure's east end using the site's sandstone blocks. If one believed the lore, it was built as a bell tower, but the hoisted bell had cracked within days. When its replacement arrived and then suffered the selfsame fate, the tower was repurposed to keep sprouting superstitions at bay.

Unlike many of England's industrial cities, the city of Sheffield, nearly 200 miles north of London near Manchester and Leeds, had seen only a smattering of German bombs fall since the start of the war. Those that had dropped caused minimal damage and just a handful of casualties, a pleasant change from the pounding that London had been taking.

Audrey and Lilli had been assigned to Sister Mary Catherine, a gentle and beauteous woman who taught language and math to nearly two dozen young girls, ages seven to ten. The rambunctious children had taken a liking to the new pair of helpers, though they didn't understand why Audrey would occasionally call Lilli by the name of Claire.

Now, after dinner, the children had eagerly assembled in the main classroom to plan their upcoming Christmas party, with Sister Mary Catherine standing in front writing ideas on the blackboard, Lilli pointing to those raising hands for a turn, and Audrey sitting in the back working to better memorize the children's names.

There was Tegan, a raven-haired child with spotted freckles and perpetually despairing eyes; Davine, a witty young thing who seemed bent on teasing anyone who ventured close; Joan, a large-boned girl with thick, tangly hair that was continually in need of a good combing.

Audrey's head tipped as a noise rudely disrupted her child-cataloging exercise. Despite the quiet of this new city, she'd been jumpy since arriving, her ears overly sensitive to every faraway beep of a car, every fading shrill of a policeman's whistle. This evening, the sound that had captured her attention, coaxing her toward the room's only window, was more subtle, more rhythmic.

She listened, waited, pressed herself closer to the glass. The hum was steady, deep, harmonic—familiar.

Lilli turned next.

The whir presently pushing itself through the windows and walls was coming from a fleet of approaching bombers.

Wes boarded the transport, settled as comfortably as he could into his seat, and then opened his letter from Audrey once again. The girl had been right: receiving a meaningful, well-written letter was much better than sharing the same message by telephone. A handwritten letter could be read, remembered, and relished over and over.

He was just unfolding her pages when a familiar drawl elbowed in.

"Well, I'll be a lazy pig in the afternoon sunshine! We meet again. I told you there was nothing to worry about going to England."

Wes scanned the welcoming eyes of Captain Jonathan Grassley, the friendly pilot who'd flown him over so many weeks ago. Wes's greeting was subdued but sincere. "Captain, it's good to see you again."

The bobbing man, in contrast, was nearly giddy. "Boy, I'm glad to see you made it through. The best part is, we'll have you home by Christmas."

"Yeah, peace on earth, good will toward men, that sort of thing," Wes answered brusquely.

"I do have to ask you," the captain said, drawing close. "London's been bombed every day since I dropped you off. That must've been something to observe firsthand. I'll bet you have stories to tell."

Wes offered the slightest of shrugs. "Not really." How could he possibly convey the carnage, the loss? They were stories he would never repeat.

The good pilot continued. "It's been something to see the British stand up like they have to the Nazis. Downright inspiring."

On that, they could agree.

Grassley followed with a friendly hand resting on Wes's

shoulder. "I'm no dummy," he said. "I can see that you're keen to get to that letter you were about to read. I'm guessing she must be pretty, so I'll leave you alone." He turned to walk away but paused. "Son, I've been in a war zone before." He took a card from his wallet and held it out. "I recognize that look. I want you to know that if there's anything you'd care to talk over, about the things you saw in London, you can call me—anytime. Here's my number."

Wes let the card hang in the air, not ready to concede that the man may have a point. When he finally reached for it, plucking it from the captain's fingers, he added words.

"Thank you, Captain Grassley. I will."

November 22, 1940

My dearest Wes,

I write, hoping that as I trace these scribbled thoughts to paper, the words will carry from my wishful heart to yours and narrow the distance between us.

On a haunting night, not long past, after you had gathered the scattered body pieces of a young couple literally torn apart by the ravages of war, you asked me if our efforts to save lives were worth it. You wondered whether all of the good in the world, all of the joy, could ever outweigh the bad, because on that day you had witnessed so much tragedy.

The dilemma pestered me, and I didn't have an answer until the night that we held each other in the dark at the warehouse after the colonel's death.

Having you sob in my arms was one of the most trying

moments of my life, as I longed to take away your hurt and heartache but could do nothing except cry with you. Strangely, that grief-filled night was also hallowed. I felt such love and concern that I would have taken away your burdens and carried them myself if such things were possible. I realized in the midst of your misery that the compassion welling inside me, which remains to this day, would not have been possible without that pain.

Wes, life isn't a scale where the good is balanced against the bad, squaring the sides to declare a winner. Rather, our experiences, both the despair and the joy, are weighed on the same side, intertwined together to create the thread that weaves the cloth of our lives.

Sadly, this truth is easily forgotten when we've been so stretched and torn that we fray at our edges, scarcely remembering what it's like to be whole, but the fact remains: the war will end, the suffering will stop, the agony will ease, and when the sun rises on that day, it will be grand and glorious. Without the pain of the past, it would otherwise be just an ordinary day.

My secret, Wes, is that I scribbled you a poem. I sometimes write to bring comfort, and as we held each other that night in the warehouse, I heard the subtle sound of rain outside tapping on the window. It reminded me that we find ourselves in unusual times, these times of rain and war.

Rain has always been a mystery. It can be so cold and menacing, and yet it also brings moisture, causing flowers to grow—sometimes even in winter. It is like a stern but loving parent, reminding us to constantly flush away life's dust and rise up. While these times are trying, they are also miraculous. Perhaps that's the true secret: love will always persist. I'm enclosing my pressed primrose petal, so that you'll remember.

Until that season, when we are at last together, I will take hope in the rain.

Love,

Audrey

Soft Falls the Rain

Soft falls the rain, bright shines the moon,
Resplendent flora shed their earthly bloom.

Our seasons turn, and birds take wing,
As winter wrests its toll from delicate things.

When petals drop, their fate fulfilled,
Don't loathe the rain or shun the season's chill.

Stand strong, grieve not the woes of men,
For buds shall rise and blossom yet again.

Spring's hope will conquer all our pain,
Have faith in love and whisper this refrain:

In time, our lives will have no war,
I'll long for such upon that distant shore.

Until that day our peace obtain,
Shine bright, grand moon; fall soft, dear rain.
Shine bright, grand moon; fall soft, dear rain.

The city of Sheffield was home to the Hadfield Steelworks, the only place in the UK where eighteen-inch armor-piercing shells were being made. For the Luftwaffe, it meant that it was time to launch operation *Schmelztiegel,* meaning "crucible." It was time at last for Sheffield to pay.

Never mind that the city was home to 560,000 innocent civilians who would also be bombed; war is war. Except this attack would take a different approach: the first wave of Heinkel 111s would drop incendiary bombs. Called the B-1E *Elektronbrandbombe,* the one-kilogram, baton-shaped devices housed a magnesium alloy that ignited on impact, burned hot, and was almost impossible to extinguish. Recent modifications added an explosive charge that could penetrate the roof of a building.

While a single bomber could hold more than a thousand B-1Es, sprinkling them like confetti over a wide swath of the city, their purpose was for more than starting fires. The incendiaries were dropped in the first surge of an attack to provide glowing targets for the additional bombers flying behind, those lugging more lethal ordnance, including the parachute mine.

Called the most fearsome weapon of the Blitz, parachute mines measured nine feet long, two feet wide, and weighed in at two tons. Half of that weight consisted of Hexanite, an explosive significantly more powerful than TNT. Originally designed to sink ships, the mines had been repurposed once the Luftwaffe realized that they could be set to explode at rooftop level and that a single bomb could decimate an entire city block.

Their downside was that they couldn't be targeted. Once released from the plane, the mines would float indiscriminately toward their victims, carried by the whims of the wind, and perhaps it was better that way, letting fate decide who would die and who would live.

Today, the breeze had shifted and was carrying the last mine from the final squadron of bombers—an ordnance to be dropped above the Darnall Wagon Works—toward an innocent building below, a building with a large tower crafted from stone taken from the nearby quarry.

The mine was drifting toward the St. Mary School.

Once the air-raid sirens had finally sounded, the three women—Sister Mary Catherine, Lilli, and Audrey—quickly herded the children down the stairs from their main classroom and into the largest of the building's cellars. Thankfully the room was lighted, so until the attack passed, the good sister in charge decided to organize a game where she would pretend to be a type of animal for the children to guess.

With the little girls timidly bunched around her in the center of the musty room, Sister Mary Catherine was flapping her arms and pecking with her head. "What am I?" she asked, trying not to tense, but failing miserably.

"A frightened nun?" Lilli whispered to Audrey in an attempt to lighten the mood, but Audrey wasn't listening. Something had roped her attention, pulled her up from the floor, and was luring her toward the stairs, where she listened more closely to the bombers overhead. It wasn't what she heard that was discomforting, but what she didn't.

"There are no explosions, no bombs," she said to Lilli, who was stepping beside her.

"Isn't that a good thing?" Lilli asked.

"No, the planes were flying too low to be moving past toward another city. Sheffield has to be their target."

"Why, then, are they not dropping anything?"

Audrey sniffed at the air. Like the anxious children raising their hands nearby, a familiar scent wafted down the stairs equally begging to be noticed. "They are!" Her worry stiffened. "Can you smell that?"

Lilli's eyes arched. "Something's on fire!"

"Children, stand up!" Audrey called out, waving them up with her arms. "We're going to go outside."

A puzzled Sister Mary Catherine edged past. "What is it?"

"We're not hearing any bombs exploding," Audrey told her, "because they aren't dropping them yet. They're dropping incendiaries!"

The good sister protested. "But the building here is made of stone. It can't burn."

Audrey draped an arm around her, pulled her in close. "That's true, but there are wooden beams in the rafters that support a wood tile roof." She lowered her voice, not wanting to startle the little ones. "It doesn't matter if the walls are stone. If the roof catches fire, this place will become an oven. We have to get the children outside, and we have to do it now!"

"Stay close, children, and be brave!" Sister Mary Catherine coaxed, knowing that although little girls are resilient, they are also fragile, especially in a war with planes overhead and visible fires burning around them—including smoke coming from the roof of the building they have just exited.

Two of the girls whimpered, three were sobbing, and the remainder were apparently too nervous to emit any sound at all. Sister Mary Catherine was doing her best to reassure while Lilli and Audrey counted, but by the children's looks, the whole group would soon be terror-stricken.

" . . . fourteen, fifteen, sixteen . . ." As Audrey touched the girls one by one, looking at each of their faces, taking a mental tally in her head, panic soon puddled. "We're missing someone!"

Sister Mary Catherine had been taking her own count. "You're right. It's Tegan!" she called out. "She must still be inside."

Audrey twisted, ready to run back into the smoky building, when Lilli seized her arm. "Look up there!" She was pointing toward the watchtower.

Audrey had noticed that the tower roof was leaking smoke, and she expected to now see that the timbers had flared into a blaze—which they had. What she didn't imagine as she followed Lilli's finger was to also see the dark outline of an enormous bomb dangling by parachute cords tangled on the tower roof.

"We need to move the children now!" Audrey screamed.

Sister Mary Catherine pointed toward the darkened field beside the school. "How about the quarry? It's been mostly filled in, but there's a bit of a gorge that could provide some protection."

"Yes, take the children there!" Audrey answered. "Lilli, go with her to help."

Lilli's worry bent into a question. "What about you?"

Audrey was already turning toward the building. "I'm going back inside to find Tegan!"

"Tegan? Tegan! It's me. If you're hiding, you need to come out. Let's get you to a safer place."

The cellars weren't as smoky as the main upstairs floor, but there were nooks and crannies, an abundance of places a scared youngster could hide. Audrey searched the largest of the rooms, moving boxes, calling, stooping to check under a stack of rusting bed frames. When sufficiently sure that the girl wasn't there, Audrey shuffled down a corridor, making her way toward the three smaller rooms—but then the lights went out.

"Oh, sod it," she grumbled, fumbling her way in the dark. She pressed her back against the moist wall, inching, inching, inching until she felt the doorknob leading to the first room. She opened it, then sniffed at the distinct odor of fermenting food. That's right; this was the root cellar where they stored vegetables. It was colder than the remaining rooms, with a pipe vented to the outside bringing in fresh air, which decreased the risk of mold and prolonged the life of the stored produce.

"Tegan? Are you in here?"

Audrey paused, listened, then turned to feel her way back out when thunder coiled around her, striking a blow to her back, her stomach, her legs, her chest, as if trying to reach inside and tear out her heart. She opened her mouth to scream, but her sound was swallowed by the fiery air. Stone cracked, the earth trembled, once-solid walls toppled inward. She tried to run, but her feet had cemented in place.

Audrey had been here before—not in the cellar of a school as the walls caved in, but in a place of dirty air with the end of life looming. She instinctively groped for her siren suit, the fabric that had once saved her, but this time broken boulders had tumbled around her legs, her arms, her body.

Audrey held her breath captive for as long as she could as the dust and rumbling settled. When she could hold her air no longer, feeling the weight of the debris surge against her, she exhaled, expecting it to be the end.

She was standing in the doorway when the building fell, leaving space around her head, above her shoulders, but trapping the rest of her body, as if she'd been buried alive in a small cave.

She inhaled a tiny quarter breath of the grubby air, let it out, and then sucked in another, each one thin and panting. Her lungs begged for more, dusty or not, but small gasps were all the pressuring mass would permit—but it was enough.

"Lilli?" she whispered, words spoken so softly she could hardly hear them herself. But of course, Lilli couldn't hear because she was in the gully with the children—wasn't she?

Please let Lilli be in the gully with the children.

Audrey tried again to move her arms, her legs. She could wiggle her fingers, that much was good, but below her waist, she felt . . . cold.

"*Tegan?*" Had the little girl also been buried, or did she make it out? Either way, everything would be okay. Lilli would find them both. Audrey just needed to hang on.

She fought the urge to cough, let her head lean forward in the dark, then smiled as she wished for a pillow. "And a ginger lemonade would also be lovely, please," she implored to the surrounding stones with the faintest moving of her lips. She would need to stay in good spirits. Keep breathing; keep battling. Still, she could also feel the pull of doubt, a whisper telling her to close her eyes and give up trying.

"I'm here, Lilli," she repeated. "I'll hang on. Please hurry and find me."

Lilli had been crouching with Sister Mary Catherine and the children, trying to keep the girls calm, when the parachute mine exploded. While their huddled human chain had been shielded from the bulk of the blast by an outcropping of rock, the explosion's wave of energy still knocked Lilli and several of the girls to the ground.

"Is everyone all right?" she asked frantically as she stood—and they seemed to be—so she turned back to face the school. Even in the dark, the sight was sickening. St. Mary School—the main hall, the annex, the tower—was no longer there. In its place lay a jagged and jarring heap of smoking rubble, a giant silhouette that looked eerily like the outline of a body lying lifeless on the ground.

Lilli's arms wrapped desperately around her body as if needing help to keep from dropping to her knees. She wanted to scream at the smoldering stones, shout at heaven, curse the despicable, cowardly Nazis who would drop bombs on innocent children, but her focus had turned elsewhere. She gestured toward Sister Mary Catherine to say, *watch the children,* and then, not considering if the place was safe, as presently she no longer cared, she sprinted toward the settling debris.

"Audrey? Audrey?" There was no reply. Next, Lilli reached down to pick up the closest fragment of warm sandstone, a fractured boulder the size of a large watermelon, grunting as she tried to move it. When it would barely budge, a panic crept across her that would have reduced most women into a helpless heap. That time might come, but it wasn't now. Instead, she turned toward the town of Sheffield, now glowing with sizable swaths of the city on fire, and screamed out into the night.

"HELP! ANYONE!" she yelled, over and over. "PLEASE, I NEED HELP!"

It took just hours for Rescue Services to gather a group of men who began removing the rubble of what was once St. Mary School, searching for survivors. They seemed to rotate in and out, new faces joining, old faces disappearing, with the single constant being Lilli working tirelessly by their side.

At first, they had insisted it was a man's job, though they learned quickly that this strong-willed woman was impossible to dissuade. Besides, she was working harder than any man on the crew and was the only one who wouldn't run for cover when a bomber flew over.

She slept in their tent, catching an hour of rest here or there. She ate their food, generally lamb stew and biscuits, and she drank their tea. She helped them carry stones and load trucks, as if she'd always been one of them, and was soon calling them by their first names.

At dawn, Sister Mary Catherine approached. She placed a kindly hand on Lilli's arm. "You should take a break."

"I'm fine," Lilli replied, reaching up to hold the good sister's hand but then lifting it aside so she could get back to work.

"I actually came to let you know that we found Tegan," Sister Mary Catherine said. "She wasn't inside the school after all. When the sirens started, she became scared, slipped out unnoticed, and scurried all the way home."

Lilli answered quietly, carefully. "That is good news, then. Thank you for letting me know."

She allowed herself a brief pause for reflection, one tinged with regret, before turning back to the still-smoking pile to hoist up another stone.

Audrey could hear sounds above her, calling her name as she drifted in and out of consciousness, though she could never be certain if the echoes overhead were the voices of rescuers beckoning from her own earthly world or a more saintly summons reaching out from beyond her dreams.

As she pondered her future and whether this occasion would be the end, a quizzical notion picked its way through the rubble and entered her brain. If voices were calling from both sides, each eager to welcome her back, was she being presented a choice? Was that what the dreams meant that she'd been having for these past many months, always seeing herself scale the same familiar mountain? In these dreams, she had imagined that her father waited on top, had wondered if these night visions were a shadow of her someday passing from her mortal life to the one that is to come—but in truth, she had never seen him.

The hefting of boulders being moved scratched overhead.

What she had to consider, having been concealed so suddenly in a stone tomb, was that mountains lift, but they can also bury. Rising above life's challenges often means climbing, but it can also mean digging.

If Lilli was working to get her out, then she owed it to her to hang on. However, if her father were also peering over the edge of the mountain, yearning to reach down and grasp his daughter's hand to pull her up for a long-awaited embrace, it would be hard to say no to that reunion as well.

Breathe, Audrey, breathe.

One way or another, she would soon have to decide.

By dusk, after the first full day of clearing, Charlie, the youngest of those helping, waved Lilli over to where he was removing debris from a bent and mangled bed. There was no sign of Audrey, alive or dead, but beneath their unearthed bed, Lilli discovered Audrey's tattered box, the one she treasured, the one her father had made that held her most important letters. It was still intact.

Lilli's first thought was to whisk it away to the tent and store it there for safekeeping, but she decided instead to prop it up on top of a pile nearby, for all the rescuers to readily see, as a reminder of why they were all working so tirelessly.

By the second day, when fatigue set in, Lilli lost hope. The box now seemed to mock rather than refresh, and she broke down sobbing twice, taking a short rest each time, only to return soon afterward to insist that she was okay.

It was on the morning of the third day, just after the sun had pushed over the horizon, while Lilli was helping Charlie steady a wheelbarrow they were carting to an outlying pile, when she heard the men's commanding officer, Owen, begin to yell.

His call was both welcome and terrifying. "I've found something!" he hollered. "Quick, I need everyone's help over here! I think I see her."

Audrey couldn't say how much time had passed—two days, or double that—but as the chorus of scraping, digging, and the removing of debris grew louder, one thing was becoming certain: they were going to find her alive.

She was weak, still fighting to breathe, struggling to hold her eyelids open, but once they'd cleared the fragments from around her upper body and back to ease the pressure, they brought in two mattresses to shield her head, nervous that the stones they'd uncovered over the doorway would give way before they could free Audrey's feet.

"You'll be fine, Audrey. Keep fighting!" Lilli commanded, though she was doing a poor job herself of battling back her tears.

It was a wonder watching Lilli work—such a good, good woman—and the way she'd taken a personal interest in Audrey's well-being these past many years, so protective and mothering to a girl whose own mother couldn't be around.

Audrey couldn't move her fingers, couldn't tell if they'd been freed yet from the rubble or if she'd merely lost feeling, so she kept trying to motion to Lilli with her head, begging her to bend down close enough so Audrey could whisper into her ear.

"Lilli?" Audrey finally muttered, the hoarse words scarcely spitting out.

Lilli lightly brushed fingertips against Audrey's bruised face. "Save your strength."

Audrey drew in another breath, as deep as her broken ribs would tolerate, but dragging fortitude with it. "No!" she called out, lassoing Lilli back, demanding she stoop close and press her ear against Audrey's cracked and bleeding lips.

"What is it?"

Every word was determined. Every word was endearing. "Lilli," she said. "I need you to listen. There's something very important that I have to tell you."

CHAPTER 22

Wes leaned with his elbows on a table in a briefing room at the new Navy Building on Constitution Avenue in Washington, D.C., huddling with six officers who specialized in munitions. While Wes would ultimately be discharged and then sent home, he was first to spend time passing along the bomb disposal methods and intelligence he'd gleaned from his service in London. The Brits had yet to send over any sample fuzes, as they were still rare to come by, so Wes was sketching out the various types, describing not only the mechanisms but also the solutions the Backroom Boys had devised to defeat them.

A staff sergeant stepped into the room, saluting the circle. "Lieutenant Bowers?"

"Yes, that's me." Wes stood.

"There is a telephone call for you from New York."

New York? Wes excused himself, then followed the sergeant to an office—gray, windowless, drab, with a telephone sitting on the desk.

He spoke into the mouthpiece. "Hello, this is Lieutenant Bowers."

"Long-distance operator. Please hold, and I'll connect you."

Minutes passed before Wes heard a scratchy voice reaching into the room, a woman's voice. "Lieutenant Bowers?"

"Yes, I'm here. Go ahead."

"Lieutenant, this is Lady Reading. We met at the Dorchester in London, the day you waited there for Audrey."

"Yes, of course, Lady Reading. How are you? How may I help?"

"I've just landed in New York. I'm spending a few days here with Eleanor, the first lady. We've been good friends for years."

"I'm glad you arrived safely."

The static-filled silence seemed to shift its weight. "I bring news about dear Audrey," Lady Reading then said, her voice cracking. "Lilli wished to tell you herself, but alas . . ."

Wes pressed his mouth against the receiver. "Is Audrey okay?"

"You know that she was staying at the St. Mary School in Sheffield? I recommended she go there since the city had barely been bombed."

"Has something happened?" Wes asked again.

"I'm sorry, Wes," Lady Reading said, her apology whistling in like the bombs over London. "There was an explosion at the school. The building tumbled in. Our Audrey didn't make it."

The news, like the real bombs, caused an eerie silence—until rubble started to rain.

"No, it can't be," Wes cried out, shaking, dodging the falling debris. "Tell me it's not true."

Words garbled and blurred—the connection perhaps, or was it the pain? Stern, stout, solid-as-stone Lady Reading was sniffling. She was speaking about a collapsing school and Audrey being buried in the rubble. But Wes quit listening—did anything in life matter without Audrey?

"Wes . . . have a letter . . . from Lilli . . . sending it by courier . . ." and then the line went dead.

Wes's hands were shivering, his head rocking, not willing to accept the news. He fell to his knees on the callous floor, his body not knowing if it should curse or cry.

Filled with torment, filled with rage, a restless and repeating thought echoed in his brain: Audrey was right. Telephones are the absolute worst kind of communication.

January 4, 1941

Dear Lieutenant Bowers,

If you're reading this, then Lady Reading has delivered the tragic news. Like you, I am broken from loss. I have spent so many years teaching and protecting our dear Audrey that it's now difficult to find meaning.

I told Lady Reading what happened at the school, how Audrey died, but I didn't tell her everything. Some details were too personal, but I will share them here with you.

Audrey was buried in the ruins of the school for three days with no food, no water, just her will to hold on. When we found her, and the debris was removed, she was weak and fevered. Still, I held her hand, and before she died, she whispered something to me.

It was strenuous for her to speak, and she worried that she wouldn't have the strength, but she was so determined. She was not always coherent, but clear enough that I knew she was speaking about her father, her brothers, her mother. She was trying to tell me that she had a choice, that she could decide for herself whether to stay or not, but that others were there beckoning to her.

She was afraid that if she chose to go with them, we would think that there wasn't enough love on our side of her existence, and she wanted us to know that wasn't true. She kept saying, 'Love is weighed together, same side of the scale.' I don't pretend to understand, but I trust you might.

By then, I was frantic, screaming, commanding that she hold on to her will to live. But in retrospect, I realized she obeyed me precisely. I should rather have demanded that she hold on to her will to stay.

Her final words before she passed were, 'No pain, only love.'

I have but a minute more to finish this note, as Lady Reading is ready to leave, so let me conclude by thanking you, Wesley Bowers, for your kindness, for touching a girl's heart and letting her touch yours. If this sad and sorry war is teaching me anything, it's that what counts are friendships and family. They will be the measure of a life well lived. To that end, I wish you all the joy in the world.

Sincerely,
Lilli Perlen

CHAPTER 23

Six Years Later

The Arizona town of Apache Junction had seldom seen a traffic jam, never had a flock of park pigeons, and if a car honked its horn along Main Street, the driver was likely trying to catch the attention of the passing parish priest. It was a barren, sun-parched plot of civilization that, in his youth, Wes had sworn to leave—but that was before the war.

True, Apache Junction remained a place with little to offer, but it was working for Wes, since it sat about as far away from England as one could get—in both miles and memories.

The sun was calling it a day as Wes pushed through the front door of the small, tidy house.

"Wes? Is that you?" Nathelle beckoned from the kitchen. "Your mother came by. She brought you a package."

Wes stepped into the room where his wife was putting the final touches on dinner. "A package?"

She pointed with her stirring spoon. "It's there on the table. It's from Germany."

"Germany?" Wes picked up the cardboard box, shook it gently, then pulled out his pocketknife and sliced the packing tape open. As he bent back the flaps to peer inside, his eyes narrowed.

"What is it?" Nathelle asked, scooting close herself to see.

He recognized it instantly—a black wooden relic from his past—the box carved by Audrey's father, the one he'd once retrieved for Audrey from her flat in London. He removed it reverently, like a priceless treasure, an envelope taped to the side.

Wes looked to Nathelle, her eyes asking questions, but what words could he possibly use to explain?

"It's a gift from Audrey . . . or I guess from Lilli." He turned it over and then back, feeling the heaviness of the letters it held inside. His next request was hushed and solemn.

"Dear, I'm going to need a little time by myself. If it's all right, I'll be in the basement." He truly didn't mean to be unkind but knew he wasn't succeeding.

Nathelle studied the box, the postmark, the anxious lines deepening in her husband's face. It seemed a familiar place for both of them, a path they'd walked before.

"Take your time," she said, stretching up on her toes to kiss him tenderly on the neck. "I'll keep your food warm."

April 6, 1947
Dear Wesley Bowers,

I hope this letter finds you well and that your life after the war has been a time of healing. I wanted to write to you sooner, but only recently secured your address in Arizona.

I think about Audrey often and know that you must do the same. After such a long war, filled with so much wretched gloom, I am finally finding peace. To that end, I am sending you Audrey's prayer box, the one she used since childhood to send letters to her father when he was away. I have felt for some time that Audrey would want you to have it. It's a bit scuffed, and there's a crack in the main cover, but I trust, like all of us, it still holds purpose.

I returned to Germany after the war, certain to find only despair. I don't know if Audrey ever told you, but when we left for Switzerland, before ultimately making our way to England, I left my love, Kaden Froe, behind. I had tried to write to him while in England, sending the letters covertly, but he never responded. The last time we'd seen each other was in Hamburg before he was forced into the war, and I longed to locate him there afterward, a likelihood that dimmed when I read in the London news that Allied forces attacked the city in 1943.

It turned out that when Hitler decided to bomb the innocent civilians of London, he opened Pandora's box, as the reciprocal bombing of Germany's innocent civilians followed. War was no longer an army clashing against an army, but now people against people, race against race, and where would it all end? We soon learned in Hamburg.

The city had not seen rain for a dreadfully long time, and the highly concentrated bombing in the dry city created fires that turned into a whirling updraft of super-heated air, a consuming tornado of fire over 1,500 feet high. I found out later that the raid, ironically, was code-named Gomorrah, taken from the Canaanite cities of Sodom and Gomorrah, whose destruction is recorded in the Bible. Indeed, it rained fire and brimstone on Hamburg that day, incinerating some 40,000 people and wounding 125,000 more. More people died in Hamburg in a single day than in all of England during the terrible Blitz. Justice, it seems, can be unforgiving.

I knew that if Kaden hadn't died in the war, he would surely have been burned in the fires. What I'm saying is that I lost all hope—something we should never do, because when I returned to Germany in 1946, I found that he was not only alive but that he had been searching for me as well. When we were at last reunited, we wept in each other's arms and then married a few short weeks later, and I am expecting a child. And if my baby is a girl, then Audrey seems like such a strong and fitting name.

Audrey always said that our best letters should contain a secret, something personal that we should share with those whom we most trust. So I will share a secret with you today, one that even Audrey didn't know.

When Audrey's father, Walther Strumpf, first began looking for a tutor to teach his young children, he learned of my credentials and availability from my brother, who had worked for him in Hamburg. Wes, my brother was Selig Perlen, the man who then betrayed Walther, who stood by and did nothing as the Nazis murdered him and his family.

What Audrey never knew is that as I held my hand over her mouth at the factory, trying to keep her quiet, she was able to scream just before she passed out. Selig told the Nazi soldiers that he would take care of us, but after finding me with Audrey in the back, helplessly struggling to get her out of the factory, he aimed his pistol directly at me and then shot twice into the ground just beyond, so that the soldiers would think we were dead. After the Nazis had gone, he helped me lift Audrey into the car to get away. It was the last time that I would see my brother, and to this day I can't reconcile his actions. At first, I assumed that he was driven by greed, but perhaps it was fear—I will never rightly know. In the end, he showed compassion, and it makes me wonder how people can carry such contradictions.

I see this happening again in Hamburg. One minute our countries are dropping bombs to blow each other up, and the next, there are Allied soldiers here in Germany helping the people to rebuild. We humans are such a funny breed!

While it's true that war creates terrible loss, beneath it, there will also be courage. I'm finding mine and trust that you are finding yours.

May you have a warm and wonderful life, Wes, and may we both trust that Audrey is looking on with her typical encouragement and love.

Herzliche Grüße (Heartfelt regards),
Lilli Perlen

P.S.: She died saving children. I can think of no better epitaph for a person's life.

Wes read through Lilli's letter once, twice, and then a third time, wanting to be sure that nothing was missed. Then, with a breath of confidence, he rifled through the drawer of his desk, found his favorite pen and a sheet of his best paper, and began to write a letter of his own—a letter he could finally send.

June 12, 1947
Dearest Audrey,

I can't count the times that I've started to write you over the past handful of years, that I tried to answer your sweet letter, but I could never finish more than a sentence, always asking, what is the point? Then, your box landed miraculously on my doorstep. I know that you believed it would carry your letters to those you loved, despite the distance, and so today, I will trust in your belief.

I should also tell you that I married Nathelle. You were right in your hunch: she is a good woman. She's been patient with my recovery, my moods, and while she doesn't have your smile or your laugh, she has her own, and it's candid and caring, and she has helped me get through the worst part.

I still recall when she first asked, who is Audrey Stocking? It caused both reflection and wonder. I said that Audrey was an extraordinary Jewish girl, without family, but who still managed to find her way home. She was someone whom few would remember, but whom I would never forget. It's true, Audrey, because your life asks the same echoing questions for us all. Do I matter? Can I make a difference? Is there more?

Nathelle didn't ask if I'd loved you, as that answer was seeping readily from my eyes. Her next question, though, was more curious, asking what your life taught me, and that, dear Audrey, I ponder to this day.

After I returned home from the war, after I heard the news about the tragedy at the St. Mary School, after I lost you, it was several months before I was able to function. I was incensed; I was depressed; I was filled with sadness over your death but also drenched with guilt for not having done more to save you.

It's peculiar, our nature to want to save others, especially when we can't even save ourselves. During the war, you worked feverishly to save the children, Lilli was doing her best to save you, I was trying to save the men in my section, and, by the time it was over, we all failed.

But Audrey, did we? Because here you are, popping up again out of nowhere, your box bringing with it a whispered feeling that you are here to prod me forward. And so, perhaps, we are all saving each other after all.

In my fairy-tale ending, we would have both survived the war and called it a miracle, but it seems that triumph in life is infinitely more subtle. I am damaged from the war, but I'm not broken. My heart is, at times, lonely, but I am still loved. Life was never meant to be as perfect as I had supposed; rather we are to adapt, make our best choices, and then live with the consequences, learning that it will all be okay.

Colonel Moore once asked if I was prepared to die, and, in looking back, I was. What I wasn't properly prepared for was to live—and that is what I'm working toward.

I visit on occasion with a support group, other men who served in the war, and we labor prudently at peeling away the layers of our shame. It's a slow process, but it's been helping. It's interesting that years later, memories of the brutality, the death, the pain that I witnessed remain as raw as the day that they happened. But slowly, I'm reconciling my circumstance.

And I shouldn't imply that all the memories are haunting. Sometimes I see you in my dreams. I hold your hand, I see the sparkle in your eyes, I let my fingers trace your smile. Then, when I wake, I am both empty, because you are not there, and full, because I imagine that you were, and I'm reminded to try harder to live a better life and to furiously love those who are still around.

Speaking of which, do you remember Driver? After leaving the section, he opened up a flower shop with his mum, and, to this day, he is terrorizing the good drivers of London as he makes his deliveries. He sends me flowers every year on November 16th, the anniversary of my surviving ten weeks in London. He says it's so that I won't forget I am living on borrowed time.

I also learned from Driver that Hastings, the only other man in my section to survive, served later at the front in North Africa and was awarded the Victoria Cross for saving the men in his platoon. I hope he had the sense to not throw it into a bog.

Now, Audrey, to my secret: while I have days that I struggle, some pretty terrible days, it means that I also have stunning days. I weigh them both on the same side of the scale, a lesson that you taught. Life is short. Life is fragile. I shall grasp it with both hands and hang on, trying always to find the joy.

If those of us still living in the world were half as compassionate as you, there would be no more Hitlers.

Until we meet again,

All my love,

Wes

CHAPTER 24

March 7, 1990
Dear Audrey,

I'm writing to let you know that Wesley passed away this week, but it was peaceful.

It may seem odd, me writing to you now, stuffing a letter into this aging box, but it brought Wesley peace, and I find it does me as well.

While I suppose I should be both jealous and angry, I am neither. On the occasional evenings when Wesley would get forlorn and hole himself up scribbling his thoughts and placing them in the box, I could have been cross, but I chose not to be. On the contrary, I have felt only gratitude.

Thank you, Audrey, for giving me Wesley. He came home from the war a different person, but we had all changed. War has a way of doing that, no matter the angle from which it's viewed.

For Wesley, it meant that he didn't do well around large

gatherings. When we would enter a room filled with people, I would watch his foreboding eyes scan for the nearest way out. He would always go to bed early on both the Fourth of July and New Year's Eve, not because he wasn't patriotic or festive, but because the noise of fireworks took him back to places he would rather never visit again. I tell you this to let you know that we had our trials.

But we also had so much joy! We were blessed with four children and twelve grandchildren, and life rolls grandly forward. Would that I could say they are all living faultless lives, but we know better. Life is seldom what we ask for, and we should thank heaven for every painful, wearisome, hurtful, joyous, amazing, gentle moment.

The annual flower deliveries from Driver that we so enjoyed quit coming a year ago. A letter arrived shortly thereafter from his three sons, letting Wesley know that Driver had passed away. In the letter, his boys called him 'the best pop any lads ever had.' For Wesley, that was a very good day. It still brings me a smile to know that when Wesley passed, Driver was surely the first one there waiting for him to arrive so he could take him to see Colonel Moore.

Wesley also said he could feel you on occasion, whispering reassurance that all would be well, and I like to think that he was right. I hold nothing but admiration for you and appreciation for the help you gave Wesley.

Until we meet, goodbye, Audrey Stocking, and may our dear Wesley Bowers rest in peace.

Sincerely,
Nathelle Bowers

AUTHOR'S NOTE

I was introduced to the bomb disposal teams of World War II by Rachel Bowers, granddaughter to Wesley Bowers. She knew all about bombs because during her service in the Iraqi conflict—Operation Iraqi Freedom—one of her tasks as Lead Vehicle Commander in her unit was to ride at the front of their convoys and spot improvised explosive devices—IEDs, the roadside bombs the insurgents would set to injure or kill our troops.

Before I tell you more about Rachel, though, let me address the most common question I'm asked about any of my books—how much of the story is true? It seems that we humans are born with a driving curiosity to separate fact from fiction, though life seldom offers easy distinctions.

Rachel's grandfather, Wesley Bowers, did serve as a bomb disposal technician during World War II, and only two other members of his team survived. Like many men who returned from war, he said little about his service; consequently, most of his account in my story has been fictionalized.

That said, my characters and their experiences are patterned after real people and situations from the war. When my fictional Colonel Moore digs the explosive out of a damaged and ticking SC 250 and by so doing discovers a new type of fuze, it was done in real life by a Brit named Stuart Archer. When 37 Section tries to steady a bomb hanging by a rope, and it explodes, the real men who lost their lives that day were William Ash, Leslie Foster, Leslie Hitchcock, Jackie Lewis, and Titchie Websdale.

Lady Reading, an extraordinary woman who founded Women's Voluntary Services, is also real. Her background is factual, as are the histories of Bob Davies, Herbert Gough, and the Backroom Boys.

And let's not forget Herbert Rühlemann, the gifted German fuze designer who tried to sell his designs to the British government before the war, but when they showed little interest, he returned to Germany, convinced his own country's leaders of their worth, and thereby changed history.

For the daily life accounts of my characters, I am indebted to many in the UK who wrote about their experiences living through the Blitz as part of a social research project that had started three years before the declaration of war. Called Mass-Observation, this project asked volunteers to journal their thoughts and feelings and mail them in to be later studied (preserved in a collection currently housed at the University of Sussex). Several of these narratives have been compiled into books (most notably ones by Simon Garfield), and they are well worth a read. Keep in mind that these are not historical glances back after the fact, but real-time diaries of individuals living and writing during these precarious wartime moments, not knowing whether they would survive. Many of my characters' situations, reactions, and attitudes were taken from or inspired by these real first-person accounts.

I hope this lengthy explanation demonstrates why, when I'm asked if the story is true, I never know how to answer. As a wise writer once said, "It's not true, but it teaches truth." If that is the case with this novel, then I will be content.

What is certain is that many brave men and women altered the course of the war and gave hope to the besieged. Modern bomb disposal technicians across the globe today owe a debt of gratitude to the brave soldiers who pioneered disposal techniques during the Blitz, as many of their early methodologies are still used.

Which brings me to Rachel Bowers, Wesley Bowers's granddaughter.

During her service in Iraq scouting for IEDs, Rachel (then Sergeant Bowers) guided convoys over 5,000 miles on the country's most dangerous roads, delivered crucial supplies that sustained twelve Forward Operating Bases, escorted more than nine hundred civilian vehicles, was hit by IEDs twice, and was ultimately responsible for over 25 percent of her company's total IED finds, saving numerous lives.

For her service, Rachel was awarded three medals: a Purple Heart, the Army Commendation Medal (for valorous actions in direct contact with an enemy), and a Bronze Star. In addition, she was later recognized in the Congressional Record by the House of Representatives in Washington, D.C.

Yet, when I met Rachel and heard her story, it wasn't her military record that I found most enthralling, but rather the profound connection she shared with her grandfather who had served in bomb disposal during World War II.

As a writer, I was staring at two compelling stories, and, like a wide-eyed child who takes too large a serving of cake, I picked up my pen and set out to write both accounts as a two-part story. The first part would take place during World War II and would be a fictionalized story (based on real people and events) detailing the exploits of the bomb disposal heroes of Wesley Bowers's generation. The second part would delve into Rachel's remarkable experiences in Iraq, weaving in the life-altering influence of her grandfather. I thought my plan to stitch the two related stories together into a single volume was brilliant.

Until it didn't work.

Although the stories do have a compelling connection, they are set in different eras and need to be told from different points of view. Moreover, they contain complex characters that demand they not be needlessly mashed together.

Admitting defeat, I separated Rachel's story out into its own book and decided to give it to you for free. Rachel will explain below how it can be downloaded.

Before we get to that, however, I need to thank the many people who helped make both stories possible, as they offered expertise in the areas where I'm lacking: Larry Dewey, whose book *War and Redemption* is one of the most informative volumes on Post-Traumatic Stress Disorder (PTSD) that I've come across, and much of his wisdom and wording has been incorporated into my associated dialogue; Mark Heilman, Project Director at Veterans Upward Bound in Boise, for his insight; Chris Schoebinger for his many story ideas, including the nudge to not kill off Driver (a wise move); Jon Weisberg and Hanna Alexander for proofing my Jewish history and facts; Steve Hunnisett and Steve Venus, two astute British military historians (schedule a tour with Steve Hunnisett in London at blitzwalkers.co.uk); Greg Young for his WWII expertise; Adele Wilkinson, a smashing editor in England who did a jolly fine job of insuring my wartime English phrasing was spot on; Brad Knutson, a skilled chess teacher (for lessons, contact him at borisspasstic@gmail.com); Emily Watts, Ken Neff, Patrice Young, Rosemary Lind, and many other patient editors and readers; and my wife, Alicyn, for encouraging me not to give up when my writing muse packed up and took a lengthy vacation.

A NOTE FROM RACHEL BOWERS

My grandfather Wesley Bowers struggled with the symptoms of PTSD—as do I. It affects not only those who have served in combat, but many others who have never been to war or put on a uniform. Most who have suffered trauma in life tend to stay quiet, not talk about it, sweep it under the rug. But that's the worst thing we can do. I know this from experience.

With help, those suffering from traumatic emotional injuries can still live rich and fulfilling lives. With my grandfather, for example, my grandmother Nathelle was very patient. I remember as a young child hearing relatives discuss my grandfather's occasional anger, but I never saw it. The emotion I remember feeling from the man was an overwhelming sense of love and acceptance.

Sadly, my grandfather was taken early in my life. He died when I was just seven, and while it's true I don't know a lot about his bomb disposal work during World War II, what I do know about the man far eclipses everything else in importance.

You see, while I was in Iraq, he saved my life.

To download my story, *Saving Rachel McCally,* for free (as well as to find a list of sources and broader material for book clubs and other interested readers), please visit Camron Wright's website at AuthorCamronWright.com and click on the link *In Times of Rain and War.*

And may your journey in life be as wonderful as mine.

—Rachel Bowers

DISCUSSION QUESTIONS

See *AuthorCamronWright.com* for additional information relative to the story, including author comments on many of these discussion topics.

1. At the beginning of the war, in a letter to Audrey written by her father, he talks about preparing for the approaching calamity, saying, "When an unexpected storm rolls over the horizon, it's prudent to board the windows, stockpile food, fill jars with water. But how does one know which storms intend destruction and which shall pass? Should one cower at every dark wisp of a cloud?" How would you answer his question? While it's prudent to prepare for difficult times in our lives, can we overprepare? How do we find the balance between spending time preparing versus spending time living?
2. Germany discovered early that the psychological damage and disruption caused by an unexploded bomb was often greater than the ultimate damage caused by a physical explosion. How might this understanding help us as we approach problems?

Is our worry over a situation sometimes worse than the consequences of the problem themselves? How can we defuse unnecessary worry in our lives?

3. As a child, Audrey placed letters in her box because her father had promised that when he was away, he would "feel the words in his heart." How might Audrey's box be a metaphor? Do you believe that Audrey's box truly worked when her father was alive? How about after he had died?
4. In the early days of bomb disposal in England, it was believed that a soldier's life expectancy in that capacity was about ten weeks. Could you work in such a dangerous job? How might such a precarious job change your daily attitudes and interactions toward others?
5. We learn that Lady Reading—a real person, whose history in the book is factual—had a bout of spinal trouble as a child that confined her to bed for months, an experience that she later called *lucky*. Why might she consider it lucky? What do we learn from her attitude about how she faced life's problems? Is her outlook naïve, or should it be admired and followed?
6. When discussing the first German bombing of London—one believed by many to be accidental—Dr. Gough explains to Colonel Moore how it may have changed the entire outcome of the war. He notes that after England's reprisal bombing on Berlin, Hitler shifted his resources from military targets to the civilian bombing of London, a move that offered the British military time to rebuild. In their discussion, Dr. Gough wonders, "What if, in the grand scheme of things, as the universe balances out good and evil, the first accidental bombing of London wasn't an accident at all? What if it was fate turning the tides of war? What if life's worst disasters—our greatest defeats—are the

beginnings of our greatest victories?" Do you believe the bombing of London was an accident? How can accidents change the course of our own lives? On a personal level, how can we turn our defeats into victories?

7. Walther Strumpf believed that "few acts of human expression are more intimate and profound as that of a hand-penned letter." Audrey added, "A well-thought-through letter whispers with sight, touch, smell—and most important, time." With today's fast-paced communications—phone, text, and email—what might be the merits in sending a handwritten letter? Do you have any letters that you keep and cherish? If so, what makes them special?
8. Audrey's primary job with WVS was to help evacuate children from London. On a particularly trying occasion, she asks, "Are we helping as we scurry these children away from their families and this wretched war, Claire? Or are we creating deeper scars from the separation?" Is she right to doubt? Does a heightened risk of death for the children staying in London outweigh the psychological harm that may come from family separation? If you had been a parent with children living in London, what would you have done?
9. When Audrey is close to death, she tells Lilli that she has a choice, that she can decide for herself whether to stay or not, and that "others were there beckoning to her." While everyone must eventually die, do you believe that some have a choice in the particular moment? Can we will ourselves to live or to die?
10. In the letter Wes writes to Colonel Moore after the man's death, Wes notes, "One of the first questions you ever asked me was if I had prepared myself for the afterlife. It seems that I never gave you a proper answer, and now find myself wondering what

an afterlife might look like. Can you see us? Can you somehow continue to make a difference in our lives?" How would you answer Wes's questions? Have you ever felt the presence of a loved one who has passed?

11. Pike offers Wes thanks for being friendly, since officers and sappers in the British army usually don't mix. He then shares that his mother sat beside a university professor in a bomb shelter and the two had a pleasant conversation, something that wouldn't have happened outside a war because of the country's societal classes. Why does it take a war or similar tragedy to bring people together? What else about war is "nice" (as Pike put it)? Bringing the concept closer to home, what benefits arose from the Covid-19 pandemic of 2020?
12. Audrey asks Wes if death scares him. She later says, "In my view, I think we place too much importance on death. And why? People have been getting maimed and killed for thousands of years, haven't they? Doesn't life end as easily as it begins? We should keep a sense of proportion about it." Is she right? Does death scare you?
13. When remembering Audrey, Lilli's says, "She died saving children. I can think of no better epitaph for a person's life." How would you like your epitaph to read? To that end, in contemplating Colonel Moore's question about being prepared to die, Wes later answered, "In looking back, I was. What I wasn't properly prepared for was to live—and that is what I'm working toward." Why is living harder than dying?
14. Wes writes that Audrey was someone whom few would remember, but whom he would never forget. He adds that her life prods us all to ask the same echoing questions. "Do I matter? Can I make a difference? Is there more?" These seem to be universal

questions that have been posed since the dawn of time. Why do these questions persist? Have you found answers to them?

15. In writing to Audrey, Wes notes, "In my fairy-tale ending, we'd have both survived the war and called it a miracle, but it seems that triumph in life is infinitely more subtle." While the book's ending might not be called a "fairy-tale ending," would you consider it a happy one? If you were the writer, how would you have ended the story? What do you suppose Wes means by calling triumph "infinitely more subtle"?
16. What kind of woman was Nathelle? If you knew your partner or spouse had once deeply loved another, would that notion bother you? Why didn't it seem to bother Nathelle? Was her approach healthy? If so, what can we do to be more like her?
17. Why do you think so many stories are set during World War II? A social media influencer in Britain said in an interview that we should teach children today *less* about World War II because "it's so intense." Do you agree? What specific lessons might today's generation learn from World War II?
18. In Wright's follow-up story, *Saving Rachel McCally* (free to download), he delves into PTSD, including the likelihood that both Wes and Audrey suffered from its symptoms. How much do you know about PTSD? Do people have to have been in a war for PTSD to touch their lives? How can someone battle its symptoms?